for Ma...

Many Xmas 6

Rough Music

'Still Warm'
(Josie King Mystery Series Book 2.)

"I really enjoyed *The Unborn,* and the second book in the series, *Still Warm* is, in my opinion, even better. If you like fast-paced thrillers with an engaging heroine, a cast of well-drawn supporting characters and a generous helping of humour, then you'll enjoy *Still Warm.* I'm looking forward to the next instalment."

Thrillerman. (Amazon reader.)

Rough Music

Robin Driscoll

Printed and bound in Great Britain by Clays Ltd, Elcograf S.p.A.

Authors Reach
www.authorsreach.co.uk

ISBN: 978-1-9160626-5-8

For Deborah, Sam and Dominic.

(And Maddie.)

"I paint fakes all the time."

Pablo Picasso.

"When you think about it, a fake, no matter how good, only has a value because the real thing exists someplace."

Rab MacBain.

Chapter One

RAB MacBain wondered, not for the first time, where Stink Bug would kill him. Not when. He already knew the when. That would be soon after he'd punched-in the requested response code a second time, confirming the wire transfer.

He watched the cursor winking in its little oblong box on his Mac's flat screen, waiting for the ten digits that would catapult a huge sum of cash out of a Citibank on Madison Avenue, across cyberspace to Banco Confianza on sunny Grand Cay. Dead certain that ten taps of the keyboard were about to get him killed, Rab reviewed the thirty-four years of his short life. He could've smoked. He wished he'd had more sex. Wished he'd been a better son to his old man but, most of all, hadn't lied to the woman he loved.

He looked about him in the glow of the flat screen, surrounded on all sides by walls of glass, the lights of Manhattan distorting as heavy rain cascaded down the sixteenth storey's floor-to-ceiling windows. Becky had dubbed his office the 'Shark Tank.' A joke, but if only she knew.

Becky.

He held his breath, steadied his hand and tapped nine digits into the waiting oblong box. His finger paused over the tenth and froze there, like that part of his body had died already. Maybe Stink Bug wouldn't kill him if he begged. He could beg. He could promise to keep his mouth shut; take a magic potion to make him forget the 'too much' he was supposed to know. Hypnosis or something. Any fucking thing.

He stared at the flashing cursor and the rushing in his ears went up a notch. He could see them watching him through the glass wall to Jeffery Hammer's office, silhouetted against the glow of his boss's own computer: Grove, Hammer & Dunn's newest client, Fedor Brunovich and a couple of his Russian goons. The huge, dark shape that would have been Stink Bug was absent from the group. Was that good? He hoped the guy had stubbed a toe and died in agony a million miles away. That would be good.

He glanced at his watch: 9.37. Over two hours since the last of GHD's employees had headed home for the night. Thirty-seven minutes late for his dinner date at Becky's place.

He studied his reflection superimposed over the Russian tableau beyond the glazed wall and, to his eyes, he looked pretty strung-out. So why were they letting him take so damn long with this wire?

He felt a hand at the nape of his neck. Blood shot to his head.

"What's the problem?" a voice whispered from behind.

And *tap!* In went the last digit of the response code. Another tap as he hit 'ENTER.'

"No problem," he said through dry lips.

A message popped-up on the screen: AUTHORIZING – PLEASE WAIT, along with a clock display counting down from 05.00.

Glancing up at his boss, the 'Hammer' in Grove, Hammer & Dunn, Attorneys at Law, he said, "Five minutes. That's pretty usual." The last word betraying a Scottish burr.

Since his dad brought him to the States some twenty years back, many had remarked that he spoke like Sean Connery, which had been great when he'd been a kid, useful when dating in high school, but now was mostly a pain in the ass. Anyway, most Americans couldn't nail a Scottish brogue whether it be from Edinburgh or Oban, and in truth, these days, neither could he.

The weight of Hammer's hand left him. Like his own, his boss's dark suit, crisp button-down and well kempt hair shouted corporate lawyer. Forty something, Jeffery Hammer's stiff coiffure was as white as Rab's was raven black. His eyes, a watery gray. He was hiding his nerves pretty well, Rab observed, as his boss watched the computer's clock click down to 04.32. *Where's he gonna kill me?*

"Can I leave you with this, Jeff? I've godda be somewhere," he said, aware of the American 'godda' rubbing shoulders with his Scottish.

"In a few minutes, Rab. Twenty-five mil's a serious

3

wire."

"It's a done deal," he said, standing and tightening his already too-tight black neck-tie. Then with a subtle challenge in his tone: "If Frank was here he'd tell you the same."

Hammer's handsome, though pinched features slackened at that. "Sorry, Rab. It's been a damned shitty day for you with the funeral and all. What the hell am I thinking?"

Yeah, thought Rab, the cremation ceremony this afternoon had become but a minor scene in this ongoing horror show. He headed for the glass office door, scooping up his black mohair coat from a low calf skin sofa on the way, his heart pumping something thick.

Hammer was on his heels. "You'll have a better evening I hope," he said, his voice too jovial.

Rab glanced back at the computer's clock: 04.18. He paused in the corridor to put on his coat, feeling the laser-stares of Fedor Brunovich and his goons; the brothers Golovko, zeroing-in on the back of his head. Quite a feat given the amount of glass between them.

All the offices on the firm's three floors had clear glass walls thanks to the re-furb completed less than a month ago. The design was to affect an open and trusting work environment, it was explained from above; sixty associate attorneys, a hundred-plus paralegals and the three ruling partners out in the open where all could see one another greasing the same wheel. He had to admit that hadn't stopped himself, Frank Holt and Jeffery Hammer

4

greasing their palms after-hours under the cover of darkness.

Hammer was shaking his hand. "Great job, Rab. Your and Frank's work on Merlin's been beyond the call," he said then lowered his voice, "to which your bonus this month will attest, I assure you. I trust you're still enjoying the Porsche." All delivered with a smile full of expensive crowns and veneers.

What a pro. Once, he'd considered this man a friend. Right now, there wasn't the time for that fact to hurt him. "Shame Frank wasn't here to see it through," he said, slipping his hand out of Hammer's damp squib, "As co-signatory, I mean."

And there was that slackening thing again with his boss's face. "Yes. Poor Frank."

Rab's senses sharpened and he became aware of the smell of stale coffee and printer ink, the concussion of water against the building's high windows and the scent of his own fear. If he could just get to the elevator and out of this damned aquarium. He needed oxygen.

The large shape of something he *didn't* need eased itself from the shadow of an office doorway to block his path.

"Ah, Rabbie, pal buddy. How things?" came Karpos 'Stink Bug' Brunovich's heavily accented growl.

The Russian had a couple of years on Rab and stood a good six-three with a barrel chest, muscle going to flab under a cheap baggy suit Rab had never seen him out of. Beige, like his buzz-cut and pockmarked complexion. The crumpled jacket failed to hide much of the pink and yellow Hawaiian shirt beneath. Ouch.

It had been Becky who'd christened him 'Stink Bug.' Why that? he'd asked and she'd said, "Because they're kind of round and ugly, and harmless if you leave them be, but step on them and they stank pretty bad." He'd taken her word on it. She'd graduated *Magna cum Laude* in entomology out of Virginia Tech. But for the record, he didn't wholly go with the insect label. Her bug wisdom aside, 'Pumpkin' was closer; right down to the eyes, nose and mouth hacked out, making a Jack-o-Lantern of his head. Minus any light in the eyes.

Karpos turned those black holes on Jeffery Hammer, who winced, keeping his dental veneers in place.

"Evening, Karpos. Rab was just leaving," he said, his eyes on Rab's computer clock.

"Yeah, you done good, pal buddy. My Uncle Fedor. He very pleased of you."

Rab knew for a fact Karpos had taught himself English from a box-set of *Sopranos* DVDs.

Forcing a grin, he said too loudly, "I glad your uncle he pleased of me, I very pleased of him as well."

He always had to be the funny guy, especially when under pressure. He caught Hammer wincing again and it struck him, not for the first time, that he'd never seen his boss laugh. No one had. It was one of those things that went round the office.

He glanced back at his computer where the clock read 03.02. When he turned back, Karpos was breathing in his face. Garlic, olives, something else. No prizes for guessing

6

the guy's cultural food of choice. He wondered if there was a Tony Soprano Cookbook out there.

Wrapping a heavy arm around Rab's shoulders, Karpos steered him toward the elevator. "Hey, Rabbie. I hear your new Porsche it banged-up good in body shop."

"You crashed it?" Hammer. High-pitched.

"I give you ride in my wheels," Karpos continued, "Take you any place you wanna get."

And there they were; those last seven words. The same deadly seven he'd whispered to Frank Holt on their way to those same BMW wheels this afternoon. No one had seen or heard from Frank since.

"Mind if I take a rain check on that ride, Karp, ol' pal buddy? My NYPD counter-terror pals are waiting for me in the lobby. You know, with guns and shit?" But he didn't say that, of course.

They'd arrived at the elevator. "You want I take you see your Becky?" said Karpos, "She some hot babe with those legs. Real cupcake." If he'd had eyebrows he would've waggled them.

Rab had wasted enough time being terrified. Hadn't given a thought to how all this could impact on the woman he loved. But maybe it wasn't too late to put his masterly plan into action. Well, half a plan if you wanted to be picky about it. And strike 'masterly.' The elevator doors slid open. Karpos must've hit the call pad already.

"Uh...great, but you know what? I kinda left something in my office," and twisting out of his hold he added, "Why you not wait for me in your wheels, ol' pal buddy?"

The Russian bristled, whether at Rab's mimicry or his neat uncoupling from the cretin, he didn't give a crap. He watched him back his reluctant beige bulk into the elevator car and waited for the doors to close on his ugly pumpkin face. He hit the call pad so the elevator would return after delivering Karpos to the lobby.

Adrenalin pumping, he turned on his heel and retraced his steps, darting a black look at Hammer as he re-entered his office. The computer's clock was reading 02.04. He had just two minutes if he was going to pull this off.

The unframed canvass was propped against a low bookcase where he'd left it this afternoon. Though small, the oil painting of water lilies was a dead ringer for one of Claude Monet's Impressionist works on the same subject. This one, though, had been painted by his father, completed the day before he died. Rab snatched it up and wedged it under his arm.

Next-door, Fedor Brunovich and the Golovko brothers had their laser-eyes zeroed on Rab's monitor clock and were taking no notice of him. He returned to the door and punched a button on its swipe-lock with his free hand. A winking LED switched from green to red as the door snapped shut behind him.

He found Hammer still lingering in the hall; a shy chambermaid waiting to clean his room. The men's eyes met and locked. Then Hammer's pooled up, but Rab had no time for whatever crap he was about to get fed.

"Look. About Frank..." his boss began before Rab cut

him off.

"I made a mistake, Jeff. I told Frank you were one of the good guys. What in God's name have you done with him?"

His boss let out a long sigh. "No, *I* made the mistake," he said to Rab's chest, "and it's one I'll no doubt pay for, if that means anything." Rab strode away down the hall. Hammer called after him. "See you in the morning!"

Yeah, right.

The elevator arrived on cue. He stepped in and hit the L button. The doors closed and the car plummeted. As he fought to slow his breathing, Frank's words came back to him in a rush, spoken five days ago at a roadside picnic spot in Great Neck Village right after the crash, their Porsches parked close-by with crumpled hoods and fenders.

"Why don't we just open a chain of Laundromats, for Christ's sake?" said Frank, his hands shaking while polishing his John Lennon specs on the bottom of a sweat-sodden *Save the Planet* T-shirt. "Jesus. I talk one time to Jeffery Hammer, tell him how this launderin' shit could really come back and bite the firm in the balls. How we could still dime the mob out to the FBI. Next thing, my phone's puttin' out tweetie noises and I feel someone tuggin' on my shirt-tails everywhere I go. I'm gettin' out, Rab. What you do's up to you."

Like a lot of little guys, Frank had to talk big a lot of the time.

"They know I want out," he continued, "so, okay, I'm

9

dead, but, hey, when they find out we had this little chat, you're dead too, my friend, with bells on."

Rab had tried to lighten him up with something funny. Given he couldn't remember the crack, it probably wasn't a belly-acher.

"Hell," Frank went on, "why d'ya think Hammer didn't make himself a signatory on this? He gave you and me that honor, remember? Said it was a measure of his trust and respect. Kinda promotion. Shit, he doesn't even have the access codes to the Merlin account. Don't ya geddit? Rab, he's coverin' his bony ass!"

"Relax, Frank. One more transfer and it's bye, bye Merlin, believe me."

"Who're ya kiddin'? After that, who the hell needs us? No, my friend, it's bye, bye, you 'n' me. It's like in the movies, man; we know too much."

One word could sum-up why he hadn't listened to Frank that day. 'Greed.' Oh, and 'stupid.' Now it was too late. Becky had Frank down as a mayfly; here today, gone tomorrow. Well, Frank was certainly gone.

As the elevator car dropped past the eighth floor, his right hand dove into a pocket and came out with a palm-sized BlackBerry 83000. Propping his dad's painting against the wall, he set both his thumbs to work on the gizmo's QWERTY keyboard and trackwheel.

He thanked the advent of wireless Internet technology and the list of passwords he carried in his head for, by the time the car reached the lobby, he had remote control of his office computer via GHD's Infranet. Its screen in miniature, depicting the same Merlin wire transfer data. Same clock. Same message: AUTHORIZING - PLEASE WAIT. But what had his attention now was the hot button below that: EDIT TRANSACTION? And with the clock showing 01.03, that's exactly what he had in mind.

*

Deep Purple's '*Smoke on the Water*' thumped out of his black 7 series BMW's stereo. Tony Soprano's favourite track, Karpos Brunovich had been pleased to learn, and now the Hard Rock classic had become his favourite too.

He thumbed a control on the steering wheel, upping the volume to cover the rain pounding the vehicle's roof. He looked to the building's entrance where Rab MacBain would soon emerge. No sign yet; just pedestrians passing on the sidewalk. Diners or late workers, coated up and wielding mostly black umbrellas.

The Makarov MP 9x18mm felt warm in his lap. The pistol, an old friend from his soldiering days in Afghanistan, was obsolete as a military sidearm now due to its magazine taking only eight rounds and its relatively low stopping power. But it was still good for a hit like this, he thought. Up-close; right where he'd have the mouthy Scottish prick when the time came. *One in the stomach. One in the head.*

He was pleased Uncle Fedor had finally given him this mission. A chance to prove himself, Matvy had told him.

Lately, Matvy and Timur Golovko had taken care of this side of business, which had galled him. The Golovkos were kids. Weren't even family, just a couple of Georgian migrants scraped off the streets of Brooklyn's Brighton Beach. Tonight, he had a chance to make his uncle proud. If he didn't screw this up, maybe Uncle Fedor would speak to him again.

It'd been half a lifetime since he'd returned home from the Soviet Afghan war in disgrace. Sixteen years since his seventy-one-year-old uncle, head of the Brunovich family, had effectively disowned him. A fact that had given him more pain than the wounds that had disfigured his left thigh and lower torso.

He produced an emery board from a jacket pocket and proceeded to file his nails; an old habit that kept him calm. Shame about the Beemer's gray leather interior, he thought, but this time cleaning it up would be down to those ass-lickers, Matvy and Timur.

His job was more important this time. A job you didn't shout about. Like in the first episode of *The Sopranos,* when the babe shrink with the legs asks Tony what line he's in, and the mobster says, "Waste Management Consultant." Yeah, he thought, like that. Tony's answer had had a double meaning, of course. He'd spotted that right away.

Okay, his English wasn't the best. There were English words that often.... uh... eluded? Yeah, eluded him. Like names of stuff, but that didn't mean he was as stupid as MacBain made out. *One in the stomach. One in the head.*

Anyway, how smart was Rab MacBain? There'd been a wiretap on his home and office phones for days. Put there by a phone company contact of Timur Golovko's. And that day at the picnic area: he and Frank Holt, his midget pal with the stupid pink shades, had they really thought their cosy chat about coughing to the Feds had been all hushy hushy? Covert listening equipment could be gotten from more than one spy store in the city. It ain't that fuckin' difficult, Rabbie, pal buddy.

Smoke on the water, fire in the sky... continued the band's lyrics.

He quit sanding his nails, lost the file in a pocket and killed the music. He'd spotted MacBain out there in the rain, approaching fast. The prick was smiling and waving, something unwieldy tucked under his arm. He checked the Makarov's silencer and safety before secreting it under his left thigh, uncomfortable there due to the still tender scar tissue.

When he looked up there was no sign of MacBain. Just a crisscrossing of black umbrellas on the sidewalk. He scanned around the windows. Nothing out there in the murk. Then it hit him. MacBain hadn't been waving to him. He'd been flagging a cab! Fuck-shit! Then came the squeal of tires on slick blacktop as a yellow cab in front shot out into traffic, heading north on Madison toward East 27th.

He could just make out MacBain in the cab's rear window giving him a cutesy finger wave. His war wounds throbbed and the veins in his neck stood out. He put the

Beemer into drive, hit the wipers, then the gas. Nothing happened. Fuck-shit! He started the engine.

*

Up in his darkened office on the sixteenth floor, Jeffery Hammer had been pouring a fine *Dom Pérignon* into a pair of fluted glasses on his antique rosewood desk, noting with surprise that his hands were steady.

In just two seconds he would've been home and dry. Fedor Brunovich would've been happy with the six times twenty-five mil' transfers he'd arranged for him over the last three months, and the mob family would've been off his back. And unbeknownst to Fedor Brunovich, the dried up sack of bones, there wouldn't be a next time.

He'd stolen a glance at the old guy, sitting and staring through the glass wall, his totally bald and wrinkled head looking too small poking out the top of an over-sized Donna Karan Kashmir coat. He'd been leaning forward, chin resting on pale, sinewy hands propped up in turn by his gold-topped cane. His watery, turtle eyes locked on Rab MacBain's computer screen next-door.

In two seconds he would've started the life he'd earned; Fedor's promised ten mil' commission, squirreled into a secret account his grabby, soon to be ex-wife, Claudia would never have found. The bitch would've been so mad he'd had the last laugh... well, not 'laugh' exactly. Laughing was something he never did. Laughter betrayed a man's vulnerability; his weakness. No. Hilarity was for lesser men.

He'd taken the drinks over to where Brunovich was sitting to find the Golovko clones spitting whispers at one another on the leather sofa. The one with the mole on his forehead, Matvy? Whatever. He'd jumped up and hissed Russian into Brunovich's ear. Fedor had blinked once, and had struggled to get upright with the aid of his cane, the end of which had the hem of his coat pinned to the floor.

The old bastard had staggered forward to lean against the glass wall, misting it with his breath. Hammer had arrived at his side with the champagne, had followed Fedor's gaze... and that's where he was now; staring at Rab's computer monitor, its clock frozen at 00.02. The four men pressing against the glass; children peering through the window of a candy store that had closed for the day. Then the clock vanished altogether.

The champagne flutes left his slick fingers and shattered on the parquet floor. He stared at Rab's screen, helpless, as the characters making-up the wire's destination: BANCO CONFIANZA - GRAND CAYMAN, deleted themselves as if by magic and something else typed across the blue void in their stead. Maybe fear was blurring his vision, but he'd swear he could see Rab's ghost sitting at his computer in the dark, tap-tap-tapping out Hammer's death warrant. Rab MacBain; always the funny guy.

He left the others and dashed into the corridor. In seconds he was pushing on Rab's office door, but the damned thing wouldn't budge, an LED winking red on its swipe-lock rubbing it in deep.

*

With the cab's windshield wipers battling with the downpour, and before the taxi had even turned left into East 39th, Rab had punched a new destination for Brunovich's millions into his BlackBerry. By the time the Iranian cab driver had gotten him across 5th Avenue, he'd entered the new account number and ten digit response and confirm codes.

He was able to carry a lot in his head but these numbers he'd scribbled on the back of a restaurant check the day he met with Frank at the Great Neck picnic area. He committed them to memory now, scrunched up the paper slip and fingered it into a tear in the passenger seat.

Frank had rattled him so much at the picnic rendezvous he'd used his Grove, Hammer & Dunn creds to get a very discrete bank in Switzerland to set him up an account. He was only ever going to use it if the brown stuff hit the fan, and it was definitely doing that now. He kicked himself for the hundredth time for not doing this sooner; for thinking he was immune to the consequences of his dicing with the Devil.

He stole a look out the rear window. Karpos's Beemer was two vehicles back. He thought about giving him another cutesy wave but that would've been childish. The cretin was out to kill him, so he stuck out his tongue and flipped him the finger instead.

A few more amendments to the BlackBerry's wire intercept and the clock would reset and count down from 05.00 again. He was still working with half a plan but, assuming he got clear of Karpos, he'd soon have dough enough to disappear.

The question was, would Becky go with him? She loved him, he knew that. On the ride back from the crematorium this afternoon she'd said she'd thought about what he'd said last weekend out on the lake. About him wanting to get them both out of the city. Move out into the sticks somewhere. She'd said she'd give him her decision tonight over dinner. She'd kissed him and said she wanted them to be together.

But then she'd had no idea that would mean doing it like this; in the middle of the night in a rain storm, taking only what she could stuff into a suitcase. Had no idea they'd have to buy new identities and live like fugitives for however long it took to shake off the bad guys.

He could do that twinkly thing with his eyes and say, "Come on, it'll be fun!" if she hadn't been ten times smarter than he was.

He pictured her response to his masterly plan: "You don't have a damned clue! Buy new identities? Where, JC Penney's, for Christ's sake? And where in hell are we gonna go? You say these guys are good enough to tap your phones but so dumb they won't find us? Jesus!"

And then she'd say what was really getting to her. "You laundered money for these monsters and you didn't once ask yourself if what you were doing was wrong. I thought I knew you, Rab." The tears and anger in those hazel eyes would say the rest. Now, he supposed, the real question was, how *much* did she love him?

Damn. Did she even own a passport? Yes, he remembered; she did Europe once. He felt his coat pocket for the comfort of his British passport; plan B if they didn't sell counterfeit IDs in JC Penney's. His dad had always insisted he maintain his dual citizenship; keep his options open. He never thought he'd need to. He glanced at the painting of water lilies on the seat beside him, streetlights strobing over it. *Thanks, Dad.*

The Iranian was scowling at him in the rear-view mirror. He knew he was Iranian because the guy had told him so less than a minute into the ride. "I Iranian," he'd said, apropos of zilch, "but I for the war!" Rab hadn't been in the mood to chitty-chat and, by the way, like so many others, since the Twin Towers came down, he didn't feel totally at ease around Middle Easterners he didn't know. He felt bad about that because it spoke to the insane state of our world. A world that could take another two thousand years to fix. This guy was staring at him hard and he guessed his behavior must've seemed pretty off to the guy; all the sweating he'd been doing; his feverish obsession with his BlackBerry.

When he'd gotten in and the driver had asked him where to, he'd pushed a handful of bills through the pay slot in the Plexiglass partition and yelled, "Anywhere!" like in the movies. To which the guy had shot back, "No destination, no ride," and had shoved the cash right back at him. Which never seemed to happen to Bruce Willis. So he'd given him Hoboken, New Jersey, for the drop, where Becky's condo was. Stupid or what?

He'd have to lose the Russian before he got too near her place; give him the idea he was headed somewhere else. He'd trodden on the stink bug and the bad smell wasn't gonna go away. He knew he should call Becky and warn her of the danger, but couldn't risk screwing with the wire transaction on his BlackBerry.

He checked out the rear window to see Karpos was narrowing the gap, but if he told the cab driver to floor the gas the good citizen would probably slow right down.

At last! The clock on his phone's display had reset and was counting down from 05.00 once more. He pictured Hammer and Co. freaking-out back at the office and laughed out loud. Too loud, maybe. Evil genius loud. He had to calm down, damnit. Had to concentrate on saving himself and protecting Becky.

The Iranian was scowling in the mirror again. Probably figured his passenger for a terrorist, for Christ's sake.

As the cab hangered right onto the Lincoln Tunnel ramp, he noted that Jersey traffic was thin for the time of night. Was that good? Bad? What? When you only had half a plan, who knew? Maybe he should just stop the cab. Take the Russian assassin to a bar and sort out this whole silly mess. What's the worst that could happen? Oh, yeah, that.

He snatched a look behind to see the BMW hugging

the cab's rear fender. He thought he saw the outline of a gun emerge from the driver's window and so hunkered down.

"Excuse me? There's a hitman on our tail, so how about you put your damn foot down?"

"No can do, my friend. I good citizen!" the Iranian chirped, and Rab would swear he felt the guy's foot give a little squeeze on the brake.

*

It'd been a stupid idea, anyway, thought Karpos. Just as the cab had entered the Lincoln Tunnel, the prick had ducked out of sight. The outline of the driver's head should've been an easy target against the taillights of a gas tanker up front but, at this speed, shooting left-handed out the window would've been tricky. Besides, whacking the driver would've just totalled the cab. And with a FedEx truck bearing down on his ass he'd have gotten himself trapped. Or dead.

Tunnel smog burned the back of his throat. He stowed the Makarov, buzzed the window up and hit air recycle. He'd have to wait until the cab entered New Jersey before he made his move. His cell phone trilled on the passenger seat, Matvy Golovko's name in the display.

Fuck-shit! What was he gonna tell him? That he was screwing up as usual? but when he picked up, with the panic in Golovko's voice, he guessed the guy's evening wasn't going any better than his own. The wire transfer was going to hell, Matvy yelled in his ear, the Georgian's accent grating on his already frazzled nerves. Someone was doing some clever shit with the Internet. Remote something or other. Was it MacBain? Did he have him? Had he whacked the guy yet?

There was nothing for it, he had to come clean. No, the Scotsman had given him the slip, but he was on top of it now. The prick was in his sights. On his mother's life! He braced himself for the usual abuse, but what he got was a long silence... "On my mother's life!" he repeated just to fill it.

Matvy came back. Change of plan. Get MacBain alive and bring him back to the office. Then the ass-wipe hung-up. But not before reminding him his mother had been in the ground for ten years. A family plot, according to Fedor Brunovich, with plenty of room for her shit-for-brains son.

*

An overweight security guard lumbered as best he could along the hall to join Hammer at Rab's office door, the sweat stains on his shirt showing a map of the world over the globe of his paunch. He grappled with a thick swatch of plastic key-cards, trying them through the swipe-lock to no avail.

Hammer watched the idiot with mounting rage, not daring to look through to his own office where he was sure his Russian client was doing likewise.

Between cartoon puffs and pants the guard managed, "We ain't got these in any kinda order yet, sir. It's a new system so…"

"Just get the fucking thing open!"

He peered through the gloom as a new entry popped up on Rab MacBain's flat screen: BANK HAASE – ZUG. A Swiss account, damn it! The clock was showing 03.22. Barely three minutes to turn this nightmare around.

"Shit!" muttered the guard, and Hammer watched in horror as he fumbled the deck of key-cards like a crap magician. They hit the floor and scattered in every direction.

*

The storm had eased and the word *'dreep'* floated up from somewhere in his childhood. A steady fall of light rain. Snatches of Scottish had been coming back to Rab lately. He put it down to that last visit with his father in the nursing home. He felt bad it hadn't gone so well; felt the old man's disappointment in him. One day he'd put that right. He really would.

Three minutes to go on the BlackBerry. He kept low in his seat whilst peering out a side window. They were moving through a gentrified neighbourhood. Pastel clapboard houses, gift stores, a florist on every block, it seemed. They'd left the toll booths and the 495 West far behind and were heading south somewhere down Willow

Avenue.

The Iranian was driving faster now, spooked at last, Rab hoped, by the big, black Beemer trying to climb into his trunk.

What if Becky wouldn't go with him? he thought, suddenly. What was plan B or C or D? Going to the cops was a no go; he was guilty of laundering several millions of dollars for organized criminals. Even if he turned State's evidence, there wouldn't be a deal on God's table that'd get him no jail time.

"Here Hoboken," the cabbie shot over his shoulder, "Where now, mister?"

Good question. They were about four blocks across from Becky's condo, but there was no way he was taking this shit to her door. Call her old fashioned but she'd be expecting flowers.

He stared down at the hand holding his phone, noting the Celtic silver rope ring on its pinkie; a birthday gift from Becky last Fall. That had been a week after they'd become lovers. Five weeks since twenty-eight-year-old Becky Gordon had become his PA. Once the office affair was out, he'd waited to be hauled up in front of the partners. When that hadn't happened he'd concluded he must've been too valuable an asset for them to fire him. It was that kind of arrogance, he knew now, that had brought this nightmare upon him.

"Hey, Cabbie!"

"Huh?"

"Floor the gas! Get us as far away as you…"

"What damn thing..!" yelled the Iranian. Rab shot a look left and saw the BMW keeping pace alongside. Saw Karpos yank its steering wheel to the right; a mere toy in his huge hands. The vehicles' flanks came together hard, metal screaming on metal. The passenger side window shattered, rain stinging his eyes. The driver was yelling words in Farsi when the cab veered off the road at around 50mph and into something solid and immovable.

Rab's face hit the Plexiglas partition, the cartilage in his nose bursting in the same instant, sending him into a world of pink pain. He gulped in air only to find himself breathing gas fumes. Something bubbled in what used to be his nostrils. He coughed and spluttered, wiping blood out of his eyes.

The Iranian's still form was slumped over the wheel. His head had punched through the windshield and Rab couldn't tell if the guy was breathing. He mustered what strength he had, shouldered the door and fell out onto the sidewalk clutching his dad's painting. The BlackBerry left his free hand and skidded across the wet paving, 01.03 glowing in its display.

He retrieved the phone and pushed himself to his feet where he rocked unsteadily, trying to focus on his surroundings. He took in the cab, belching steam, concertinaed against a Victoria Secret's storefront. The store's window was miraculously intact, as were the lingerie-clad mannequins behind it; the half-naked women seemingly staring with disapproval at the Iranian's head protruding through the cab's windshield, one of its wipers impaled in the guy's right eye-socket.

Rab re-focused beyond the gore to where the crunched Beemer had come to a halt twenty yards down the street. It must've hit something on the driver's side because Stink Bug was fighting off airbags to get out through its badly buckled passenger door, yelling muffled oaths as he wrestled with it. In Russian, if Rab had to guess.

Karpos looked up and the men's eyes met through the rain; the Russian's bulging out of his pumpkin head. *If my dog was as ugly as that I'd shave its ass and make it walk backwards.*

He decided to reserve judgement on that until he'd seen his own face in a mirror: Handsome guy. Black hair and blue eyes. Oh, and look, an exploded pimento where his nose should be!

There was blood in his eyes again from a gash in his forehead, he discovered. Vehicles drove by in a neon haze without stopping. If there were people on the street or nearby he hadn't seen them. He turned to face the mouth of an alley between the lingerie store and a nondescript eatery. His pimento had gone numb along with the rest of his body and he wanted to just lie down and sleep; dream all this bad stuff away... but he had to move now or get killed. The choice was a no brainer. He headed into the alley with his oil painting, thinking how the night had turned from *dreich* to *smirr*.

*

Jeffery Hammer swung the chrome and leather chair with all his might at the office door, which exploded in a plume of splintered glass, sending millions of shards skidding across the polished floor.

They crunched like ice underfoot as he dashed to Rab's computer, its clock counting down: 00.09...00.08... He stabbed at the keyboard with a finger to make it stop. Why wouldn't the fucking thing stop? 00.04...00.03...00.02... Thumping it now with his fists... 00.01...00.00. Up popped a message: TRANSACTION COMPLETED – HAVE A NICE DAY!

He stood, transfixed in the monitor's glow as the display was replaced by a FLASH animation of a stupid looking cartoon bird. He leant closer, incredulous, as the creature repeatedly hit itself over the head with a ridiculously large hammer. "Ouch! Ouch! Ouch!" it screeched.

He could feel the coldness of Fedor Brunovich's eyes on him through the glass wall, but as the cartoon character continued to mock him, something he didn't recognise rose inside and caused his lungs to convulse. Nothing fatal, as it turned out. He was simply laughing his head off.

*

The cartoon buzzard had been a nice touch, Rab thought. A video clip Frank had emailed him in another life. The oversized hammer had been the point of it, its namesake the butt of an office joke he'd long since forgotten. He watched it playing in miniature on the BlackBerry's tiny screen and hoped Hammer was getting the message. The one that said, "fuck you".

Becky had dubbed his boss 'Firefly' for reasons he also couldn't recall. 'Glow-worm' suited him better, minus the glow.

He turned the gadget off and tried to manoeuvre it into his coat pocket. Difficult in these cramped conditions. Something cold and cloying slopped onto the back of his hand. Tomato sauce? He was using his neck-tie to staunch the gash on his forehead with his other hand. The pain in his nose had come back but was bearable, allowing him to listen out for the Russian's footfall.

He now had twenty-five million dollars stashed on the other side of the world. Which meant nothing all the while he was holed-up in this Dumpster in the pitch dark, up to his chest in the kind of yucky stuff he didn't want to think about. Meant nothing if he died in here tonight. And talk about opting for the economy casket.

His head was jammed against the Dumpster's lid, blood tasting like tannin on the back of his tongue. Even with his screwed olfactory system he could smell well enough to realize he'd picked the Dumpster owned by the nondescript eatery on the corner. Garlic? Olive oil? Definitely burnt cheese. Karpos Soprano's kind of place.

There was a lot he regretted about the last few months, but if he could've lived them over he'd have chosen

Victoria Secret's Dumpster. A heavy scraping sound from the alley stopped him breathing.

*

The empty wood crate moved easily and Karpos covered the space behind with his pocket Maglite and pistol. Nothing but rat shit and cockroaches. The Prick had to be here somewhere. The alley had a dead end so he couldn't have gotten far, he decided.

Pistol raised, he scanned around with the flashlight, thin rain squalling in its beam. There was crap everywhere he looked: sodden packing cases, broken restaurant tables, and piles of trash bags spilling their guts out onto the ground. There should be a law against it, thought the hitman.

He crept forward three paces, squinting against the rain and stopped by one of those things. Not trashcan... Dumpster!

He was doing this all too slow. The cops would get to the wrecked taxi sometime soon, finding its driver dead for sure. And the Beemer all scraped up and wrapped around that damned fire hydrant. They'd reckon its driver had fled the scene after the crash, would run its tag, but that wouldn't get them anywhere, of course. He wasn't that stupid. No. If he kept his cool he'd probably have time to finish what he'd started here.

He poked the pistol's silencer into a gap under the Dumpster's lid, got control of his breathing then flipped it up. He shone in the flashlight. Zero. Just cardboard and shit; boxes depicting women's bras and frilly sex stuff. One with a photo of a girl modelling pantyhose made his balls clench. He liked legs.

He sensed something move behind him and spun around to catch a shadow moving from behind a Dumpster opposite. It was heading for a fire-door he'd missed before, screened, as it was, by shredded packing plastic. He shot low, needing the prick alive now.

The shadow moaned and crumpled to the ground. He'd shot it through the heart, but that was okay. The guy was dead because he was shorter than Rab MacBain; a teenage vagrant. Long matted hair and rancid wind-breaker, his Maglite revealed.

That was the good news. The bad news was that there was a… whippet? A skinny gray dog on a leash, tethered to the dead loser's needle-pocked wrist. The damn thing was straining to get at him; snarling and yapping like crazy, its pointy teeth snapping just inches from his war-ravaged thigh.

Moving pictures popped into his head. Ones he didn't want to see again but which played out anyway. An Afghan mountain village six miles from the Pakistan border. The *Mujahedeen* rebel detachment had obviously been tipped-off; were long gone with their pack mules laden with munitions. Just women and children left. Low threat, the *Khad* rat informer had told them.

A weapons search of the village was ordered by the Comr'd Senior Lieutenant just the same. Karpos was first in. The greenhorn. Shiny brass buttons and AK assault rifle strapped across his chest.

The women wailed behind *burqas* and the children cried. Low threat. Except the *Khad* snitch hadn't mentioned the street dogs the villagers used as perimeter alarms. Up to twelve of the fuckers appeared out from behind rocks and over craggy ridges. A hungry pack of mange-ridden Afghan hounds coming at him fast, kicking up dust. He flipped the AK's safety but couldn't get off a shot before they were on him, tearing his flesh off in pieces.

"Police! Drop the weapon!"

He wrenched his attention from the crazed whippet's jaws to the mouth of the alley. Two NYPD uniforms were approaching, stooped with weapons drawn. Fuckshit! He killed the Maglite and dove in the direction of the curtained doorway, his three hundred pounds making short work of the fire-door behind.

The whippet got crazier and so, though totally unnecessary, he turned, raised the silenced Makarov and, *piff!* The barking ceased and he was gone before the dog hit the ground.

*

Rab pushed the lid of the Dumpster open a crack, then all the way. He clambered out with his painting and took-in what he could of the dead kid in the dark and the dog with no head. His guts loosened.

"Stay where you are, asshole, and lose the weapon!"

A female voice this time. The cops couldn't see much with the rain and no light, he guessed. He spotted the splintered fire-door and headed for it, one word screaming through his brain. *Becky!*

Chapter Two

BECKY Gordon blew out the second candle on the table laid for two. They'd been all but stumps anyway, their flames guttering and spitting red wax onto the white tablecloth. Last time she'd looked, the watch-face on her silver Gucci bracelet showed a quarter after Midnight. It seemed her dragonfly wasn't going to make it.

Her eyes sought out the cordless phone on the drinks stand across the room knowing it wasn't going to ring. She'd tried calling him at the Shark Tank over an hour ago but had been put straight through to voicemail. His cell phone had been tied-up too.

She looked to the curtainless window, vaguely noting the rain had turned to drizzle. She was past hunger. The risotto had dried-out on the hotplate in the corner, where the kitchen area's muted down-lighting presently supplied the only illumination for the open-planned condo.

She reached back and removed a Spanish style hair slide so that straight fair hair dropped past her exposed shoulders, the strands honey-colored in the low glow from the kitchen halogens.

She'd been going for romantic, obviously, which was a joke when you found yourself sitting across from an empty chair. No one to tell you how great you looked in your killer black cocktail dress and seven hundred dollar Jimmy Choo stilettos. She laughed out loud. Drinking alone was never good, her mother would say. She wrung the last of the tepid *Blue Peaks Chardonnay* from its bottle and knocked it back in one.

She put down the empty glass, dipped a manicured finger in the dregs and ran it around its rim to make it sing. She'd be sleeping alone tonight and the prospect saddened her.

There was so much she needed to say to him. Her eyes returned to the phone and she thought about trying his apartment again. Thought better of it because, after all, the words she'd rehearsed for her after dinner speech had been, still were, too important to say over the phone. Because they'd be very different from the ones she'd spoken to him four days ago, laying on the deck of a rowboat at the feet of the Catskill Mountains.

Rab had rented them a cabin on Swan Lake for the weekend. Cute and oldie-worldie with its own jetty and rowboat. She'd driven them up there. Two hours out of Manhattan, that's all. Rab's new Porsche was in for body repairs or something. He hadn't been clear about that. Secretive, in retrospect.

There'd been no sign of the promised rain and she remembered the sun warming her closed eyelids. They'd just made love, the rowboat adrift on a mirror of pine forested mountains and sky, Rab's hand feeling just right, nestled beneath her T-shirt. Her cheek slightly sticky against his bare chest. She knew he wasn't dozing because his heart was beating too fast.

She opened her eyes in time to see a pure white feather descend, see-sawing through the air, to land by his head. She searched the sky for its owner but the bird, whatever its make, was long gone. Retrieving the feather, she ran its tip down the bridge of his nose. He opened his eyes. They looked young and troubled. She grinned into them.

"A white feather," she said, "An appropriate symbol, wouldn't you say?"

"Symbolic of what?"

"Cowardice?"

"I think you'll find it's betrayal," he said, closing his eyes again.

"Uh, uh. Cowardice. I'll put money on it."

She snuggled into his neck and bit his ear. Hooked a bare leg across his midriff, where she felt a stirring against her thigh. He made a low noise in his throat and said, "It's definitely betrayal."

"It's positively, indisputably and irrefutably cowardice. Look it up, Rab."

"So what's there left to be scared of? I've already seen you shave your armpits."

"Living together," she laughed. "You're terrified I'll monopolize your bathroom and blunt your razorblades."

He took the feather from her and studied it. "It's not that…" was all he got out before her lips were on his, the tip of her tongue flicking and teasing. The kiss was long and warm, until they both opened their eyes, Rab's made bluer by the sky.

"You've always said your apartment's too big with only you in it."

"As much as I hate to disappoint," he said, dead-pan, "I'm looking after a friend's elephant for a couple of years. It likes to sleep on the bed, so my place is kinda... you know."

"No problem. Jumbo can take the couch."

He smiled then frowned one of his frowns. "Becky, I've been thinking."

"Oh God, he's been thinking," she said to keep it light, disappointed the stirring beneath her thigh had gone south.

"We can be together, sure, I want that," he said, "but why's it have to be New York?"

"What're you getting at? It's where we work. Where we live."

"Look around you, Becky, breathe it in."

She pushed up on one elbow to take a cursory glance over the edge of the boat.

"Great water. Great trees. Get to the point." Then she read his expression. "Jesus. You wanna quit the city? We had a plan, Rab!"

"Well here's the thing. It's the same plan. Just somewhere else, okay?"

"Oh, I get it, so it's the same plan except it's not *our* plan anymore. It's all yours?"

"That's right. Do you like sheep?"

"Great idea. Quit our jobs and move out into the

sticks... Sheep?"

"Diversionary tactic."

He was twinkling his eyes at her but that wasn't going to work this time. She'd *done* the sticks. *Lived* them. She'd grown up on a small cattle farm in Virginia's Shenandoah Valley. A largely agricultural region saddled between the Blue Ridge Mountains and the Alleghenies. Her parents had worked hard to pay for the college education that would get her the hell out of there. Her dad, especially, had spotted early that bib overalls, cowgirl boots and pigtails were never gonna cut it for this girl. Back then she'd wanted to be a scientist and maybe fly into Space.

On her sixteenth birthday, Dad had taken her for a breakfast of pancakes in Standing, their nearest small town. Aptly named, went the local joke, because during the Civil War it'd been one of the few places left standing after Major General H. Hunter and his Union troops had rampaged through in 1864.

Sixteenth birthday. Pancakes. John Gordon had noticed his daughter swapping flirty looks with the young guy working breakfast behind the counter. He was a kind man. He'd simply said, "Rebecca, sweetie, you ain't never noticed? There ain't no pretty girls in this town, 'cept you and your ma. The rest are just, well, plain somewhere else."

She never got to fly into Space but graduated *Magna cum Laude* in biochemistry from Virginia Tech. Her major had been entomology, a life-long passion. She'd kept black widows in jars as a kid. Pinned moths to balsa boards and displayed them alongside her Barbie dolls.

She hadn't gotten around to using that degree yet. Not too many jobs out there for entomologists starting-out except on lowly paid post-grad research projects. So she'd had to bust her butt to earn a living for six years, and to that end had switched tracks to study for the Virginia State Bar exam. She'd failed it, so paralegal work was all she was deemed equipped to handle. She'd sit the exam again the following year, she'd promised herself.

There'd been a spell in Washington DC, then New York, where she'd temped for a while. Until last Fall when she'd turned up at Grove, Hammer & Dunn to take shorthand, type and make coffee for a day or two, and had ended up getting promoted as Rab's PA and sleeping with him. Oh, and definitely in that order, by the way. It was his eyes that had won her, and she'd instantly dubbed him 'Dragonfly.' *Rhionaeschna multicolor,* the Blue-eyed Darner. Handsome. Territorial. Hunts on the wing.

Dad had a stroke and died before she reached seventeen. She hoped that wasn't the reason she'd always preferred to date older men. Rab included. Because that would be just too pathetic.

Billie, her mom, struggled with the cattle farm as long as she was able with Becky away at Tech. When it became too much, she auctioned the hundred-odd head of Black Angus and planted grapevines. The tiny population of Standing thought she was crazy, but less than ten years on, her *Blue Peaks* winery label was thriving, and Billie Gordon was doing just fine. And since she'd left home, graduated and moved to New York City, so was her daughter.

So, that day on Swan Lake, she told Rab she'd so done the sticks. That she was Personal Assistant to a handsome attorney in a respected corporate law firm in the City. A city where she liked to attend art galleries, museums, movie theatres and to shop at stores that sold more than bib overalls, bug-spray and electrified fencing. She'd 'done' Europe, for crying out loud, and now he wanted her to live with sheep?

"There doesn't have to be sheep," he said, "diversionary tactic, remember? I'll even shoot the elephant."

"Do I look like I'm laughing myself to death?"

"Hey, look, no biggie, we're just talking here..."

She pushed herself off him and stood unsteadily. "I'm done with talking, okay? I'm done with the great water and the great trees!"

"Becky, sit down! You'll turn us over!" He stood, causing the craft to rock even more.

"Sit down yourself!" And she snatched up one of the oars. Rab grabbed its blade and the two played tug o' war, the vessel rolling side to side under them. She gave the paddle a hefty yank and... spla-doosh! Rab was no longer in the boat. No sign of him in the lake either when she looked. She dropped to the deck and laughed so much it hurt, until it crossed her mind he'd been under water too long. She scanned the lake's surface. No bubbles.

She stood, filled her lungs and swallow-dived overboard, making hardly a splash. Seconds later, she resurfaced and pulled him, coughing and spluttering, into the boat. They lay there, getting their breath back, until eventually she asked, "And where were *you* the day the other boys learnt to swim?"

"Drilling peepholes into the girls' locker room."

She moved to sit astride him, took his face in her hands and smiled into it. "Look, about us moving to somewhere with great water and great trees. . ."

"No. *You* look." He kissed her, sliding his hands under her soaked T-shirt and unfastening the clasp of her bra with practiced fingers. And just as he had her breasts cupped in his palms, a cell phone rang somewhere.

"Leave it," she purred, "It'll be my mom telling you to get your filthy hands off my body." Which he did, too readily in her opinion, and retrieved the ringing BlackBerry from his neatly folded jeans. She feigned disgust. "We agreed to dump the damned phones for the weekend and you just…"

"Sorry, I told Frank he could get me in an emergency." He frowned at the display as if not recognizing the caller's ID and picked up anyway.

"MacBain."

She felt him tense-up under her but was stuck in mischief-mode.

"Why didn't you just bring your office desk? There's plenty of room back here for it."

"Shut the hell up!"

Suddenly her face was on fire. In all the time they'd been together, he'd never spoken to her that way. She thought she was going to cry then noticed he'd beaten her to it. Tears streamed down his cheeks as he asked of the phone, "Was anyone with him?"

The funeral had taken place this afternoon. Poor, poor Rab. She removed her finger from the rim of the wine glass and it stopped singing. She'd been playing it for what, a minute? Two? She thought how much she wanted to comfort him. Make him better. Maybe she just needed to be needed. No, strike that. She needed to ease his pain. She was past wondering why she loved him. What was important now was that she'd chosen to live with him. *Chosen.*

And that notion, fuelled by too much of her mother's *Blue Peaks Chardonnay*, prompted what she did next. She sought out her reflection in the large, chrome-framed mirror across the room and asked it a question she'd often asked: *What was the choice you made that brought you to this?* Her reflection looked back and, as always, gave no reply.

She was making a monumental choice now, she realized, because the words that would be so different from those she'd spoken on Swan Lake, the words too important to be spoken over the phone, were these: *"Yes Rab, I'll follow you wherever you want to go."*

The door buzzer sounded. She ran to it, tripped the latch and turned the handle. "Jesus, Rab, what is it with your damn phones?"

The door flew open with such force it smashed into her forehead and sent her reeling. The back of her skull cannoned off the wall and she welcomed the numb nothingness that followed.

*

Dawn brought with it a cold mist that hugged the ground. Way off in the distance, she could make out her dad astride his beaten-up quad bike, herding cattle into the top field. He must've spotted her sitting on the gate where she waited with his breakfast, warm and wrapped in a cloth, because he waved to her. But then the mist rose up and he disappeared behind a veil.

*

With no idea how long she'd been out, the first thing she sensed was the faint scent of garbage. And sweat. She could feel her face pressing against the pine flooring, a sea of pain lapping to and fro inside her head. Next came the vague sensation of strange hands touching her. Someone stroking her legs. Large hands caressing her calves, moving up to fondle her knees and the insides of her thighs. *Please God, no…* She needed to throw-up. She squeezed her legs tightly together and turned her head; forced herself to open her eyes. The hands went away and a hard slap stung her face.

"Rise 'n' shine, Cupcake. Where is piece of shit?"

*

While MacBain's girlfriend had been napping on the floor, Karpos, gun raised, had been through the place. There was no sign of the guy. The table had two places set so she'd been expecting him. And maybe to get laid. Did that mean she hadn't known MacBain had ripped-off the Merlin account and was gonna do a runner?

He'd staked the building from a doorway across the street for a couple of hours, but if MacBain had made it here, he could've used the rear entrance. The Golovkos had that covered now.

The prick's cab had been heading for her place. That was for sure, but he'd spotted no packed suitcases in the bedroom. No smoking airline tickets on the dresser. And Bonnie and Clyde were gonna stick around and do dinner?

It hadn't made sense. If MacBain had wanted to raid the Merlin account, as a... oh yeah, signatory, with the access codes at his fingertips, he could've done that anytime. No, it must've been last minute. If something had spooked him, the wiretaps on his phones hadn't caught it. So, yeah, last minute. And now he was running, maybe dumping the girlfriend into the bargain.

What a waste, he'd thought, stroking her legs, his balls tingling, his breaths getting shorter. What a damned waste.

When she'd opened her eyes he'd felt ashamed. Like a kid caught playing with himself in the tub. That's why he'd hit her, of course. He knew that. Maybe he should get himself a shrink to help him out with this shit. Yeah, a looker; a babe shrink like Tony Soprano's. He might think about that later, but now he had to get back to work. The girl might still know something.

He grabbed her by the front of her dress and flung her onto the sofa. Clamped a hand over her mouth before she could scream, badly smudging her lipstick.

"I out of patience," he hissed, "Where is he?"

He loosened his grip to let her speak. She was trembling and her eyes showed bewilderment.

"I... I don't know... Please don't hurt me..."

He gripped her jaw with one hand and pressed the Makarov's silencer to her temple with the other. When he flipped off the safety he felt a jolt go through her body. He got close to her ear and whispered, "Is last chance."

The room lights came on. In the same instant, even before his eyes adjusted to the brightness, he spun around to aim his weapon at the doorway.

How the hell had it come to this? Fuck-shit. It was meant to have been so damned simple. Get the prick across the river, one in the stomach, one in the head. The body gets transferred to the hearse and the Golovko ass-wipes clean up the mess. The whole thing should've been wrapped-up in under an hour. *Badda bing, badda boom!* as Tony Soprano would say. There should've been plenty of time for him to make Tony's favourite place: Holsten's ice cream parlour in Bloomfield. Great food. Great atmosphere. He'd had his heart set on a tuna melt and lemon fizz. Maybe there'd still be time. The joint was only a half hour away.

Jeffery Hammer's suit looked damp and rumpled. He was trying to appear confident. In command. Pretending he wasn't looking down the barrel of a gun. To Karpos, though, the asshole was clearly out of his depth.

The lawyer nodded to the table laid for two and said, in that superior tone that always pissed Karpos off, "He obviously didn't get here. I'll talk to her."

Karpos tossed the girl aside and flew at the lawyer, whipped him hard across the cheek with the grip of his pistol, grasped his neck-tie and dragged him out into the hall by it. A dog on a leash. He slammed him against the hall wall and held him there by the throat. Forced the gun's silencer into the roof of his mouth and hissed into his ear.

"You damn right you talk to her. Twenty-five mil'. You find. Or I find you." Releasing him, he pocketed the Makarov and headed down the hall.

*

 Hammer watched him go, gulped in air and leant heavily against the wall. He called out in a small voice, "Frank Holt. Is he dead?"

The Russian paused, thumbed a number into his cell, and went down the stairs in silence.

"But you didn't have to, damn it! I was shipping him out!"

How could he have been so stupid? All he'd had to do was keep Rab in his office for five damn minutes while the wire went through. If Becky couldn't help him find MacBain tonight he'd be going the same way as Frank Holt.

His hand went to the swelling on his cheek where he'd been pistol-whipped. His face felt hot and wet. Not with blood, he was surprised to discover, but with tears. He turned and headed for Becky's apartment, only to be frozen by the sight that met him from the doorway. Becky was standing by the window, clutching her cordless phone. Her hands were shaking badly but she managed to punch in two digits before he blurted, "What are you doing?"

"Sending out for Chinese." He didn't get it so she helped him out. "Calling the cops, you idiot!"

He made it across the room in three strides, snatched the handset from her and tossed it on the sofa where it bounced once and slid to the wood floor.

"That's out of the question," he said.

*

Karpos exited the girlfriend's building and lingered on the wet sidewalk, filing his nails with a fresh emery board. He'd have to do Holsten's ice cream parlour another night. The Golovko brothers would be here any minute with the VW van. They'd nicknamed the vehicle 'The Hearse' on account of some of the jobs they used it for. It should've done one of those jobs tonight.

There'd be no point hanging around, he reasoned. Hammer wasn't gonna get anywhere with the girl. MacBain had cut and run, trading his hot piece of ass for a Swiss bank account. Timur would set up surveillance on her and the prick's Central Park apartment anyway. Because you never knew.

He watched, unmoved, as a cop car cruised by on the otherwise deserted street. It slowed down to get a look at him. He gave the uniforms a friendly wave and the patrol cruised on by. *Assholes.*

It had stopped raining. That was good. Fuck-shit, what was he thinking? Nothing was ever gonna be 'good' again! Uncle Fedor wouldn't use him to wipe his bony backside after this. He'd blown it again. Same old, same old.

When they'd helivaced him out of the mountains to the medical aid station in Jalalabad, he'd thought his life couldn't have gotten any worse. The field surgeons had patched him up best they could before air-vacing him via Kabul to a military hospital on the outskirts of Moscow. Word reached Uncle Fedor that he'd been invalided home after only two weeks on the ground, having never once fired his weapon. Heard his war wounds were, in fact, doggie bites.

Just eighteen-years-old, he'd pissed on the Brunovich family's honor, as far as the old man was concerned, and he hadn't once visited Karpos during the five agonizing months of intensive skin-grafting.

But it wasn't so much the cause of his injuries that had

embarrassed and enraged Fedor Brunovich as the nature of the damage. Because, when those Afghan hounds had torn chunks out of his left leg and lower torso, they'd also gnawed off his penis. Once he'd reached conscription age, his uncle had expected the war to make a man of him, not a fuckin'... what was it? Oh yeah. Eunuch.

He'd dishonored the family name and had been paying for it ever since. Part of that price had been his uncle practically disowning him. Another, the taunting he'd received, and still did, by those too foolish to fear him. Matvy Golovko, for one.

He'd met many wounded veterans whilst in hospital; guys who'd lost arms or legs, and some had told how they could still feel them even though they were no longer there. Ghosts, the nurses had called them. Phantom limbs. That's the way it was with him these days. Like when he got turned on. He still felt a nice tingling in his balls and non-existent dick, though the latter tingled less and less as time went by.

He paused sanding his nails having noticed a dark smudge in the palm of his left hand. He sucked it and tasted lipstick.

A battered, tan Volkswagen van pulled up in front of him, Timur at the wheel. The dented passenger door creaked open and cigarette smoke plumed out of the vehicle. Matvy glared down at him, a lit Marlboro hanging from his mouth.

"Get in, phantom dick," he said in Russian.

Which hurt so bad inside he thought again about a

shrink. Maybe it wouldn't matter if she was ugly. A man, even. He snapped the nail-file in two, tossed the pieces and climbed into the hearse.

*

Rab had found another fire door at the rear of the lingerie store which let out onto an adjacent alley, the route Karpos had taken seconds before, he figured. There'd been no sign of the hitman but he knew where he'd be headed.

With the store's alarms wailing behind him, he'd zigzagged through back streets and alleyways in the direction of Becky's condo, the bridge of his nose hurting like hell. He'd stopped to rinse crusted blood from his face in a puddle. An extraordinary act of vanity, he'd think later, when beating Karpos to Becky's door had been all that mattered.

He'd gotten to his feet and passed-out. Had come-to hours later face-down on a stinking pile of trash. His evening was definitely taking-on a theme. He hoped he'd laugh about that one day.

On the move again, he'd gotten himself lost in a labyrinth behind houses and stores, losing more valuable time. There'd been a couple of messages from Becky on his BlackBerry and he'd tried calling her on the hoof, but had gotten no signal. He was doing everything wrong and he hated himself for it. He'd always trusted himself to improvise under pressure. To hunt on the wing, as Becky would say, but not tonight. Tonight, he was totally screwing up.

He'd eventually found himself in the dead end of a narrow alley and by sheer chance had recognised the logos on a vac-pack of take-out cartons by a rear door. They'd all been printed with the name, *'Beanies'*, and he realized he was behind the vegetarian restaurant situated right across from Becky's building.

Warning her was all he could do now so he put down his dad's painting, jumped up and grabbed the bottom rung of a rusted fire escape. His weight brought the spring-loaded section screeching down. He clambered up the iron steps, searching for a phone signal as he went. He got one four storeys up as he made the flat roof.

He dialled. Her line was in use. When he reached the front edge of the roof, and looked down across the street to her second storey apartment, he understood why. She was standing at the window, phone in hand, and he prayed if the Russian had gotten to her she was calling 911, because he was too far away to be a movie hero.

Movement caught his attention down at the building's entrance. Stink Bug appeared and strolled out onto the street, doing that effeminate thing he did with his nails. Difficult to tell from this distance, but he seemed calm. Too leisurely. Things weren't adding up. Why the hell was he leaving?

He looked back to the window but Becky had moved back into the room. He dialled again. Her line was still busy and his brain wanted to burst. There was no point calling her cell. She always switched it off at home.

He thought about trying it anyway when a cop car appeared in the street below. Perhaps she'd called them after all, thank Christ, but then the Russian gave the uniforms a wave and the patrol drove on by.

A van arrived and pulled-up at the kerb. Orange. Brown. Could've been either in the sulphur street lighting. Whatever, Karpos got in and the vehicle sped away.

He checked Becky's window again. There was a man standing in it, looking out. He was holding a bottle of something and a glass. Ramrod back. Raised chin. There was no mistaking the posture. What the fuck was Jeffery Hammer doing in his girlfriend's apartment?

Of course, he realized, calming himself, Hammer had turned up to play good cop to Karpos's bad cop. Using his lizard charm to pry from Becky anything she might know, which would be zilch. But was she still in danger? He struggled to think it through but his head was a mess. Concussion from the car crash? And something was distracting him. A sound. The sound of pigeons cooing. Then he spotted them.

The makeshift coop had been just feet from where he'd been crouched the whole time. Sometimes people did that in the city when they had no back yard. The roof scene in 'On the Waterfront' came to him. Why couldn't life be like a movie, he thought, where getting killed just meant you knocked-off early for lunch?

Looking closer at the birds, he saw they weren't pigeons

after all; but white doves. About a dozen of them, all fluffed-up against the damp night. Clumps of feathers poked through the wire at the bottom of the coop and he teased out a tail feather. Something about it nagged at him until he remembered the day with Becky on Swan Lake. The last time they'd made love, and the phone call that had inflicted a pain he knew would never leave him. But enough. He was getting side-tracked. He had to concentrate. *Becky. Hammer.*

He looked down to her apartment and experienced a new kind of pain. Not numb and enduring like the phone call had brought him, but sharp, like the stab of a knife. Because the only woman he'd ever loved was framed in her apartment window with Jeffery Hammer, and they were embracing and kissing deeply.

He wanted to yell at them to stop, but the pain wouldn't let go of his voice. His vision blurred as Hammer's hand moved to caress Becky's breast through her dress.

It was no trick of the light. No waking dream. Everything he'd trusted as real in his life; all he had treasured, just slipped away, his world rendered meaningless in an instant by a kiss.

The present shut-down, his mind sending him to a safer place. Just five days ago, where he'd felt uncomfortable sitting in the long grass wearing a suit.

*

Why he hadn't changed out of it after that morning's meeting he had no idea. He'd meant this visit to be short, that was it.

He observed Charlie Whistler on a low canvass stool by the lily pond, engrossed in his work. Applying the last delicate touches, master strokes, to the pastel colored painting on his easel. Rab was confident most would never tell it from an original by the French Impressionist, Claude Monet.

"I can't stay long, Dad. You know how it is."

Charlie adjusted his paint-smeared Yankees cap, leant down and turned up the volume on his transistor radio. Not so much to hear the commentary on his team versus the Boston Red Sox, Rab guessed, as to tune him out. The Yankees were batting and the bases were loaded. Spectators were going wild. He'd never gotten into the game.

He studied the sixty-two-year-old for a while, surrounded by the trappings of his craft. That's craft, not art, because Charlie had never considered himself an artist. What he relished most was the challenge of producing works that could fool experts. Their subject matter had never been important to him.

The sports commentator went crazy. Someone had hit a homer and cleared the bases. Rodriguez? Charlie chuckled and slapped his leg with the same hand that held his paintbrush. Light-blue splashed down his bathrobe, adding to his coat of many colors. Something else to piss off the nurses, thought Rab. They'd already stopped him painting in his room because he'd stunk the place up with turpentine.

What had made his old man clam-up this time had been the sight of Rab's new Porsche. He didn't want to hear how his son made his dough these days. Well, if Charlie wanted to be childish, then fine.

"You were proud enough when I made law school," he pitched up over the radio, and Charlie surprised him with a response.

"Sure I was. But you'd've made a better painter if you'd stuck at it. It ain't too late, by the way."

Charlie had made an effort to lose his Scottish accent over time and had succeeded. Like everything else about his past, including his real name, Fergus MacBain. His dad was an American now.

"You know I don't get time to paint," said Rab.

Charlie ran his brush hand through his Einstein hair under the faded baseball cap, leaving a pastel-blue streak. "Just time enough to suck up to the bully-boys your firm has as its clients!" The corporate world had always been a matter of contention between them. His dad, once a fisherman on a remote Scottish island, had come from poor beginnings.

"Sometimes you have to sleep with the enemy," he heard himself say.

"And ya think that don't make ya one of 'em?"

Rab was grateful Charlie was lucid for a change, but he'd had enough of the same old crap.

"Hey, this place doesn't come cheap, by the way."

Charlie turned up the ballgame a notch and went back to his water lilies. At only sixty-two his dad's features, once the mirror of his own, appeared drained. The man himself somehow diminished. He could see anger in his old man but no fight.

Rab snatched up a handful of grass and grappled with Charlie's disappointment in him. Then looked up beyond the pond where an old woman in a nightgown and cardigan was playing Frisbee with a male nurse among the trees; the three cedars that gave the modern, purpose-built care home its name. The woman was shrieking with laughter and could've been mistaken for a teenager at this distance.

For this latest Monet, he noticed, Charlie was using store-bought oils. No longer having access to his laboratory; the Brooklyn basement apartment where he'd once made his own pigments by grinding minerals and colored clays. Cooked up resins and plant matter, pastes and gums. Where he'd collected and concocted the base materials essential to the art forger's alchemy.

The radio announced another big hit from the Yankees. The ball was leaving the field.

"Did ya see it, Rabbie?" Charlie blurted, looking skyward, "Did ya see the blue-tailed falcon? Just swooped down and… where'd it go?"

Rab knew where this was headed. They'd followed this script countless times in the months since Charlie's dementia had worsened.

"They don't exist, Dad. I told you, not with blue tails.

We checked in all the books, remember?"

"I know what I saw."

"You imagined it, for Christ's sake!"

Why couldn't he just go along with the old guy? Charlie turned to page two in the script.

"Me and ya mom knew where to find 'em. A pair of blue-tailed peregrine falcons. First saw 'em on the island summer of nineteen fifty… shit, I dunno. We were the only ones knew where they nested, mind. It was our secret!"

Rab felt queasy lately at the mention of his mother.

"We must've been thirteen, fourteen-years-old," Charlie was saying, eyes twinkling, "Miss her these days. Even miss that damned island, can ya believe that?"

"We shouldn't have left her."

His dad ignored that. Instead, he swivelled on his stool to face him. "You think I'm losin' it, don't ya? The blue-tailed falcons. Well let me tell you somethin', mister. It ain't *me* frickin' lies to himself. Look at the scum ya work for!"

The commentator went crazy again along with the crowd and Rab was close to dumping the damn radio in the pond.

"You're the last person to lecture me on lying, old man."

"Christ sakes!"

"I wasn't even ten-years-old."

"Bringin' you here was the best thing I ever did for ya."

"A vacation, you said."

55

"So ya got home-sick for your mom. Get over it!"

"You said she was dead. No point going home."

"Change the frickin' record."

"You never even let me say good-bye. How evil is that?"

"She didn't wanna come! There was nothin' left for us on that fucked-up rock in the sea! The fishin' was dead, how many times? I brought ya up good, didn't I? Look at ya! You're a swanky lawyer with a fancy sports car! What's your problem for cryin' out loud?"

Okay, he'd always known his dad was a fraud. Everything about the guy was fake, right down to his name, but he'd grown-up loving those quirks and eccentricities. They'd made his dad different.

Until a year ago, around the time he'd started dating Becky, when the dementia first kicked in. Doctors had been optimistic, though. Charlie had responded well to drugs, they'd said, and future 'episodes' aside, he had every chance of living to a ripe old age. Nevertheless, he'd come out with plenty of weird stuff back then and one thing he'd said had shaken Rab to the core.

At first, he thought it was Charlie's memory screwing up; part of the disease, but then, in a moment of lucidity, his dad told him his mom *hadn't* died back in 1983. The old man had lied to stop him pining for her.

More than twenty years on and he had no idea whether his mother was still alive or what family, if any, remained on the island. For the first time, he was ashamed of his father, but what he hated more than the old man's wicked deceit, was that he hadn't tried to find out himself. Another day, he'd been saying for too long. He'd find Clair MacBain another day. The woman who'd sung to him in Gaelic when he was small.

He looked at his dad, wrapped in his paint-smeared bathrobe, streaks of color through his hair and across his face, and saw a worn-out clown in a baseball cap.

"You chose to fake your life, old man. Why'd you have to fake mine?"

Charlie got back to his painting and said in a voice barely audible, "You're right. Should've left ya behind."

The ballgame must have ended because the commentator had shut-up at last. Neither father nor son had caught the score.

Chapter Three

RAB sped away down Three Cedars' drive too fast, hating himself for hating his dad. Trying to summon the good times; when he'd been proud to be The Alchemist's apprentice.

At age fourteen, one of his jobs had been to crawl around under antique furniture, secretly collecting the 'tells' while Charlie kept auctioneers, dealers in European antiquities, and the like, talking in side rooms. On his back in the dust, scraping centuries-old debris and fibres from crevices and wood joints into little brown envelopes with his penknife. Sometimes easing rusted screws and tacks from furniture whose age might've corresponded with whichever fake Charlie had waiting on his easel.

Then there was the fun they'd had in the Brooklyn basement; studying his findings under a microscope, picking out the foreign dirt particles and possible plant pollens. Boning-up from library books and dusty magazines.

They'd mix these tells into Charlie's pigments and varnishes or tuck them into cracks between a canvass and its stretcher. The latter held together with Rab's rusty screws and tacks.

He remembered his dad's patience when teaching him to draw and paint; the manipulation of light and shade and the tricks of perspective. Spending quality time with his son after a gruelling day mixing inks at the printing factory where he worked.

Rab realized he was driving too fast toward the high iron gates at the end of the drive and, as they opened automatically, a blood-red Porsche swerve through them, fishtailing and throwing up gravel. He hit the brake too late and the vehicles collided head-on. *Shit!*

He got out in a fury. The other driver was out too. Jeans, T-shirt and John Lennon shades. The little guy was shaking.

"Frank?"

"It's Friday, right? Knew you'd be here, man."

Rab surveyed the mangled fender on his brand new Porsche 911 Turbo Coupe. "Remind me to take a cab on Fridays."

*

The picnic area was on the edge of Great Neck's District Park, where he'd brought Charlie to watch baseball on occasion. Now he studied his friend and colleague across an oak bench-table.

Frank finished polishing his specs on the bottom of his *'Save the Planet'* T-shirt, then put them on. He hadn't stopped shaking.

"I don't have to be Jim Rockford to know when I'm

being followed, Rab," he said, his eyes flicking once more to a patch of dense woodland to his left.

"Come on, Frank, that mafia crap's *so* last year. Like your T-shirt."

"Last year's still with us, man. Believe it."

"I take it you weren't impressed with our bonuses this month," he said, nodding to their coupes at the roadside, their fenders crumpled-up like candy wrappers.

"You ain't makin' me proud of you, man."

Rab pictured a clown painting water lilies. "It's a character flaw. I'm working on it."

Then Frank gave him the speech about phone-taps and 'dropping a dime' to the FBI that had forced Rab to take a reality check. Made him realize maybe he was up to his neck in something that could get him killed. He'd just been bowling along, trusting Jeffery Hammer had known what he was doing and if anything was going to blow up in anyone's face it would be his boss's.

Later, Frank got into his vehicle and fired it up. Rab leaned down to the open window.

"Look, talk to Jeff again," he said, "he's one of the good guys, I promise."

"I dunno, Rab. He was the only one I spoke to about this shit. Now look at me. I'm goin' crazy here. I'm dead, Rab, I know it."

"Look, me and Becky are up in the Catskills for the weekend. You need to talk, just buzz me, okay? Use a callbox if you have to."

"Sure."

"And Frank. How're you gonna save the planet driving a Porsche 911 Turbo?"

As his friend hit the gas and sped away, he found himself staring into the patch of forest Frank hadn't been able to tear his eyes from. The little guy's paranoia didn't mean he hadn't been right about there being a tail on him.

That's when Rab first thought about the insurance of a Swiss bank account. About preparing Becky for pulling up and starting over somewhere remote. And something else. How young his mother must've been last time he'd seen her.

Next day, the worst phone call of his life would find him on a lake at the feet of the Catskill Mountains.

*

As the wood casket descended on its elevator platform to the strains of Art Garfunkel's *Bright Eyes*, Rab wondered who in God's name had chosen that. Meanwhile, a priest he'd never seen before assured the small congregation that the deceased had gone to a far, far better place.

He closed his eyes and let the stranger's second-hand eulogy, the taped music, everything out there, become distant to him. All but the lifeline that was Becky's hand holding his.

Afterwards, while the funeral party huddled by the crematorium's side exit in subdued conversation, he broke away to stroll along the short line of floral tributes, all with message cards telling him the same thing in different ways: "*The guy's dead. Get used to it.*"

He came to one which looked out of place among the otherwise tasteful arrangements. A wreath made from gaudy red, white and blue synthetic fabric. He'd seen them selling half price in Kmart. He knelt to search the message for its author.

"Look, man, I uh…" Rab stood to face the speaker. "I never knew your pop but I came to, you know."

"It's okay Frank. Thanks for coming."

Frank removed his specs and proceeded to clean them on the bottom of his black neck-tie. Becky had apparently informed Jeff of his dad's death, which explained the presence today of a few of his closer colleagues. It was just like her to muster support for him like that. An act of love he didn't deserve given he'd blatantly lied to her about Charlie. The only person in the firm he'd confided in about him had been Frank.

When he and Becky had started dating, she'd been keen to learn about his family, and it had been easier to make something up. Their relationship was in its infancy. Telling how his dad had robbed him of his mother's love as surely as if he'd killed her hardly made for romantic dinner conversation.

And then the call had come on Swan Lake and he'd found himself owing to his father living in a nursing home on Long Island. Becky hadn't understood why he'd needed to lie about it but, given his obvious distress and fragility, hadn't pushed it. He'd promised her he'd explain another time. And he would, tonight, over dinner at her place. Explain how his dad had been a fake his whole life and how he was terrified he was taking after him. Jesus. Lying to the woman he loved was a case in point, wasn't it?

"And sorry about the other day," Frank went on, "I just kinda, you know, flipped. You get ya wheels fixed?"

"It's in the shop."

"Mine too."

"I've been trying to call you, Frank."

His friend smiled, replacing his glasses. "I talked to Jeff again like you said and he's shipping me out. Satellite office; off-shore maybe. Don't know where yet but, hey, it's a done deal. No more trips to the Laundromat, know what I'm sayin'?"

Jeffery Hammer and Stink Bug ambushed them out of nowhere, which was pretty clever given there wasn't a tree or shrub in miles. Their smiles were too wide for a funeral.

"Rab. How're you holding up?" came Hammer's stunningly original line.

"I'm fine, Jeff. Really." Which was all it deserved.

Karpos had a fat arm around Frank's shoulders, and was steering him away.

"Hey, Frankie, pal buddy, how go it with you?"

Frankie pal buddy didn't look happy. Rab felt Hammer's fatherly hand on his arm, squeezing too hard.

"Anything. Just shout, you know that, right?"

But Rab's eyes were on the Russian leading Frank to his black BMW and, even at this distance, heard him say, "I hear your wheels banged up good, my friend. I give you ride in mine."

"Uh, it's okay, I can get a cab," Frank insisted.

Rab strained to hear as Karpos spoke close to Frank's ear. "Take you any place you wanna get." Those deadly seven words. Frank's speech after the crash came back to him in a rush: *They know I want out so okay, I'm dead. But when they find out we had this cosy little chat, you're dead too, my friend, with bells on.*

Rab had become detached again; like he was at the controls of a heavy truck where he could see out the windshield but couldn't steer the wheel. He was aware of Hammer speaking but the words were distant: "...know Frank has expressed reservations recently, regarding Merlin, but..."

He tuned-out his boss completely when he spotted Becky by the chapel's exit, chatting to one of Charlie's old poker pals. She looked radiant in a small black hat and veil and he found himself smiling for the first time in days. Four, to be exact, since the call out on the lake.

Charlie's doctor: The Alchemist had finally succumbed to the effects of long-term exposure to the poisons of his craft. Lead and mercury had been essential ingredients for a number of his precious pigments, Rab knew, and the neurologist believed, a contributing factor in the cause of Charlie's dementia. Finally, a growing lack of oxygen to the brain had triggered a massive seizure in his sleep.

Whatever the technical terminology, in the end it's death that kills you.

Hammer's lips were still moving and he'd become angry for some reason: "...and your snout's in the trough as deep as the rest of us. The last twenty-five mil. Tonight. Be there!" He gave Rab a wide smile before swanning off in Becky's direction.

"How long've you been tapping my phone, Jeff?" he called after him, but his boss kept moving.

Rab knelt again to read the message card on the synthetic wreath: *'You always knew when to do the right thing.'* No signature.

He didn't get it for a moment... then shot upright, scanning the faces around him. Finally, he stared toward the road. There was no sign of Stink Bug's BMW. A black stretch Lincoln had parked in its place. Its rear window buzzed down. Fedor Brunovich raised his gold-topped cane in salute and bowed respectfully. The tinted window buzzed closed and the vehicle glided away.

He felt someone tugging his elbow and looked into a familiar face, but with so much blood pumping to his head he couldn't place it. The kindly black woman was smiling and pressing something into his hands. Her mouth was moving but he still couldn't hear the words. Then she was gone before he remembered who she'd been. Miss Gloria Hails, the superintendent at the Three Cedars nursing home. He looked down at the things she'd given him. One hand held a dog-eared paperback: *'The Pocket Book of Baseball Heroes.'* And in the other,

Charlie's paint-smeared Yankees cap.

The hurt finally rose up and he wept for his dad. Wept, too, because forgiving his old man wouldn't bring him back.

*

These were different tears now, by the dove coop on the roof, where he watched Becky kissing Hammer in her apartment window. He could feel the baseball cap and book pressing against his chest, in the same coat pocket as his passport. The object he had clasped in his fingers now was a pure, white tail feather.

*

An hour later found him at her door. He placed his key in the lock, turned it and slipped into the apartment.

The place was low-lit, sickly sepia, courtesy of streetlights and the naked window. The effect did nothing to help his fragile hold on reality. He was trapped on the ocean floor in a sepia-tinted movie where his character was past the point of drowning, his lungs breathing heavy liquid slowly in, then slowly out. *Why* had he never learned to swim? Even underwater, he could smell something bad. A Dumpster smell, and figured it was coming from him.

He took-in the candle stumps on the table. The empty wine bottle, pondered the two place settings. The still-life meant something but he couldn't recall what. Couldn't even remember what he was doing here.

He scanned the room until his eyes fell upon the sofa, ten feet away. It faced Becky's bedroom so he could only see the back of it. A man's clothes had been neatly folded and placed on its headrest. He recognised Hammer's neck-tie. The one with light stripes, not the black silk one he'd worn at the funeral that afternoon. He recalled him heading to talk to Becky afterwards. Had the bastard kissed her on the cheek or the lips?

And with a jolt he remembered why he'd come. Beyond the sofa, the bedroom door was open halfway. He could make out Becky's bare leg, hooked over the comforter. Something she didn't know she did, her thigh tinted green by the time-display on her clock-radio: 03.12. She was sleeping on her usual side of the bed. The half-open door obscured his side of it. *My side.*

He took an unsteady step toward the bedroom… and froze, because if he allowed himself to complete the picture he might truly lose his mind. He breathed-in heavy liquid. Slowly breathed it out. He was treading water, trying to make sense of everything. If Becky had been screwing Hammer all along, did that mean she'd known about the money laundering?

He'd never told her about it, of course. Only that Merlin Holdings was in deep shit with the IRS and the Russians were paying the firm top dollar to iron things out. Which was partly true.

Once, when she'd found the presence of Karpos and

the Golovko goons unsettling in the office, he'd explained that the client, Fedor Brunovich, was paranoid about personal security. Felt better having muscle around. Which was certainly true. Forget about them, he'd told her. Not her problem. He'd kept her away from Merlin; getting her to concentrate on his more *bona fide* clients.

So now the twenty-five million dollar question: If she'd been expecting him for dinner tonight, why was Jeffery Hammer in her bed? Because she *hadn't* been expecting him for dinner? Because dead men don't eat? He almost laughed and had to clap a hand to his mouth, which sent a jolt of pain through his broken nose. Blood came away on his fingers.

Answers to the above would have to wait until he was out of this nightmare and on dry land. He had no idea where that would be yet, just that he'd never see his Central Park apartment again. Today had become a day for goodbyes. Just one more to go.

He caught movement in the bed. Becky's leg shifted and disappeared under the bedclothes. A muted police siren approached and receded a couple of blocks away. He considered why he'd risked coming here. Thought maybe what he had in mind was stupid; childish. Yeah, he decided. It was both. *But you know what? Fuck it.*

*

Something woke her. A familiar sound. Her head felt heavy on the pillow, damp from her tears. The back of her skull still throbbed from its collision with the wall. Something cold might ease it, she thought, and remembered she had a pack of frozen peas in the icebox. She slid her feet to the floor and sat upright. When she turned on the bedside lamp she found her reflection studying her in the dresser mirror. *What was the choice you made that brought you to this?*

When Jeff had snatched the phone from her and thrown it across the room she'd flinched, expecting him to hit her, but he'd taken her hand and led her to the sofa where they perched on its edge. The guy had been trembling, she recalled, a sign he was in shock. Whatever, she'd held on to his hand because she'd needed to.

He'd been crying and that had struck her as odd. He'd never been one to show his emotions. Then she recalled the other odd thing he'd done that day. He'd cracked a joke!

After the funeral, he'd walked up and surprised her with a kiss on the cheek.

"Becky, you've been working for Rab for what, almost a year?" He beamed with perfect teeth. "How do you *stand* it?"

"That's easy. I answer his phone, type his letters and get to spy on him every day."

"And that's enough for you? Career-wise, I mean."

His gaze had become intense and she'd looked away. "Uh... how's the lovely Mrs. Hammer? Well, I hope."

"Suing for divorce."

"Oh, Jeff, I'm sorry..."

"It's okay. Really. I just thank God it wasn't her golf coach she ran off with. He's my coach too!" The joke.

Holding her hand on the sofa, he'd explained why she couldn't call the cops. The reason Stink Bug had been so 'brusque' with her was because the asshole had suspected her of being an accomplice in a crime. Someone in the firm had embezzled a huge sum from Merlin Holdings, a reputable import/export business.

He'd explained how GHD had been embarrassed by the theft and had opted to keep the knowledge in-house. Standard practice in such cases, apparently. Bad for business, she had to understand. Then his eyes had met hers with a burning intensity and she felt the bomb drop at last.

"No. Not Rab!"

The lawyer had gone straight to the drinks stand and poured himself a large Jack Daniels, then moved to the window and gazed out.

"I was *there*, Becky, I saw it. Squirreled twenty-five mil' into a Swiss bank account right under our fucking noses." He knocked-back the contents of his glass and refilled it. "Becky, please... if he contacts you in any way... Please, you must..."

"Rab wouldn't do this." Then more to herself, "We had a plan, Jeff."

"Looks like the bastard had one of his own."

It had finally become too much. She'd clutched her bruised head and screwed her eyes shut. A sob had come. Followed by another. She rewound and replayed Rab's behaviour lately: his sudden need to get out of the city. The lies he'd told about his father. He'd always made out his dad was a successful painter living in Los Angeles and hadn't seen him in years. A family rift it hurt to speak about.

Then after the phone call on Swan Lake he'd let the truth flood out. His father had just died in a nursing home on Long Island. He'd been too ashamed of the guy to let her meet him. Something about his dad being a fake and fearing he was turning into one too.

Had he done what Jeff was saying? Had he really upped and left her for all those millions? Their relationship; had he faked that? She wondered if she'd ever really known him.

A new wave of distress had overtaken her and she'd risen involuntarily from the sofa to find herself in Jeff's arms at the window. All she'd needed was to be held, and she somehow knew Jeff needed that too. As she wept on his shoulder, she felt him trembling, his face buried in her hair.

The guy had been just as shaken as her by the night's violence. She'd stopped crying when Jeff began kissing the tears from her cheeks. Something her dad used to do and which had never failed to make her feel safe and loved. Then his lips had found her mouth, which hadn't felt right. She'd wanted to pull away but had been torn. To've done so would've left her vulnerable and scared again. So she responded and lost herself in a luscious fantasy, where Jeff had become Rab, her beautiful dragonfly. And that had made everything okay; kissing him hungrily on the deck of a rowboat adrift on a mirror of mountains and sky.

They'd moved as one from the window when reality slapped her harder than Karpos had done.

"No," she'd said, breaking free.

"Becky…"

She'd already made the other side of the room. "I'm sorry," she'd told him through more tears, "It was my fault."

He'd reached for the bottle of JD again and had taken a pull from its neck, gulping it down like water.

"But you'll stay?" she almost whispered. He looked back with red-rimmed eyes, read her fear and nodded assent.

So now, with still no answer from her reflection in the dresser mirror, she rose and moved unsteadily to the bedroom door, needing to stop the pounding in her head with something cold.

There was that sound again. The one that had woken her. A faint beeping from somewhere.

She took a pack of frozen peas from the icebox, causing light from the refrigerator to wash over the sofa where Jeff slept beneath a blanket, his clothes laying neatly folded on the sofa back. She was grateful he'd stayed in case Stink Bug had come back. Grateful, too, he'd remained the whole time on the sofa and not tried to join her in the bedroom. Perhaps she'd been wrong about the law firm's senior partner.

She hadn't worked a week at GHD before she'd christened him, *Lampyroidia Lucifer*. A species of firefly found only on Cyprus, and it had struck her from the get-go the guy was mostly show. He glowed to attract potential mates and allies and to maybe warn would-be predators to stay clear of his unappetizing taste. She suddenly felt bad all over again for letting things get out of hand earlier.

She pressed the pack of peas to the swelling at the back of her skull and relished its coldness, then noticed her cordless phone tucked under the sofa next to Jeff's spent liquor bottle. Its little green indicator light was winking, telling her the phone was off the hook. *That's* where the muted beeping had been coming from!

Panic took a hold. Her number had been unavailable since Jeff tossed the phone there earlier. She discarded the frozen pack on the drainer and crept toward the winking light, not wanting to wake the lawyer. What if Rab had tried to call her? She knew in her heart he couldn't be responsible for the hell she'd been through. He'd tell her so. Her lover would reassure her and want to take the pain away. All she had to do was talk to him.

She snatched up the handset and speed-dialled his cell… then almost let out a scream when a phone rang in the room! She recognised the ring-tone. It was the theme from 'The Third Man.' Oh, Rab. Ever the movie buff.

Jeff stirred on the sofa but remained asleep as the ringing continued. Her eyes and ears traced its source to the dining table where she could see the BlackBerry's display aglow. She hit 'END CALL' on her handset and the ringing ceased.

"Rab!" she whispered, scanning the apartment, but there was no response. It seemed there was only one place he could be hiding. The bathroom door creaked as she pushed it open.

"Rab!" she whispered into the near-darkness. She flicked the switch outside the bathroom door, flooding the tiny room with bright halogens. There was no one there but her reflection in the bathroom mirror. No time for a question or an answer that wouldn't come, because something was missing here.

It came to her at once. His toothbrush was gone from the glass on the shelf! So were his blades and spare razor! And, oh God... there were spatters of blood in the wash basin. She backed out of there, shaking, and was hit by a familiar scent. One she'd smelt a few hours ago. Garbage. The stench was stronger than before and a jolt of fear went through her at the thought Karpos could be concealed somewhere near.

"Jeff!" she screamed, "Jeff!"

No good. The guy was out for the count. She had to calm herself. She'd already looked everywhere someone could hide in the apartment. There really was no one here but herself and the lawyer.

She slowed her breathing and returned to the dining table; to Rab's BlackBerry, propped against a candle holder, its display no longer aglow. On closer inspection, squinting hard, she could make out a missed caller ID:

BECKY - HOME.

Then she spotted the other two objects Rab had left besides the discarded phone and fought the violent urge to vomit. Not because he'd also left the spare key to her condo, but because she remembered lying with him in a rowboat on Swan Lake, and what had symbolized 'betrayal' to his mistaken mind. She plucked up the white feather from the table cloth, and the whole of her world caved-in.

Chapter Four

GRAHAME Warrick had warned him the islanders might not welcome him with open arms. Small communities held long memories, he'd admonished. They might wonder why it had taken so long for a son to do right by his mother.

He and Gray had been friends in law school, had shared a frat house and later roomed together for a time in Manhattan. Though balding early and being on the podgy side, he'd always managed to date fantastically beautiful women. And the reason for his success, Rab knew, was his innate, unerring honesty. A trait that had also served him well as a lawyer, fast-tracking him to the top of a profession often renowned for its cynicism, double-dealing and shady politics. Rab wished *he'd* stayed as clean.

Criminal law had been Gray's thing back then and it hadn't taken him long to secure a desk in the Prosecutor's Office. Now he lived in Canada where he held an exulted position as one of Ottawa's Assistant Crown Attorneys. He was married to ex-beauty queen, Carmel and father to toddlers, Tod and Chelsea. In short, the guy had a perfect life and could do without the kind of shit Rab had turned up reeking of.

"You're putting me in a bad position here, ol' beer-buddy," he'd told Rab quietly, taking him by the arm and leading him out of the Irish bar in the heart of Ottawa's city center.

It was around nine at night and the place had been buzzing with lawyer types and journos. Gray flagged a cab which dropped them at a Dunkin' Donuts eight blocks away, where he'd ordered coffees and a plate of Boston Creams. Rab had made a huge deal of paying for them.

"Consider it a bribe," he'd joked, but Grahame hadn't laughed.

Business had looked slow in the place. Just a few dating pairs; college kids on stools at the counter and a couple of hookers at a front table by the steamed-up window. They'd both worn tiny leather skirts above fish-nets. The younger of the two's had been laddered badly at the knees and her cheeks had been streaked with mascara. Her friend had been holding her hand.

Gray slurped some coffee and dabbed his mouth with a napkin. He'd looked bigger, balder and rounder than Rab remembered. He'd picked up where he'd left-off in the bar; spilling his guts about Becky's affair with his boss and the Russian mob out for his blood. He'd told his honest friend everything. Except the bit about the embezzled twenty-five mil' tucked away in Switzerland. Gray wouldn't't've liked the sound of that. Instead, he'd strung him a tale where he was Tom Cruise starring in *The Firm*, drowning in a sea of corporate corruption and in too deep to be rescued.

He'd left-out the dead Iranian cabbie too, and the murdered kid in the alley, keeping to hitmen wielding guns, phone-taps and Slavic eyes being everywhere.

The Assistant Crown Attorney had then gone through the script Rab had expected of him. About Rab's duty to help New York's FBI bring down Fedor Brunovich and maybe a couple of his big-name associates. He still knew people in The Apple, he'd said, who could get Rab into witness protection. All of which Rab had argued against as the six beers he'd downed earlier had begun to take their toll.

He'd become maudlin then, and found himself talking about Charlie's death, and how he intended to find his mother after near on twenty-five years. Prodigal son and all that. That's when Gray said the stuff about small communities having long memories. Said Rab should leave the past be and move on.

But Rab could only see his problem one way. He was bound for the Isle of Garg, no getting away from that, and to get there he needed to create a new identity. Obtain a phoney passport, driver's licence, anything to help put himself out of Fedor Brunovich's reach. His British passport had gotten him this far but he couldn't risk leaving a trail with his real name to the Scottish Isles.

His frat brother knew the criminal underbelly of this city. All he'd asked of him had been a nudge in the right direction.

"I've already told you what you need to do, Rab. You

can't get me into this."

"I know. Your job."

"Screw the job, buddy. I got Carmel. The kids."

There was nothing much to say after that. Gray had stood, shaken his hand and had told him to see a doctor and get his nose fixed. Said he'd meet him the next night, same time, same place, with a couple of ideas. Nothing illegal, he'd stressed. He'd do some thinking out of the box, was all. Then he was gone, leaving Rab with the perceived bribe; an untouched plate of Boston Cream doughnuts.

And so here he was. Same time, same place, but Gray was a no-show and Rab couldn't blame him. He took time over his coffee, trying to figure his next move; how he was going to lay his hands on those false documents. Money wasn't a problem, but how do you gain access to the kind of underworld service provider he so desperately needed?

He imagined trawling the shadier downtown drinking dives and approaching big guys with scars and tattooed knuckles: "Hey, good buddy, let me stick another shot in that glass. You know, you strike me as the kind of unsavoury, bottom-feeding individual who could hook me up with a similarly lowlife document forger, so how about it, chum?"

Even if those weren't his words, that's what the guy would be hearing. Result? A rearrangement of his face and/or body parts. Or worse. So, okay, plan B, The Yellow Pages. He wasn't making himself laugh.

The place was busier tonight, and he noticed the hookers from last night sitting at the same table in the window. The younger one's fish-nets were intact this time but both her hands were bandaged. She was laughing while her friend tried to fix her lipstick for her, the stuff going everywhere but on her mouth.

Even with his own problems stacking up, he thought how lucky he'd been in life. He'd made *some* good choices, hadn't he? Nevertheless, if he couldn't think himself out of this mess soon he'd be dead. So much for his ability to hunt on the wing. Then he remembered who'd called it that. Christ, he needed a drink.

He took a slurp of coffee and gagged. His brain had expected something stronger.

Chair legs scraped on linoleum. He looked up with a jolt to find a skinny guy with long, filthy hair sitting opposite. He had piercings in his eyebrows, nose and lips, a diamond stud in each cheek and a goatee. The newcomer leaned forward to within an inch of Rab's face as if to kiss him.

"Fuck, you is ugly," he said with an accent and stale breath, "Mister, you godda get that snoot in a sling!"

His hand slid inside his grubby denim jacket and Rab's bowels turned to juice. *Please, not here! Not now! Not ever!*

He thought he'd been so careful; opting for a Greyhound red-eye over a plane flight to get him across the Canadian border, gambling Fedor's goons would be staking-out airports and train stations.

That morning, he'd had just enough cash to check out

of a downtown boarding house that charged by the hour. Using credit cards or ATMs had been a no-no. Brunovich probably had ways of tracing those transactions, like in the movies. So, okay, Rab had made it into Canada, but the old bastard was bound to have connections here. If the mob boss wanted to find him in Ottawa it probably wouldn't take him long. The thing was, Rab hadn't planned on sticking around. Two days, maybe. Three, tops.

He'd used a callbox on the street and gotten Bank Haase to wire a large sum to a Bank of Nova Scotia in the financial district. He also took the opportunity of converting the remaining dollars into gold, given the current volatility of the currency markets. He'd shopped for necessities: fresh clothing, toiletries and a holdall to carry them in.

He'd killed time in a couple of anonymous bars before the planned rendezvous with Grahame. He'd stayed alert; on the look-out for suspicious types paying him too much attention, confident that if they sent Stink Bug he'd see the dumbass coming for miles.

It had been around mid-morning, after his third bottle of Bud, when a thought had hit him like a train. His personnel file at GHD! He knew for a fact it contained the resume he'd presented at his job interview, citing Gray as a principal reference. The guy's Ottawa address was even in there!

He'd snatched the handset from a wall phone, shoved in a couple of quarters and had dialled two wrong numbers before: "Warrick residence." A woman's voice.

"Mrs. Warrick? Carmel?"

Silence the other end... then, "Look. Grahame's not here."

"I guessed that. I didn't want to risk calling his office. I need you to get a message to him. I'm sorry but it's urgent." Another pause in which he heard a small child laughing in the background. "Please. We met a few times, remember? Back when Gray was living in Manhattan."

When they'd come, her words had been cool and brittle. "If you're who I think you are, please don't call this number again." Followed by a *click*. Then nothing.

Well, Gray and his family were out of danger now. Fedor Brunovich wouldn't need to bother them because, tonight, he'd reached across the Canadian border and stuck one of his goons in the seat opposite.

The hitman brought his hand out of the denim jacket clutching a crumpled business card. There was a phone number under the name. Veggie Ménard. French Canadian, Rab guessed and let out a long breath. Veggie? he queried. A nickname on account of his cauliflower ears, the guy explained. Trophies from his early days on the bare-knuckle fight scene. The weasel looked to be in his fifties but was probably younger than Rab.

Ménard returned the business card (probably the only one he possessed) to a greasy breast pocket and surveyed his surroundings, his lime-green studded tongue moistening narrow lips.

"I can get you what you need."

"Did Grahame send you?"

"I don't know no names. Maybe mine ain't even Veggie."

"I understand."

"I doubt it. You got dough?"

"Uh, yeah," said Rab, nodding toward the counter, "What do you want, coffee?"

"Fer a phoney ID, ya peckerhead."

*

Veggie Ménard, whoever, was as good as his word, and so, two days and four thousand dollars later, Rab boarded a plane at Ottawa International Airport as Timothy Santry, a financial adviser on business out of Montreal. His Canadian passport, incidentally, would've more than impressed The Alchemist. When he'd asked the French Canadian how he'd obtained it for him he hadn't expected an answer, but the guy had surprised him. He'd given a Gallic shrug and had whispered one word: "Internet."

A seven hour flight winged him direct to Glasgow, where Tim Santry's driver's licence got him a Hertz rental to Oban on the west coast. Then to the Isle of Mull aboard a Caledonian MacBrayne ferry.

Before he could go further, he had to ditch the vehicle. Captain Angus's smaller craft, *The Mishnish*, carried only foot passengers, sheep, kegs of beer and store supplies. The seven mile journey was pretty hairy, the horizon disappearing behind towering waves with the wind increasing in strength the further from Mull the tiny vessel chugged.

Angus must've been in his late seventies now, Rab reckoned. He easily recognised him from his childhood and wondered if his own face rang bells in the captain's mind.

The Royal Navy veteran kept eyeing him over his shoulder. And 'eyeing' in the most accurate sense given the empty pink hollow of his left eye-socket. He steered the ferry single-handed through the rolling green mass and spray. 'Single-handed' again precise as Angus's right arm had been severed at the elbow.

When at last Rab glimpsed the cliffs of Garg's craggy coastline, he waited for the surge of emotion that would tell him he'd finally come home. An emotion, as it turned out, that was very slow in coming.

*

My darling boy,

Today is your twenty-first birthday and you've become a man! How I long to be with you on this special day. To hold you and feel your grown strength. To smell your scent and run these fingers through your soft hair.

The wind is up and scowthering as I write, the sea throwing up waves thirty foot or more. Do you recall how funny the birds can be in such weather? The crows tossed about like black rags in the wind? I can see a murder of them now, out the parlour window, flying backwards over Ben Wrath's craggy peak.

The gales have been up to force-eight and Captain Angus's wee ferry's been harbour-bound this past fortnight. But he's as happy as can be, as you would guess, holed-up in Mrs. Drum's the whole time with his crossword book and never-ending bottle of Oban malt.

Is it true you must be twenty-one before they let you drink in America? Will you have your first tonight? Promise you'll have one for me!

With no ferry, supplies are short just now, so I'm afraid your birthday cake lacks your favourite dark cocoa filling. Oh, and my goodness! Twenty-one candles! Greda and I will need all our puff to blow them out! Your sister will be so excited when she comes home from school. She says it's like having two birthdays every year. The wee thing has no idea how that saddens me.

Ignore my rambling, now. Instead, you must enjoy this important day, and remember that the future is always bright. Be good. Be strong. And, until God returns you to these arms, try to think kindly of me, Rabbie.

All my love, Mam.

The ballpoint ink was bottle-green, the handwriting an elegant copperplate typical of Clair MacBain's generation, Rab observed, his heart pounding as he worked his tongue to return saliva to his mouth.

The East Wind was bearable today, the sea a mere choppy lead-gray carpet, though a sudden gust tried to snatch the precious letter from his hand. And so he returned it to the tartan shortbread tin where nestled the other twenty-two sheets of thin, cream, notepaper. One for each of his birthdays since he left. This year's would never be written, of course, because his mother had died age sixty-two and, at the time of his arrival three weeks ago, he'd missed her by just five months.

He placed the letter chronologically in the wad and retied the yellow ribbon that kept them in order. The tin's lid depicted a Black Watch piper amid a luminous sea of heather. He remembered the tin box from his childhood and the buttery sweetness of the shortbread it once contained. Remembered, too, the shelf above the cast-iron cooking range where it used to live.

He tried to imagine his sister, Greda - born six months after he'd left the island - every year, blowing out birthday candles for a brother she'd never known. When small, she'd admitted, she'd seen Rab as an imaginary friend popping round for tea once every autumn. It had been fun until, in her teens, she'd come to see those strange birthday rituals for what they were. A mother's pining for her lost boy. Greda told how she'd come to hate Rabbie, the birthday ghost, who'd haunted her growing up.

Rab felt chilled here, in the shadow of Ben Wrath; the granite mountain that dominated the island's interior, until the charcoal clouds parted over its peak allowing a rare ray of sunlight to find him in the long, sharp grass where he lay on his belly.

A shriek startled him, and he looked up to see a peregrine falcon plummet from nowhere and disappear below the cliff's edge, six feet away, something large and bleeding in its beak. The sight of which prompted him to explore the new shape of what Charlie would've called a pugilist's nose. No pain these days but resetting it would have to wait.

After a while, he took up the cookie tin and pushed himself to his feet, the wind batting his black mohair coat, frayed and the worse for wear since its softer life in Manhattan.

The glen, lush and bleak, was dotted with sheep; the small Hebridean kind: black and brown with most sporting four long horns.

He looked to the mountain where six or so lime-washed crofters' cottages clung on for their lives, then turned north and headed down the cliff path toward Garg's tiny fishing harbor. He was headed for Mrs. Drum's, one of the few habitations on the island with electricity, where an open fire and a full bottle of single malt awaited him. He hoped the place would be empty, because he had twelve more of his mother's un-mailed letters to read and needed to be alone with them.

*

Faint laughter lines fanned from the corners of her pale-green eyes, but the twenty-four-year-old hadn't shown him a smile once in the three weeks since his arrival. She was seated opposite Rab now, her expression neutral.

The oak-beamed pub, lit by too few wall-lamps, hadn't been as quiet as he'd hoped. A half-dozen bodies slouched at tables, keeping warm near the inglenook at the far end of the oak-beamed room. A couple of visiting birdwatchers, Large Stanley, the shepherd and the small crew of the fishing vessel, *Sea Cry*. The silver-haired proprietor, Mrs. Drum, surely in her eighties, busily polished glasses close-by, pretending not to eavesdrop on his and Greda's conversation.

He'd finished with the birthday letters and so slid the tartan tin box across the small table. Greda slid it back to him with slender, freckled fingers. "Keep 'em," she said, "Me mam meant fer ye ta have 'em."

Not *our* mam, he noted but thanked her with a nod. Her gaze was probing and he found himself averting his eyes. Her copper, shoulder-length hair, wide mouth and pretty chin still caused him pain. And shame. Because he couldn't look into his young sister's freckled face without seeing his mother. *Their* mother.

Stuck for a response, he gestured to the third-full bottle of malt at his elbow, nearly knocking it over. "Drink?" he said, the 'r' in the word softened by the missing two-thirds.

Little sparks of yellow appeared in her eyes and her brows furrowed. She stood, buttoned her ragged sheepskin jacket, placed her hands in tight jean pockets and opened her mouth to speak.

Mrs. Drum ceased polishing glasses and leaned in to catch Greda's words, but the younger woman said nothing. Instead, she turned on her heel and walked into the shadows.

"Night, lass," Mrs. Drum called after her but got no reply. Rab heard his newfound sister exit the bar and close the heavy oak door behind her.

He poured out the last of the whisky, added a drop of water from a small earthenware jug and downed it in one. He thought back to the day he'd spotted Garg's craggy coastline, waiting for the surge of emotion that would tell him he'd finally come home. With a spent whisky bottle and a shortbread tin containing his dead mother's un-mailed letters, he was still waiting.

*

Mrs. Drum locked the street door on the last of her customers and returned to Rab at the bar. "Ye'll be away ta yer bed then?"

"Yeah, I hadn't realized the time," he said, placing his empty bottle and glass on the counter.

"Aye, past midnight. Ah'll bring ye up a jug o' hot water at half-seven sharp, Rabbie." The place had no running hot water in the upstairs rooms.

"Thanks, Mrs. D. Goodnight," he said, strangely touched at her using his real name. When he'd arrived on Garg he'd heeded Gray's advice and had kept a low profile as Tim Santry, the quiet tourist. In truth, he hadn't expected anyone in the tiny community to recognise him and, indeed, no one had shown any interest in him. Sometimes even ignoring him to the point of rudeness. At first, he'd put it down to his sounding too American to their ears; America's unpopularity abroad with the Iraq and Afghanistan mess. Iran looming. But then it became clear the islanders were uncomfortable with strangers, period.

After about a week, and he'd let it be known who he was, a few uncles and cousins had emerged from the woodwork. He'd remembered names but not many of the aging faces. Then it had been Mrs. Drum who'd been the first to change her attitude toward him. She who'd stunned him with the news he had a sister, and had cajoled Greda into meeting him at her small cottage in the glen. The place he'd once called home.

Clutching the shortbread tin to his chest, he headed for the door that lead to his rented room. The wind was up again, rattling the pub's leaded windows.

"She was a good woman was yer mam," Mrs. Drum blurted, halting him in his tracks. "I knew her, so I did."

He'd drunk too much, as usual, and Clair MacBain was the last person he needed to talk about.

"Yeah, well, it's a small island," he said, alcohol displacing his manners.

"A grand woman, if a wee confused at times."

He pictured his mother making her little girl blow out candles for the birthday ghost. The old woman became agitated, pulling at a loose button on her Aran cardigan.

"And I remember ye 'n' yer da. He was a good'n tae, so he was."

Though there were some who now spoke to Rab, none had mentioned his father. "You knew him? Fergus MacBain?"

"Oh, aye, he fished wi' yer Uncle Dugald on *The Midas Touch* until... well, ye must know how things turned out."

Her voice tapered-off as she lifted the counter flap, squeezed through and flicked a row of brass switches behind the bar. The room's wall-lights died, leaving just the glow from embers in the inglenook.

"Well, no, I don't," he said, "How *did* things turn out?"

She had her back to him. Her shoulders slumped and he thought he heard her sigh.

"Well, I'm sure Greda can put ye in the picture there. Is nae mah business."

She plucked a shot glass from a shelf and put it to an optic. "Nightcap?" she said. Rab shook his head, which made it ache. "At my age, ah dinnae sleep wi'out a tot o' rum. Slainte," she said, raising her glass and knocking it back. Then her eyes met his, weighing him up. "Naebody blamed him fer leavin' yer mam like he did. And nae many were shocked at him takin' ye wi' him."

He found it hard to believe her on that score. He'd been as good as kidnapped, for Christ's sake. People must've realized that. His pulse thumped in his temples, heralding the hangover he'd been expecting. He thumbed the latch on the oak door marked *'Private,'* to the right of the counter hatch, opening it to reveal a narrow wood staircase leading up, but the old woman hadn't finished her piece.

"He loved Clair, I'm sure, but there's only so much a man can take. Ye think life's hard here now. Back then, well…"

Rab found himself getting defensive though unsure on whose behalf. He retraced his steps and leaned across the counter, which seemed to unsettle the old woman.

"Look, whatever happened between them, Dad did what he thought was best. Best for me. The fishing was dying, right? His livelihood slipping away. Mom wouldn't emigrate to the States and nothing could change her mind, but I'm sure if he'd known Mom was three months pregnant with Greda he'd never have deserted them."

He was about to head upstairs but saw the old woman's face pale in the room's amber glow, the fire's embers reflecting in her intelligent, milky-blue eyes. A loud gust of wind buffeted the leaded windows, causing the curtains to billow out.

"But o'coarse yer da knew she was pregnant," she said, "It's why he left!" She became flustered, losing the glass and picking at her cardigan again. "Ah've said tae much."

The pounding at his temples worsened. "What're you talking about?"

She reached up and took his face in her warm hands, at

once making him sleepy. "Were ye so very young, Rabbie, ye dinnae remember the Rough Music?"

*

...and I made it all the way down to St. Donan's Bay today. With Greda's help of course, and the damned stick your Uncle Dugald whittled for me. The one with the handle carved in the shape of a sandpiper's head.

But I mustn't bore you with an old woman's aches and pains on this special day. Suffice it to say, getting old isn't for sissies.

If you could only see your sister now. Fully bloomed and turning men's heads much as I did in my day, though she has an elegance and lightness of step these limbs, when young, could never have carried off.

And you should hear her play the fiddle! She's the best on the island by far, everyone says so, with her jigs and reels. She beats the socks off them, too, with the spoons and bones! Oh, and her voice!

And the way she has with animals, Rabbie. Down at the bay today, a family of sea otters wriggled out of the kelp and scampered up to within feet of us, and you know how shy the wee things are! I'll swear it's because of your sister they have no fear. It's the same with those birds of hers.

Which reminds me. Our favourite programme is about to start on BBC2 and we never miss it. Aye, it's the truth! Thanks to the fuel generator Greda bought at a car-boot on the mainland, we can now run a telly! I can't think why we've waited so long to join the 21st Century.

We watch only the wildlife, of course, the rest is rubbish. But I did see a Western once and swore I saw you in the background. Greda says I'm mad but I still hope it was you. You looked so handsome.

I must away now. But not before telling you how much I love you, and to wish you a happy birthday.

Try to think kindly of me, Rabbie.

All my love, Mam.

Those were her last words to him in this world, and all the more precious for that, but there was that one phrase again that had been bugging him. The way she'd signed-off most of her letters. *'Try to think kindly of me.'* As if she'd felt guilty for hurting him in some way when it was he who deserved the guilt in spades.

The huge bird of prey flapped and screeched. One of its wings might've broken a man's arm but Greda seemed unperturbed.

"Bob Fletcher was mah faither. He shagged our mam a couple o' times then nae one saw or heard o' him after the Rough Music."

'Our' mam. Progress. She coaxed the Golden eagle onto her leather gauntlet and crossed the wire-net enclosure to place it on a high perch.

"He snuffed-it years ago, by all accounts. An accident on an oil rig."

"I'm sorry," Rab said and meant it.

"It's unimportant." She removed the glove and continued mopping the concrete floor, disinfectant overpowering the scent of fresh rainfall and guano.

The falconry had surprised him, extending as it did from the rear of the single-storey cottage and running its entire breadth. Its walk-in cages housed an array of raptors: British buzzards, Harris hawks, merlins, peregrine falcons, a long-eared owl and a pair of American bald eagles.

Greda had explained how falconries weren't just for show. They were a way of preserving endangered species; safeguarding future generations through specialized breeding programs.

Many of the healthy young would eventually be set free in the wild. He wondered if the bald eagles' offspring would be flying home or going FedEx. The falconry was open to visitors to the island and he could imagine Greda being more than engaging as a guide.

He'd arrived at the crofter's cottage that afternoon unannounced, and Greda had not been surprised to see him. Though she'd asked him to keep it short; she'd had the birds to tend to.

"She must've been forty-something when she had you," he said to keep her talking.

She stopped work and turned to read his eyes. Hers were cold. "It's nae secret I was an accident. A love-child often is, I'm told."

"I meant nothing. Mom had me at thirty-three, which was pretty late back then."

"Your point?"

He shrugged. What *was* his point? Greda patted feather down from the sleeves of her sheep-skin jacket and he resisted the urge to pluck some from her hair.

"Ye didnae come ta impress me wi' yer maths, so what dae ye want?"

"Fletcher. Your dad. Where did he…?"

"Told ye. Dead. End of."

He watched her take her mop and bucket into the next cage, occupied by a pair of Harris hawks. Their mother had been right, he thought, the birds were easy around her. She looked back at him through the wire.

"Want the truth? Fer practically mah whole life, ah've dreaded ye showing up."

That stung him though he had no idea why. He hardly knew this young woman.

"Look, Greda…"

Her eyes flared. "I knew ye'd come back ta punish us. Mam, fer cheating on yer da and me for takin' yer place here."

"Believe me, I had no intention…"

"Well, ye've a wasted journey. I dinnae give a shite what ye think o' me. As fer Mam, ye punished her fer nigh-on a quarter century. That's enough fer anyone, dae ye nae think?" She shoved the mop aside and folded her arms across her chest. He took a step toward the wire, went to speak but she cut him off. "So now it's said, what's left fer ye here, exactly?"

"Tea would be good. No sugar." He tried the twinkly

thing with his eyes. Her expression took time to soften before she showed him a smile for the first time ever. Grudging but, just as he'd guessed it would be, beautiful and well worth the wait.

*

"The milk's goat. Dinnae choke."

"It's fine," Rab said, sipping from a chipped mug and hating the cloudy concoction. At home, he'd gotten used to having it straight-up with lemon. *Home. Christ, where was that now?*

His mother's parlour had hardly changed. There were still the old cooking range, Welsh dresser and stone sink; the latter fed through the wall from a cast-iron stand-pump in the yard. Something bleated out-front. Probably the goat. Clair MacBain's pride and joy, the 21st Century TV, dominated one corner looking out of place. The world's huge eye peering into a time capsule, it seemed to him, rather than peering out.

He spotted a couple more new additions. A violin and a set of small, Irish bagpipes. Uilleann pipes, as they were called. The only music he remembered hearing in this house had been his mother's voice singing to him.

Charlie's painting of water lilies was leaning against a far wall. He'd given it to Greda on his first visit, thinking she might've liked something from her father. Insensitive of him at the time. Stupid, even. It didn't matter now, of course, Charlie wasn't her dad, and he wondered if she'd ask him to take it back.

They were sitting at the parlour table where Greda toyed with the tassel on a tea cosy. They'd flipped a ten pence coin to decide who'd go first. Greda had lost the toss.

"The Rough Music's been wi' us nigh-on three hundred years," she said, "and isnae unique ta these isles, by the way. The wretched custom was also practiced on mainland Scotland and in the North o' England. Its forms may've varied but they served the same basic function fer small communities."

He put the mug of filthy tea aside. "Which was?"

"A collective expression o' disapproval. A weapon o' humiliation. A shamin', if ye like." She read his eyes. "Ye have a question."

"This stuff still go on here?"

She straightened in her chair, cupped a fist in her lap and sighed. "From time ta time, sadly." She turned to gaze out the window where evening was drawing in. After a moment she turned back, her eyes cool with fury. "Mam was able ta describe it in vivid detail, as ye'd imagine."

But he didn't have to. Since Mrs. Drum's first mention of the Rough Music, he'd been putting it together. Greda was merely providing the last few pieces of the puzzle.

He'd remembered the Saturday he'd been out fishing with his dad and Uncle Dugald and bad weather had forced *The Midas Touch* back to shore. The wind, *snell* and *scowthering*, as his mother would have described it.

He'd recalled, too, the cold wetness of his socks and the warmth of his dad's hand holding his as they'd climbed the cliff path against the driving rain.

They'd reached the brow of the hill by the old cemetery when Fergus MacBain had halted and squeezed his hand so hard it hurt.

"Hear that?" he'd said.

And Rab could, through the howling gale and stinging rain; a distant metallic roar, intermittent between the gusts.

His instinct had been to search the sky but all he'd found there were crows performing the trick of flapping backwards over the Ben. Then his breath had caught, and his young mind had thrilled to the idea a battle was being fought nearby.

He'd heard axes and pikes crashing on armor. Claymores and halberds hacking at shields. Pictured clansmen setting blade to blade, roused to the kill by fife and drum.

But then, squinting through the downpour, he'd seen something stranger. What must've been the island's entire population - up to two hundred back then - had surrounded his home in the glen.

They must've been five, six bodies deep. And stranger still, they were striking pots and pans together, belting old tin tubs with ladles, hammers, anything that made a noise. Wood spoons bashed biscuit tins. Angry fists thumped tea-chests while bells clanged and tuneless whistles shrilled. Today, he'd describe the sight and sound as sinister. Primeval. He'd tried to look up to read his dad's expression but had gotten rain in his eyes.

"What is it, Da?"

"Just a wee bit o' fun, Rabbie," he'd said without joy, "Just a wee bit o' fun."

Then he'd turned and led his son back down the cliff path, the spiteful storm mercifully to their backs.

The following few days at his godmother, Elleen's place was a half memory of low voices in lamp-lit corners. Doors slamming in other rooms and the occasional muted sound of women weeping. Then the tiny ferry leaving Garg and his mother *'tae unwell ta see ye aff,'* as Elleen had put it between tearful hugs and kisses.

More vague days staying with strangers in Glasgow, perhaps, or Liverpool, where his dad must've arranged their passports and tickets for the ocean liner.

"Mam said the shamin' lasted over an hour. The din enough ta send a person bats," Greda said, lighting an oil-lamp between them on the table. Fuel for the generator would be expensive, Rab guessed. "Stupid thing was, the only reason Fletcher was in the house that day was 'cause she'd called him round tae end the damned affair, and ta tell him she was away the trip wi' me."

"Er... translation?"

"Pregnant. Once the mob had disbanded, mah brave faither slunk out the house and away o'er the sea. And that was the last o' him." She looked to Rab's mug where a skin had formed on its contents and frowned with irritation. "Yer brew's gone cold."

"Don't worry about it. Go on."

"Next day, yer da was willin' ta take her back, so he was, until he twigged the bairn could nae've been his." Rab watched as she adjusted the lamp's wick. Saw the hurt in her eyes. "Poor Mam," she said, biting her bottom lip.

"She loved you very much, Greda. Her letters. They're full of you."

All she said was, "Well," and gazed at the table-top, waiting for more from him, perhaps.

So he took a breath and asked the question that'd been burning in his chest since he'd arrived on the island. "What about me?"

That must've come out too raw, or needy, because she looked to the low beamed ceiling before couching her answer.

"Mam said she was tae ashamed ta stop yer faither takin' ye away. And as time went by, she convinced herself ye'd have a better life wherever ye were, okay? Ne'er tried ta track ye 'n' yer da down because she felt she'd lost the right ta be yer mam. There." She sighed and softened. "Look, Rab, I'm sorry, so I am, but…"

His eyes misted and his voice caught. "Twenty-three letters. Nowhere to send them. She must've been…"

"Madder than a sack full o' friggin' owls!" said Greda.

Suddenly, it couldn't be helped, and the two burst out laughing together, Rab feeling for the first time what it was like to have a sister, and instantly mourning the years he'd missed of her growing up.

"More like charmingly eccentric," she was saying. "I loved her, mind, dinnae think I didnae, Rabbie. I miss her ta buggery."

A silence hung between them for a while before she rolled the ten pence piece toward him across the table, the cue it was his turn.

He picked it up and toyed with it for a few moments. It felt hot because she'd had it clenched in her lap the whole time. Then out it all came. Rab MacBain's life in pursuit of an American Dream he hadn't chosen. The initial weirdness of starting every school day, hand on heart, pledging allegiance to the flag of a nation not his own.

High-school proms and wooing girls with his Sean Connery accent at parties or on the rear seats of cars if he was lucky. Law school and living in Brooklyn with his dad.

Then the life of a corporate lawyer turning a buck in the cut-throat jungle of Manhattan. He caught Greda glance at the Monet look-alike at the end of the room, so went on to describe Fergus MacBain's reincarnation as Charlie Whistler, The Alchemist, and his own early role as his apprentice. She was intrigued that his dad's forged masterpieces had remained undetected in such places as New York's Frick Collection, Washington DC's National Gallery and London's Tate Britain.

He told her everything, right up to the damned lie that his mother was dead when he hadn't even reached age ten. And as he did so, he found himself having to rewrite history. Because now he understood why Charlie had lied. And how Fergus MacBain must've felt; married to the woman he'd loved from childhood and with whom, as a boy, he'd shared secrets of blue-tailed falcons. Shared a hard life with her that had endured in spite of the island dying under their feet. Then, finally, to be cuckolded, and worse; another man's seed growing in his wife's belly.

What could there've been left for him? Rab now saw, that for Charlie, Clair's death had been no lie. His dad had needed her to be dead to *him*. He hadn't faked his life, he'd simply traded it for a blank canvass. And wasn't that what America, the New World, the land of hope and opportunity, was all about?

Then came the hard part, admitting to Greda that once he'd learned the truth about his mom, he'd left it far too long before setting out to find her. And for that he could give no excuse. Not even to himself.

When the words stopped coming, he stared into the orange flame of the lamp where he saw twenty-five million dollars in gold bullion sitting in the vault of Bank Haase, Zug, Switzerland.

"Is that all o' it?" Greda asked, her face open and trusting.

"That's everything," he lied, then noticed her hand holding his across the table. Noticed, too, his cheeks were wet and stinging.

She smiled. "What will ye dae now ye've come home?"

He didn't even need to think about that one. "I'll be moving-on in a day or two. Godda get back to my job in the States."

Lie number two. He had no idea where in the world his next stop would be, but it had struck him, only in the last forty-eight hours, that all the time he'd worried about Grahame Warwick's name being in his resume, so would his own place of birth, for Christ's sake. Stupid or What?

"But it's Christmas in a few weeks," she said, "Why dae ye nae stay just…"

There came a *clack!* Metal on wood, and he shot a look to the low latched front-door. The stocky shadow of a man entered and closed it. It hung its oiled canvas satchel on a peg and approached the table, its features at once distinct in the lamplight.

Greda looked up and grinned. "Calum, I expected ye earlier."

"Aye, ah've been helpin' out at Mrs. Drum's."

He looked down at her hand holding Rab's on the table and his dark eyes blinked once; a pair of silent camera shutters.

"Am I interruptin' somethin'?" he said, turning to Rab.

"Not at all. I was just telling my sister…"

"*Half*-sister," Calum corrected.

Greda rose and moved to the range, but not before giving Rab's hand a light squeeze.

"Ah've nae started supper, pet."

"Nae matter," her man said, taking her place at the table. Rab could smell the sea on him, and tobacco, and strong beer.

The fact that, over the weeks, Calum had been the least

104

welcoming of the islanders he'd put down to simple jealousy. The fisherman had apparently lived with Greda since Clair MacBain's death and the two planned to marry one day. His sibling could've done better was Rab's only opinion of him.

He smiled to keep it light. "I was just telling Greda. I'll be out of everyone's hair in a couple of days."

The younger man was glaring at him and he found himself looking at the guy's gnarled and scarred knuckles, no doubt from years trawling nets. His hair was as black as Rab's, but short and spiky. He had a small gold ring in his left ear and a faded tattoo on the right side of his neck. A mermaid? Dolphin?

"What's yer real business here, Mister Yankee Bollocks?" he said suddenly.

"I... don't get you."

"Ye watch tae many spy films, so ye dae."

"Films. Right."

"Yer room at the pub. The mahogany chest. Somethin' taped to the underside o' the second draw down."

Rab's face burned and his breath became short. Greda had turned from the range and was looking at him, puzzlement in her eyes.

"Trouble is," Calum was saying, "I watch tae many spy films masell."

With that he pulled something from his jeans pocket and slammed it down on the table. His hand withdrew, revealing a Canadian passport. Greda arrived at her man's side and snatched it up. She opened it and studied the mug-shot. "Who the hell's Timothy Santry?"

Hunt on the wing. Sparkly eyes. Big grin... "Oh, he's just some schmuck I know who looks like me."

Lie number three. And lame, yeah, but he'd been going for humor. He was only vaguely aware of Calum's quick movement. He heard a chair topple and hit the flagstone floor and had just enough time to think, *"Yup, I probably deserve this,"* before something hard and flat slammed into his jaw, casting him adrift for a moment, then finally to the bottom of a deep, dark ocean.

Chaper Five

SHE clicked her kitten heels toward the chrome and marble reception desk where a young, attractive, bespectacled African-American woman looked up and beamed.

"Good morning Ms. Gordon and how are you today?"

"I'm good, Gabby. You and Harold manage to get the kids out to the beach?"

"We did, thank you. Had a fantastic time in spite of this awful heat."

Which was an understatement. Temperatures this summer had climbed to record highs in the State. It'd been over a hundred degrees this weekend and people had flocked to the ocean in search of cooler air.

"Did Deb get in yet?" Becky asked.

"Yep, a half-hour ago."

"Thanks, Gabby," she smiled, and set her heels clicking toward her corner office on the first of GHD's three storeys.

The building's air-conditioning had been losing the battle lately and she'd opted again to leave her suit jacket at home. Power dressing was one thing, suffocation was another. The navy knee-length skirt and white silk blouse would have to show they meant business on their own.

The floor housed mostly paralegal staff and was a hive of activity this morning. A glass hive, and not with bees, she mused, more like worker ants. She smiled, recalling the ant farm she'd kept under her bed when she'd been six or seven.

Deb Perry, her assistant, was on the phone in the office adjoining hers. She was an attractive brunette and had a brain to match her looks. The women exchanged smiles through glass as Becky ran her card through a swipe-lock and entered. She placed her attaché case on her desk and went to the window as she did every morning. The view toward Madison Park was just one of the perks her new job afforded her.

Jeff had doubled her salary and she'd gotten to travel, which she loved. Last week, she'd flown up to GHD's satellite office in Chicago. A negative media problem one of their clients was experiencing in the midst of a company takeover. And two weeks before that she'd been treating a couple of news agency execs to the joys of skiing in Aspen.

Which reminded her she had a lunch appointment today with Reuters chief, Paddy Kehoe. He was cute and interesting and she wondered when he'd get around to asking her out to dinner.

What time was that lunch, by the way? She hit a button on her desk consol.

"Deb, you have my diary in there?"

Her assistant, still on the phone, turned and shook her

head through the glass. The diary was usually on her desk. She scanned the office and spotted it on the coffee table by the leather couch. She crossed the room to get it. Jesus, it was hot, and the AC maintenance guy had said they were days away from getting cool air into the building. Tomorrow she'd bring her portable air con unit from home.

With the better salary, she'd been renting a small, waterside apartment on Long Island Sound, where the sea breeze made the present heat-wave bearable. She'd been in the place eight months, she calculated, which meant around thirty-two weeks since she'd dated anyone. She thought again about Paddy Kehoe. A nice thought. Whatever happened there, the really great thing was that Becky Gordon's life was turning out just fine.

After the night of horror Rab had put her through, she'd fled to the only place she knew she'd feel safe. Her mother's arms. Billie had tended to her bruises with herbal remedies passed down by her own mom. The wounds she couldn't see, she'd treated with love and the best of her vintage *Blue Peaks Chardonnay*. She'd stayed a week at the winery, helping-out with the bottling and winter pruning. It'd take time to get Rab out of her system but working outdoors had been a healer in itself.

On the drive back to New York, she'd made a detour to Standing and had stayed the night with an old classmate. When John Gordon had said there were no pretty girls in the town, he'd forgotten Donna DeMilt. She had amazing dimples and blonde hair so long she could sit on it.

The girls had been friends through high-school and had graduated the same year out of Blacksburg's Virginia Tech. Donna had stayed close to home and had taken-over her father's equine veterinary practice. The money wasn't great, but that was because she was a horse doctor in a one-horse-town, she'd joked.

They'd laughed a lot that night, but eventually there was no avoiding the heart-breaking tragedy that had hit Blacksburg that April when a deranged Korean student shot and killed thirty-two people on the campus. Donna had said whoever you spoke to from Tech, they'd either known one of the victims or knew someone who had. The massacre hadn't just destroyed thirty-two young lives and the lives of countless loved-ones, but had broken the hearts of at least two generations of the Tech's alumni. Blacksburg derived its name from a Pioneer preacher. Now its place-name would be synonymous with the color of perpetual mourning.

The girls had raised a glass and had sent their hearts out to the town, its people and the victims' families. That evening, Becky promised herself she'd leave her own insignificant pain and loss behind in Standing. The time had come to move on.

She opened her desk diary at today's page and was surprised her lunch with Paddy Kehoe had been crossed-out. Had Deb done that because he'd cancelled? Her first afternoon appointment had also been scratched-out. She felt rising unease as she checked her appointments for the rest of the week. The rest of the month. They'd all been run through with neat red lines.

"I don't get it either," came Deb Perry's voice.

She looked up with a start to see the brunette in the doorway. "Mr. Hammer instructed me to ditch your whole schedule. Wants you in his office, like, yesterday. What the hell's going on?"

Becky didn't have an answer for her. She'd have to ride the elevator up two floors to get one. She wondered if it got hotter the further up the building you went.

*

She was finding her boss's office icy cold and it wasn't due to favouritism on the part of the AC maintenance guy. She was shivering on the sofa, her thighs aching as she kept them squeezed together.

In reality, the room was probably sweltering as much as anywhere else in the building, but the monster was in the room again and the agonizing ordeal of eight months ago was starting over. She concentrated on not gagging, fearful she might yark-up on her boss's Persian rug.

She'd arrived at his door, tapped twice on the glass and had entered.

"I'm sorry Jeff, just got your message. What's with cancelling…?"

"Becky," Jeff had interrupted from behind his rosewood desk.

He'd refused to part with it along with the rug when

the building had its facelift last year. He'd gotten to his feet and she could tell he was stressed. Then he'd gestured to a far corner.

"I believe you already know Mr. Brunovich, our security consultant?"

Stink Bug had been standing by a giant flat screen TV, dwarfing it whilst filing his nails. Same baggy beige suit. Different Hawaiian shirt. Same bastard. He hadn't looked up since she'd come into the office. She'd instinctively moved to the low sofa furthest from him. Had tried to cover the fact her legs were giving way as she sat down. She fought to appear casual, now. Forced her mouth into a brilliant smile and said, "Wow. Security consultant. Congratulations, that's quite a step-up."

"Oh, yeah?" Karpos growled, concentrating on his nails, "From what, Cupcake?"

"How about the swamp?"

He snapped the file in two, tossed the pieces and glowered at her, his face slick with sweat. Jeff sat, staged a cough and said too quickly, "Becky heads-up our liaison office these days. Press, media, that kind of…"

"Wow, is quite a step-up!"

His English hadn't improved. She glared at her boss. "What is this, Jeff?"

His smile was so wide his ears glowed pink and she remembered why she'd christened him 'Firefly.' All show.

Sweat trickled into his left eye and he wiped it away with a fist. "Look, let's all calm down a little".

She got to her feet, steadier now. "I didn't go to the

cops that night because…"

He cut her off. "Because of your loyalty to the firm, I know, and believe me, your discretion was greatly appreciated after that… extremely unfortunate episode at your home. I assure you, we're all very much in your debt, young lady."

But that wasn't strictly true, was it? she thought. Last New Year's Eve the firm had thrown a bash for clients and employees at the Waldorf Astoria and she'd been in light-hearted conversation with the wife of GHD's founding partner, Ted Grove. The woman was in her early sixties, she estimated, but had great skin. Too much body and not enough evening gown for her age but she'd been charming in spite of being a little juiced up.

Eventually she'd alluded to her husband's high regard for Becky, which had been odd as she'd never had much to do with the guy. His wife had gone on to say she'd heard how well Becky had dealt with Rab MacBain's sudden disappearance.

Maybe she'd had a glass of champagne too many herself, but she'd taken the woman to mean her keeping her mouth shut about Rab's multi-million embezzlement. And she'd said as much. To which the partner's wife had looked blank and responded with, "Embezzlement?"

Jeff had magically appeared up through a trap-door or down a rope or something, and had excused Becky's apparent intoxication before steering her toward the ice sculptures.

That's how she knew the only person in the firm

keeping the lid on the Merlin theft was Jeffery Hammer, and that his partners, Ted Grove and Harvey Dunn, had been kept in the dark about the whole affair.

It also became clear that her new job and salary rise had been nothing more than shut-up money, and at first, that had made her feel somewhat queasy, but then she'd remember the beating she'd taken from Stink Bug that night and preferred to see her good fortune as Jeff's idea of compensation, though it certainly wasn't enough, she thought, to compensate for the bullshit she was being asked to swallow now.

"Karpos will agree, I'm sure," he was saying, "that he was somewhat over-zealous in the execution of his duties at that time."

She wanted to laugh out loud at that one. The asshole had sexually assaulted her and put a gun to her head. She sat, looked her boss in the eye and forced a sweet smile.

"Water under the bridge, Jeff. So what's the deal here?"

He suddenly looked smug, like he'd just settled a domestic dispute between Beauty and the Beast. He shot the Russian a look that read, *Told you she was a fluffy kitten,* and she had to resist the urge to throw the sofa at him. He staged another cough. This one to signal showtime.

"Karpos?"

The Beast glared at her and Jeff in turn, wiped sweat from his jowls with a large paw and reached for the TV's remote. What the hell was going on here? Why had Jeff ditched her month's schedule? She scanned the office for clues and found one on his desk. A clear plastic DVD case. It sported a green sticker along its spine upon which was written one word in black marker pen: *'Hammer.'*

She fought to show disinterest as Karpos zapped the TV with the remote, then the DVD player beneath it. The plasma screen fizzed to life and showed the head and shoulders of a news anchor-man she didn't recognise. To the left of screen was a photograph of an oil refinery and the channel's logo: 'STV.' A Scottish outfit, she guessed, if the white haired newsreader's accent was anything to go by.

"…to be granted by the Energy Commission next week…"

Becky watched, unmoved, as the refinery dissolved into an aerial shot of a small island; lush green and bounded by a rugged coastline. A caption appeared: *'The Isle of Garg.'*

Suddenly, the ground fell away and a wave of nausea coursed through her for a second time in twenty minutes. She tried to slow her breathing.

The anchor guy grinned like an idiot and shuffled papers like he teeing-up for a quirky end-of-news item about a tap-dancing poodle or similar.

"…and finally, did ye know there was big money to be made in birds' eggs? Well, ah certainly didnae until Maureen Anderson brought us this report from the Isle of Garg."

"The disc was sent anonymously," Jeff pitched-in for her benefit, "The postmark suggests by someone on the island. Garg's off the west of Scotland."

"I know where it is," she snapped.

She glanced at Karpos and found him watching her. She looked back at the screen where, as promised, STV journalist Maureen Anderson was perched high on the island's cliffs, the wind playing havoc with the young woman's auburn hair and green tartan shawl. Her eyes were too close together and she was overly bubbly, giving the impression a grown-up had let her loose with a hand-mic for the first time.

"The blue-tailed peregrine falcon has ta be the rarest bird on the planet."

The picture cut to a cliff ledge where the stars of the show were on their eyrie, the wind buffeting their light-gray speckled breasts. Their backs and wing feathers were darker but the tail feathers were a vivid blue, which was what all the apparent fuss was about. Hopefully, they could tap-dance.

"Accordin' ta experts, the pair nestin' here on the Isle o' Garg are the *only* members o' the species known tae exist!" Maureen looked ready to orgasm. Blue feathers really must do it for the girl.

"Come on, come on! Fuck-shit!" barked Karpos, zapping the picture into fast-forward. Jeff was gnawing his knuckles. The Russian hit 'play' and Maureen Anderson was back with more gripping stuff about the blue eagles, whatever.

"…illegal fer many years. Nevertheless, unscrupulous collectors'll pay thousands o' pounds on the Black Market fer such a rare birds' egg."

The picture widened to include a huge old guy standing to Ms. Anderson's right. He could've been Santa Clause moonlighting as a shepherd. The crook in his hand gave that part away. He had a nose like an over-ripe strawberry and his shabby, maroon overcoat was tied around with string. He looked like he'd just come off worse in a fight and sported a large bandage on his forehead to prove it.

"But, Stanley, you fought off the egg thieves this time, isn't that right, now?" Maureen asked before poking her hand-mic into the big guy's whiskers.

When it came, Becky found his Highland brogue barely penetrable.

"Aye!" boomed the old timer, "they'll nae be back those two! Ah got one in the bawbag wi' mah hook!" He shook the implement for emphasis.

"What is bawbag?" Karpos asked the room with a frown. Getting no reply, he nodded to the screen, "Anytime now."

Becky found herself clenching her fists as the shot widened to reveal the journalist with Stanley amid a group of Garg islanders. They were absurdly huddled in front of a rustic lime-washed building. A painted sign under its slate-tiled roof identified it as 'Mrs. Drum's.' A pub? Guesthouse?

The group, of mostly fishermen, she guessed, were looking uncomfortable in front of the camera. Maureen went for melodramatic.

"Let's hope Stanley's right about that. What kind o' world do we live in when the price o' a rare bird's egg costs us all the extinction o' a rare and beautiful species?"

The picture froze. Karpos had hit 'pause.' He stabbed at the screen with an oversized index finger. "There!"

He was pointing to the face of a guy exiting Mrs. Drum's, seemingly unaware of the news crew.

"Is no doubt."

He zapped the picture to life again and the guy walked out of shot.

Maureen strolled away from the group and the camera panned with her. "The Isle o' Garg first drew media attention last month havin' achieved its independence after…"

And then she vanished as the picture snapped to static and white noise. Karpos zapped it off.

"It ends right there," said Jeff, "The rest of the disc's a blank. Becky, are you alright?"

She felt a bead of sweat trickle from an armpit, her shirt sticking to her back. She wanted to be sick. "Sure," she lied.

Karpos lost the remote on the desk and snatched up the Jiffy bag. He slid out a sheet and held it up. It was a blow-up of the guy caught in the background on the TV. He had longer hair now and was unshaven. Unkempt. There was something about his nose too, but the Russian was right; there was no doubt she was looking at her ex-lover, Rab MacBain.

"Who sent the disc?" she shot at Jeff, her voice tight.

"Like I said, it came anonymously. Sent from the island."

"Someone close to him," Karpos added, "Someone he blab to and have grudge. Is obvious. I squirrel 'em out when I get there."

He leant over, both hands on the desk, his mouth inches from Jeff's ear.

"This is way it go. I send her in to soften up prick. Find-out where he hide the gold..."

"What the hell are you talking about? What gold?" she snapped, but the monster was on a roll.

"That don't do it, I get it out of him old fashioned way. Is cinch." She finally woke up to what was being proposed here. "There's no way I'm going anywhere with this animal!"

"What is problem, Cupcake? This scumbag throw you over for money. He must've like you hellava lot."

He straightened and puffed out his chest, still clutching the blow-up of Rab which he'd managed to crumple. She couldn't take her eyes off it. Jeff could see she was hurting.

"Karpos," he said smoothly, "Give us a few moments would you?"

His eyes communicated he'd get further with the fluffy kitten on his own. Karpos bristled and jabbed a finger at him.

"I saving your ass, here!"

"And your own. Let's not forget that small detail."

The Russian seemed surprised by the steel in Jeff's

voice. He glared at him, then at her, before lumbering out of the room. He hadn't gone far, though; she could feel him staring at the back of her head through the glass wall. Jeff pressed a button on his desk console and a heavy fabric blind descended, giving them privacy.

After a while, staring at the floor, she whispered, "Rab was born on that island."

"It's all in here," he said quietly," gesturing to a buff file on his desk she hadn't noticed. "It was the first place Karpos and his people looked for him seven months ago. Back then the natives were giving nothing away."

Becky wasn't surprised, picturing Karpos and those other two Slavic apes trying to intimidate the likes of the burly fishermen she'd just seen on the screen.

"Something else. A lead," Jeff said, removing from the file a small sheet of lined note paper. "Came with the disc."

He rose, glided over and held up the note for her to read. Which she did. Reluctantly.

'I know what you want. Come, and we'll talk.'

"So," said Hammer, "there's at least *one* native willing to give something away. Looks like MacBain's made himself an enemy. Look, Karpos and his clowns screwed up last time, but Becky, you know Rab. You know how he ticks. You can do better." He sat too close and took her hand. "*Find* him. *Reason* with him before…"

"No Jeff."

"Before Karpos 'reasons' with him. Whatever Rab did,

to any of us, he doesn't deserve that to happen."

She was over Rab, she reminded herself. The guy was a crook. A fake, and she didn't want to think about him anymore. Nevertheless, her eyes welled with tears for the first time in eight months.

"You fly out this afternoon."

He went to embrace her but she pushed him away.

*

Karpos looked up from the drop-off bay to enjoy the sight of Matvy Golovko, framed in the hearse's passenger window, fighting to stem the flow of blood from a split lip with newspaper. The asshole was losing the battle, rivulets pooling in his shirt collar, turning it crimson.

The Georgian had called him phantom dick one time too many, so he'd hammered his elbow into the ass-wipe's face. Which had felt pretty good as goodbyes go.

Timur avoided his gaze as he placed Karpos's bags on an airport luggage trolley. The little guy couldn't wait to get away. He jumped back into the driver's seat and drove off without so much as a wave, and Karpos had so wanted to give him a goodbye too. He took hold of the trolley and pushed it toward JFK's International Departures, feeling perky now he had MacBain in his sights once more.

Just inside the busy concourse, a smart middle-aged lady was yacking on her phone. She had a Chihuahua on one of those extendable flexi-leash things. He eyeballed the dog as he went by, then paused to get his bearings. He must've spooked the pooch because it leapt and sank its needle teeth into the material of his pant leg.

The woman was jabbering so much on the phone she was oblivious. He grabbed the little mutt around the throat and yanked it free, wound the leash around its pointy nose six or seven times and tossed it in a nearby trashcan. He heard a gasp.

The owner was staring at him in horror, her face strangely resembling her dog's.

"Any lip, lady, you get same fuckin' treatment."

He held her stare for a few moments, turned and pushed his trolley across the concourse.

He reached into his jacket and brought out his passport just as the Gordon woman arrived at his side, panting hard.

"We have to hurry," she said, "I got the check-in time wrong. They're about to close the flight."

"You crap at new job, Cupcake. What, you bangin' the boss?"

She snatched his passport from him and took hold of the trolley. Sped it away toward a bank of electronic check-in machines. She was wearing that suit with the knee-length skirt and inch and a half heels that showed-off her calves. Her ass looked pretty good too.

By the time he'd caught it up, the machine had already spat out his boarding pass. Something struck him as odd.

"Why this, anyway? Where is private jet?"

"Change of plan. Mr. Grove had to fly it out to

Chicago last minute. Hurry up, I checked in already."

She set-off toward a nondescript baggage check-in, making him work to keep up. All this bossy shit was getting to him.

"Look, you better got First Class. Is no way I…"

"Relax. You got the last seat. I have to go coach."

That was something. At least he didn't have to fly three and a half thousand miles sitting next to the bitch, putting up with the smart mouth and sour looks. Shame about the corporate jet, though.

GHD leased a Bombardier Challenger 604 and he and the Golovko brothers had flown it to Scotland the last time they'd gone after MacBain. The plane had a luxury interior with armchairs and shit. Even had a bar.

Oh well, he was lucky to be going on this mission at all. Last time, Uncle Fedor hadn't been too happy about them coming home with nothing but their dicks in their hands, or in his case, as Matvy had pointed-out, nothing at all. This time would be different. He'd function better without the Georgian ass-wipes, and this time he'd have the girl as bait.

The check-in lady was asking him something while Cupcake loaded his Samsonite suitcase onto the belt. "What's that, lady?"

"I said, did you pack these bags yourself, sir?"

"Sure, do I get prize?"

The women exchanged a funny look, whatever that was about, then Cupcake picked up his mid-sized aluminium case from the trolley. He snatched it from her.

"Not that," he snapped, "Hand luggage!"

Another weird look from the Bitch Sisters. Maybe his grabbing the case like that had looked suspicious, so he joked, "Is parachute." Which didn't get the girls howling.

In truth, his toy box contained nothing technically illegal, and even in the event its contents showed up in the X-ray scanner there was nothing explosive or harmful in it. Just his fold-down parabolic dish with integral shotgun microphone; the long range listening device he'd used to eavesdrop on MacBain and his midget pal at that Break Neck picnic spot last year. Also there was a mini audio recorder and miniature binoculars in the case, and if quizzed by security, he'd give them the bullshit about going birdwatching in the Scottish Highlands. Cinch.

Of course, he'd had to leave the Makarov behind but no big deal, he'd pick up a piece somewhere along the way. These days, Britain was as awash with guns as the United States, Matvy had assured him before he'd opened the prick's lip with his elbow.

They had no problem getting through security and ten minutes later found them crossing an empty departure lounge at a brisk trot, Cupcake setting the pace. He was letting her carry the aluminium case to give her something subordinate to do while he told her how this was gonna play out.

"I don't know what fuck-shit fairy-tale Hammer spin you, but when we get to damn island, I let you squirrel-out prick. Then you get fuck-out my way before I fry your sweet ass along with ya fuck-shit boyfriend's."

"Do you write poetry, Karpos?"

"Huh?"

They'd arrived at a desk where a skinny black steward complained in a sing-song voice, "You're cutting it fine, people!"

He had a funny accent, Caribbean, maybe and was flapping his hands as he spoke. "Faggot," he thought, but must've said it out-loud because the guy was giving him a shitty look and the Gordon bitch had stiffened at his side.

"Sorry to keep you, really," she said, handing the fairy a fistful of documents.

He gave them a cursory glance and handed them back, doing the tight-lipped thing. Then the bitch practically frogmarched him down the walkway onto the plane, giving him more smart mouth.

"You didn't have to be so rude, back there."

"So? I hate faggots. I your boss, now. Show me respect."

*

Most of the passengers in First Class were businessmen in suits. The guy across the aisle from Karpos was letting the side down, though, with a yellow T-shirt and a head piled up with dreadlocks under a yellow, green and black wool hat. Must've been a... yeah, Rastafarian.

He tidied his own suit wishing he'd ditched the Hawaiian shirt for this trip and worn a neck-tie.

A black stewardess with great legs was dealing out

drinks up front. She'd be getting to him soon, he hoped. Okay, so it wasn't the private jet but he could live with that. Plenty of legroom. The seat even fitted his bulk, and there was a button you could push to turn the seat into a bed! Cupcake leant down to him with his metal case.

"Mr. Brunovich?" That was better. Bit of respect. "I'll stow this for you and take my seat in coach. Have a good flight."

"Whatever," he mumbled as he watched her perfect ass mince away up the aisle. Peace at last.

There was a miniature TV housed in the back of the seat in front and it came on of its own accord. A couple of the suits were plugging-in headphones so he rummaged in the seat pocket until he found some. He tore them out of the plastic, put them on and plugged the jack into the armrest. There was a little wash bag in the pocket too but he'd save the fun of checking out its goodies for later. He hoped there were some of those cosy bootie things so he could get out of his size 13 loafers.

The plane was on the move at last. 'Taxiing', he remembered and felt proud at how great his English was getting. These days, he even thought in the language, kind of.

The TV was doing the shit about safety exits and oxygen masks, but, come on, if this crate was goin' down it was goin' down all the damn way. Ha! He took out an emery board and filed his nails.

"Hey, mon, they're lovely enough." It was the Rastafarian across the aisle, irritated by him sanding his nails. He gave him his best Tony Soprano 'fuck you' look and started on the other hand. The clown looked away.

He could hear the engines screaming over the safety info; time for lift-off. Some of the suits were reading newspapers or watching TV. The Rasta had his eyes clenched shut and was gripping both armrests. Karpos let out a snort. Flying didn't bother him. He'd done enough of it in the war. Well, while training. In fact, heights turned him on. He'd been a champion rock-climber in his teens and had even conquered Caucasus's Mount Elbrus. Climbing was a skill he'd hoped would've gotten him into *Spetsnaz*; the Soviet equivalent of America's Special Forces.

He found himself rubbing the scar tissue on his thigh through his pants. Damned mutts. That Chihuahua had gotten off lightly. Should've bitten the little fucker's head off.

A *bong* sounded over the speakers and the cabin lights dimmed. The leggy stewardess was checking seatbelts. He'd have to ask her for a drink and a massage, maybe.

An in-flight movie was starting and he thought you could choose those, so he hunted around for the TV control. He found it in the armrest, but before he could locate the menu button, one of his favourite tunes filled his headphones, though not a version he'd heard before. The TV was showing people dancing on a sandy beach among palm trees. Up popped a title caption, and as he felt the aircraft leave the runway, two thoughts struck him. One: how come *'Fly Me to the Moon'* was being played on steel drums by a bunch of Rastafarians on a sunny beach? And two: why was he watching an in-flight promotional documentary entitled: *Welcome to Beautiful Jamaica?*

*

Becky's heels were sticking to the melting black-top as she pushed her luggage trolley toward the waiting Bombardier Challenger 604. The corporate jet was parked in a corner of the airfield, well away from JFK's busy commercial terminals. Even so, the stench of aviation fuel stung her nostrils.

She looked up in time to see Air Jamaica flight 16 leave the runway through shimmering heat-haze and wished it *bon voyage.*

As she neared the private aircraft, its uniformed pilot stepped up to greet her. He had to yell over the noise of the jet's twin turbofan engines. "Good afternoon, Ms. Gordon! Another hot one, huh?"

"It certainly is, Paul!" she yelled back, "Can't wait to get onboard!"

The co-pilot appeared and took her luggage from the trolley, which now included Karpos's aluminium case. Captain Paul checked a docket slip before shouting, "I was told we were taking you and a Mr. Brunovich!"

She smiled and yelled, "Mr. Brunovich had an accident with a soda bottle! His boyfriend had to rush him to hospital!"

"Ouch! He cut himself bad?"

"I don't think it was that kind of accident, Paul!"

Cheap, yeah, but she wished the homophobe had been there to hear it. She boarded the jet, leaving Captain Paul wincing as he got her meaning. A half-hour later, with the aircraft cruising around 550mph, she sat back in her tan, leather armchair and sipped from a glass of chilled *Moët Brut*. She took-in the jet's luxury wood veneer interior and felt wicked to be flying the six-seater alone.

Duping Karpos had been simpler than she'd hoped. Jeff had scheduled the firm's corporate jet for that afternoon, giving her only a few hours to get Stink Bug out of the way for a few days and to pack for the trip. It hadn't mattered where she sent him or on what flight. Just as long as he turned up late for it.

Booking him an e-ticket online and collecting his boarding pass from the electronic check-in herself meant the Russian didn't get to read any documentation. They'd gone through the same passport and security checks together only, once airside, she would be taking a different flight.

A prior conversation with a cabin crew supervisor had enabled her to accompany her 'acutely aerophobic' boss to his seat in First and get him tucked-in. No one had had a problem with that, even with the heightened security since 9/11. After all, her passport had already been checked and she had no luggage stowed aboard Air Jamaica flight 16.

She took another sip of champagne, kicked off her

kitten heels and wriggled her toes. They ached and she'd forgotten to pack anything more sensible in the rush. She took a buff colored file from her briefcase, opened it and studied the photo of Rab MacBain clipped to the front page. She reminded herself why she'd decided to get the jump on Karpos and go it alone. "That's right," she said out-loud, "Unfinished business."

The Challenger hit a pocket of turbulence, causing her stomach to do a flip. Captain Paul's voice came over the speaker. "Sorry about that, Ms. Gordon, best fasten your seat belt." But she already had.

Chapter Six

NO school tomorrow so he'd be able to work late. Fab-a-rooney or what? Zachariah placed a half-dozen pint pots in the washer, squeezed the lemon-scented detergent into the little drawer on its front and turned the machine on. Piece o' pish, he thought. Easy money. Thinking of which, Mrs. Drum still owed him for Wednesday so he'd be taking home a fat tenner come closing tonight.

He shut his eyes against the hubbub and did the arithmetic. Add the dosh Mam gave him last week for his eleventh birthday and he'd just enough to get 'Backyard Baseball' for his Sony PlayStation 2. Well, stroll on! Right. He needed an excuse for a wee wander. How's the log situation?

Short for his age, he had to get on tip-toe to peer between the ale pumps. Aye, the log-pile was getting low by the inglenook. If Mrs. Drum noticed him gone from behind the bar the dozy hen would assume he was off fetching wood.

The place was heaving tonight and he could see her dishing-out pies and tatties to a group of camouflaged Germans seated in the midst of the scrum. The old hag must be raking it in, he reckoned, what with the thirty-odd birdwatchers in from the campsite again. 'Beak sniffers', his Grandfather, called them. Ha! Right enough, Granfer Dugald.

Numpties of all nationalities had been crossing the water in droves since that bit on the telly about the blue-tailed falcons, and practically everyone on the island was getting something out of the daft bastards. Even himself, Zac Moore, Chief Pot Collector, Bottler-upper and General Gofer (Bar Department). The first the pub had employed in living memory, Granfer had told him. And Zac even liked the job; liked the noise and bustle, the stink of stale booze, and ear-wigging the bollocks grown-ups blathered about when on the swally.

Logs, and time for a fag-a-roo. He pulled the hood of his sweater up over his paint-spattered Yankees cap (proud to be the only hoodie on the island, by the way) and slipped down the passage and out into the alley.

His stubby fingers reached into the bottom of the cast-iron drainpipe and teased out a ten-pack of Marlboro Lite and chuck-away lighter. A dry a place as any with the pub's gutters clogged with moss and gull shite. He showed the inside of the pack to the moonlight that streamed from the direction of the harbour front. Only two cigs left, fuckit. Oh well, he'd have to pinch some more from behind the bar later. The old girl was clueless when it came to her stock levels.

He dropped to his haunches between the log-stack and a tower of lobster pots, shook out a ciggie, lit-up and sucked hard on it. He exhaled through his nostrils long and slow, making a pair of smoke cones in the chilled air. Days on Garg were warming up but the nights still bit. Mmm, he thought, he was getting good at fags, his eyes watering and his mouth tasting like total shite-a-roo. He took another deep drag anyway and relived for the billionth time his moment of glory, his humongous act of heroism last Christmas in this very alley. The day he saved Rab MacBain's arse from a gang of Russian bear shaggers.

Nobody had given the Yank much mind when he'd first arrived and put-up at the pub. The islanders were used to occasional strangers; outward-bounders, beak sniffers and the like, but the American hadn't fitted that bill at all. Just skulked about the place with a face as long as a horse's dick, keeping himself to himself and getting pished on the malt all times of the day.

Then things took a turn the night Calum smacked Rab a right good'n in the gob. And how, exactly, was Zac privy to this? Well, for that you'd have to know that Greda MacBain possessed the most fantazmic pair of tits on God's planet.

He knew, right enough, because he'd keeked through her parlour window a few nights when she'd been in the tub. Watched her soaping those freckled beasties in the warmth and glow of the cooking range. Sometimes pinching her nipples on purpose, making them stiff. Or spending more time than was decent with the soap down below. And if anyone wanted to bet him the colour of her minge he'd win hands down, because he knew for a fact it in no way matched the copper shock on her head.

Greda's parlour window had been his private cinema for a while now, and priceless, with every showing rating an 18 certificate. Except the night he'd keeked in to see Greda holding Rab's hand across the parlour table, fuckit, and neither in a rush to get their kecks off.

Well, why would they be, with Rab being the son of Great Aunt Clair MacBain who croaked last year, making him Greda's brother and some kind of cousin to Zac, with Granfer Dugald being Clair's brother on the Moores' side of the family? All of which did his head in trying to figure out, by the way.

He'd been about to give up and head home for his tea when the sound of boots on gravel sent him scurrying under Greda's trap parked near-by. Calum had emerged from the darkness and gone inside the cottage. Then came raised voices and Zac had peered in again in time to see Calum lamp one right on Rab's jaw, knocking him as cold as a skittle. Jesus knows what that had been about, but it couldn't've been serious, mind, because the following night both men got slaughtered together and laughed-up a riot in Mrs. Drum's until past midnight... which has fuck-all to do with Zachariah Moore's humungous act of heroism the week before Christmas seven months ago.

He drew a final drag on his fag, dropped the dog-end down the drain and lit-up another. A low putting sound, rising in volume, drifted from the harbour. A couple of the tiny fleet's fishing boats. Calum's or Granfer

Dugald's, perhaps, returning with the day's haul. A meagre catch, most like.

So anyway, Captain Angus had radioed the post office from the ferry, warning he had three Russkies aboard and described them. Word reached Rabbie in minutes, sending him straight into hiding up at the old cemetery.

Soon after, the Russians stepped off *The Mishnish* amid a group of day trippers, sticking-out like tits on a bull. Dressed all wrong, see? No boots, Barbours, camouflaged smocks or khakis. Not a camera, spotting scope or pair of bins between them. Not even a rucksack. Instead, they wore suits and carried suitcases that looked too new.

They'd been friendly enough at first. Right Jokers, and quick to buy drinks-all-round in the boozer. Then came the questions. Had anyone seen or heard of Rab MacBain? Born here, they said, making-out they were long lost mates of his.

"He my pal buddy," the big one said. Which everyone knew was a load of raw bollocks because Rabbie had given the islanders the heads-up these numpties would come looking for him with a grudge.

Anyway, no one was going to grass him up. People liked him, and after all, he was family, wasn't he?

Day three and the Russkies were getting pushy, throwing their weight around like bampots, and so Calum and a bunch of the bigger lads took them aside and told them where to go and how fast. Even Mrs. Drum, to give the hag her due, chucked them out the two rooms they'd taken for the week.

But before they boarded the ferry back to Mull, they'd ambushed Zac in this very alley. It was before he worked in the pub. Before the beak sniffer invasion.

He'd had a stupid ding-dong with his mam about being late for school and had stormed out without having a pish. Loath to go inside again, he'd nipped in here to take one behind the lobster pots.

He'd just unzipped when the fat one with a face like a skelped arse had grabbed him by the scruff with a mammoth mit, and had smacked his head against a door jamb. "MacBain! Where is piece of shit?"

"Up mah granny's arse, hangin' on a nail, ye fat bassa!" had been Zac's reply, earning him a back-hander that had split his lip and sent a gallon of blood down his front.

His vision had whited-out and his face had gone numb. The bastard's mouth had breathed heat into his ear. "Is last chance, little one."

He'd had Zac's nuts clamped in a fist, but he didn't cry. Didn't make a sound. He'd never grass anyone up, certainly not Rabbie, damn it.

One of the other shites muttered something Russian. A few moments passed and he found himself face-down on the frosted ground with a mouthful of cold dirt and the bear shaggers nowhere in sight.

He cried then, when no-one could see, his bladder emptying into his kecks. It had been Granfer Dugald who'd found him, taken him inside and had cleaned him up by the fire.

The ferry had set sail before fear finally let him tell his

tale. And that afternoon, Rabbie had hugged him and given him the paint-spattered Yankees cap and 'The Pocketbook of Baseball Heroes', which was pretty grand, by the way, and had told him he was a hero too.

He was stubbing-out his last ciggie when the blow came fast and stung his ear. "Get in there wi' the logs before ah skin ye!"

He scrambled to his feet before Mrs. Drum could get another hand to him.

"Slaves get it better," he whined, rubbing the side of his face through his hood, "and ye still owe me a fiver from Wednesday, missus!"

The old woman's features softened. She smiled down at him, her eyes made milky by the moon. "Aye, but ah'll be dockin' that, won't ah, laddie, fer the fags ye've been thievin'!" And he was sure he heard a low chuckle as she shuffled back inside.

"Shite-a-roony," he muttered, still cupping his ear and bending to the wood-pile, "What's a hero godda dae ta get some respect 'round here?"

*

Atlantic gales had given-way to a light breeze this July morning and Rab wondered how long the calm would last, seated, as he was, at his easel in the south-west corner of the crumbling cemetery.

The fourteenth century kirk it belonged to had given itself up to the sea, the last stones of the ruin having plummeted to the foot of the fast eroding cliff face thirty years or so before he'd been born. At the going rate, he calculated, the remaining headstones, and the graves they marked, would go the same way before another thirty storm-cursed winters had come and gone.

He leant to dip his sable brush into a Marmite pot of water at his feet, then mixed white with blue-gray on the ceramic pallet housed in the lid of his wooden paint box.

The Windsor & Newton watercolors were probably left behind by his father, Greda had told him. She remembered their mother letting her play with them as a kid. The folding easel too, which now held an eight by ten inch sheet of watercolor paper taped to a board.

His strokes were practiced and certain, the color true to the darker breast feathers of a peregrine falcon. He looked up past the work in progress to the real thing; a female, perched on a lichen-encrusted tombstone some seven yards from the cliff's edge. Her bright-blue tail feathers no longer a surprise to him. *Way to go, Dad.*

He worked quickly, as the blue-tailed falcons rarely lingered. Then, as if reading his thought, the bird lifted her powder-gray wings to catch a sudden gust.

He reached into a coat pocket, brought out a stillborn chick, fresh from Greda's chicken coop this morning and tossed it through the air. The falcon caught it in a razor beak, shook it once and clamped it to the tombstone with her talons. She shredded the morsel and gobbled it down, feathers, feet and all.

Feeding her, as he knew it would, stole him a few more

seconds with the brush before another gust became too tempting and she took off, spiralled up, then dove over the edge of the cliff. Returning, Rab knew, to her mate and their three juvenile offspring on the eyrie twelve feet below.

Enough. He packed away his paints, planning to finish the picture tonight at the cottage, where, on Greda's parlour table, with Indian ink and mapping pen, he would cross-hatch over the watercolor wash just as Charlie had taught him in another life.

Male voices reached him on the breeze and he turned to see a couple of birdwatchers, Germans or Dutch by the sound of them, approaching Large Stanley's dry-stone shelter. The open-fronted structure had a grass-turfed roof and, backing onto the cemetery's rear wall, looked all the way up to Ben Wrath.

This was where Stanley, one of the last shepherds on the island, kept watch over his flock in the glen. But not today, though. The refuge was unoccupied and the black sheep were fending for themselves, scattered way-off along the slow-running burn amid rocky outcrops and cairns.

The birdwatchers had arrived at the shelter and were taking snapshots with their cell phones. All the devices were good for with no signal on the island. He hoped they hadn't seen him with the falcon just now. Seen how tame she'd been with him. But then the men turned away and headed up into the glen and he relaxed.

He rose, collapsed his canvass stool, took up the folded

easel, paint box and his dad's leather folio and headed for a gap in the cemetery's decrepit dry-stone wall.

He paused for a few moments by his mother's grave, its headstone still painfully new, then set off down the cliff path toward Garg's tiny harbor. And the tourist trap.

*

Looking about her in this comic excuse for a ferry-boat, Becky could only liken the scene to something out of 'Gulliver's Travels' or maybe a surreal European art-house flick.

Okay, she thought, the dozen or so hardcore bird enthusiasts seemed normal enough. But only in contrast to the ferry's one-armed, one-eyed captain and the chickens pecking the backs of her knees through the wicker cage she'd been forced to sit on the whole way. Oh yeah, and the handful of dung-encrusted sheep and the curly-horned ram which kept clomping on her feet.

The ram and his girls looked like something out of 'Dante's Inferno.' A strange looking breed. Small and dark with four horns apiece, they looked like little black devils.

But the star of the show had to be the real life giant with an oversized strawberry where his nose should be, sitting on a beer keg next to her. In fact, she'd been quick to recognise the old guy as the Santa-faced shepherd from the DVD recording she'd viewed in Jeffery Hammer's office. Stanley? Yes, Stanley. Same patched, maroon coat tied around with string. Same booze-boiled eyes.

This time, though, as well as his badge of office; the shepherd's crook, he had a large duck tucked under his arm. If, indeed, that's what it was meant to be. For it looked like a school kid's art assignment with its leaf-shaped feathers, probably cut from Polythene sacks, and its beak; half a plastic banana stuck on the front of a *papier mache* head. It had ping-pong balls for eyes, with pupils drawn so off-center you'd think it had an overactive thyroid.

The couple of times she'd complained to the shepherd about his ram treading on her toes, she'd received stony stares and ditto silence. So she'd tried a different tack and had said, nodding to his handiwork, "Hey! Nice duck. Does it do tricks?" Which had caused his eyes to pop wider than his model bird's.

Garg's charcoal coastline appeared on the horizon against a slate sky flecked with seabirds and she sighed inside. *What the hell am I doing here?*

Captain One-arm One-eye turned to scowl at her from the wheelhouse so she flashed him her butter-wouldn't-melt smile, which got a wink from him. She winked back then thought, whoops! For this guy a wink was probably a regular blink.

The travelling freak-show aside, she was finding the crossing invigorating. It'd been years since she'd been at sea and she savored the salt on her lips, the prickling spray on her cheeks and the easy side-to-side sway of the little open boat.

The sea breeze carried little warmth with it, though,

and she wondered if summer ever really made it this far west of the Scottish mainland. Nothing of New York's heatwave seemed to have made it across the Atlantic. From the get-go, she'd had to button her suit jacket and keep her arms folded against it. There'd been no time during the non-stop trip to shop for outdoor clothing or to even swap her skirt for the slacks in her bag.

And, Jesus, she couldn't wait to kick off her city shoes and put her feet into warm, soapy water. She hoped with all her being Mrs. Drum's would have the basic mod-cons, because otherwise she'd have to shoot herself. Ouch! Another attack of chicken pecks to the backs of her knees, for Christ's sake!

One of the bird guys shouted something and pointed over the side. She followed his gaze and was rewarded by the sight of dorsal fins cutting through silver-green water close enough to touch. Dolphins? Porpoises? *Welcome to the circus, fellas.* She smiled as a rare joy stirred deep within her. But then it died when she remembered where she was and why she'd come.

*

Rab MacBain paused at the foot of the gravelled slope where the cliff path met the black-top which skirted the harbor wall. The road had been lain after the island had won its independence; freeing itself from a blood-sucking line of lairds on the mainland who, over centuries, with the demise of its sheep farming and fishing, had choked the isle to near-death with extortionate rents.

"There was nothin' left for us on that fucked-up rock in the sea..." It's okay, Dad.

Another welcome improvement had been the restoration of a red, public call-box out-front of Mrs. Drum's. Which reminded him of his favourite scenes from *'Local Hero,'* where the young oil rep had to describe constellations in the night sky down the transatlantic line to an enraptured Burt Lancaster.

Then there was the new generator house which supplied electricity enough for the clutch of dwellings nearest the harbor, and the stone chapel, still under construction, to replace the converted Nissen hut that had served as church, morgue and meeting house right back to World War II.

There was also a glass and timber-framed construction underway, destined to become a wildlife center-cum-whale watching station. Sightings of the magnificent creatures were abundant in these waters: Minke, Orcas and Humpbacks. Future tourist draws to aid the island's precarious economy, and a venture Greda was gearing-up to run along with the falconry. After all, *Blue-tailed-falconmania* wasn't going to last for ever.

A cacophony of screaming gulls snatched his attention, heralding the arrival of *The Mishnish* as she chugged through the harbor mouth on a high tide. The birds wheeling and dive-bombing the craft in the hope of fish scraps, no doubt. Unlike a disinterested family of gray seals, their dog-like heads bobbing some way off, canny enough to tell it from one of the island's few fishing boats.

He was glad to see the ferry packed to the gunwales, promising welcome additions to the multi-colored speckling of tents on the campsite, and more much needed currency all round.

By the time he'd reached Mrs. Drum's and off-loaded his painting gear inside the pub's doorway for safekeeping, the ferry had docked at the foot of the harbor's cobblestone hard.

He took up his folio and went in search of the Dunlop sisters; joint proprietors of the Boathouse Cafe, thinking how every day here had come to feel more and more like home.

*

"Katie Beardie had a coo
Black and white aboot the mou'
Wasnae that a dainty coo?
Dance Katie Beardie."

Zac was feeling a right wassock, singing the nursery rhyme midway up the cobblestone ramp. It wasn't the actual singing that got to him, he quite liked a sing-song. It was that Miss Tonbridge had lined up the entire school, sixteen pupils in all, tallest to shortest. Which, though he was eleven, put him on the end with the wee brats. Even Lizzie Drum towered an inch above him in her plimmies, and she was only nine, fuckit. By rights he should be at Tobermory High School on Mull. But with his 'special needs' as Mam had explained, he'd had to hang back with the bairns for a year. Roll on next September, though.

> *"Katie Beardie had a hen,*
> *Cackled but and cackled ben.*
> *Wasnae that a dainty hen?*
> *Dance Katie Beardie."*

At least, being the eldest, he'd been entrusted with the plastic bucket. He'd decorated it himself with a scrap of tatty tinsel from home and a handwritten sign that read, *'SCHOOL FUND',* which looked pretty grand, by the way.

The Mishnish had docked and the beak sniffers were climbing the ramp. Which had been Miss Tonbridge's cue to start pummelling Ol' Wheezer, her portable harmonium on the back of the school's multi-coloured wagon. And for her sweet, wee angels to start belting it out about Katie and her stupid cow.

The first of the new arrivals were getting near, humping rucksacks and whatnot. Their free hands dipping into pockets, searching for change with faces beaming at the line of children like numpties. He straightened and took a step forward to distance himself from the wee brats, bucket out-stretched with a grin.

> *"Katie Beardie had a wean*
> *Widnae play oot in the rain.*
> *Wasn't that a dainty wean?*
> *Dance Katie Beardie."*

Lizzie Drum, barely a *wean* herself, stopped singing, crept up and tried to prise his hands from the bucket so she could hold it.

"Let go and sing, ye wee dobber!" he hissed, which made her bottom lip jut-out and quiver. Jesus Christ-a-roony.

Chink, chink, went the coins in the bucket as beak sniffers passed-by in a gaggle of green and khaki. *Chink, chink, chink, chink…* "Thank ye, thank ye," he beamed, "All in a good cause, and welcome, by the way." *Ye numpties.*

Out the corner of his eye, he caught sight of Maddie; Large Stanley's black and white Border collie, as she scampered down to greet her master. She'd waited all night at the top of the hard and, just like Greyfriars Bobby, hadn't budged for nothin' or no one. She took charge of the big man's wee flock in a jiffy, nipping at the animals' hind legs to buck them up. A sight that made him smile as their bleating and the reek of them followed the newcomers to the top of the ramp. Sheep leading sheep. Ha!

> *Katie Beardie had a cat,*
> *Sleek and sly and unco fat.*

Wasnae that a dainty cat?
Dance, Katie Beardie.

And, as it happens, that old Scots word, *'unco'*, which their teacher had taught them meant 'surprising' or 'uncanny', could accurately describe what he saw next. Then again, 'funny as fuck' described it better. For there was a blonde lass, bit of a babe, actually, in a tight skirt, struggling up the hard with her suitcases, her ankles looking ready to snap in high-heels on the cobbles.

He wanted to hoot out-loud at the spectacle as huge black-backed gulls swooped and shrieked around her. The poor hen had to be bonkers, he reckoned. Or American.

On spotting the sign on his bucket, the woman paused, swaying back and forth like a drunkard. She dropped her luggage to fight with the clasp of her handbag, all the while cursing under her breath.

"Damn-it... Damn-it... Shit... Damn-it..."

Well, there you go then. American.

He found himself laughing his guts up and at once felt guilty. Then realised the whole school had deserted *'Katie Beardie'* and was howling along with him, ignoring Miss Tonbridge's bashing of Ol' Wheezer's lid in an appeal for calm.

Meanwhile, the lass staggered towards him and tossed some coins into his bucket, *chink, chink, chink.* She spun on unsteady feet to shoot daggers up and down the line, causing the kids to clam-up in an instant. Then, to give the lovely lady her due, she burst out laughing as well.

Which was the moment he fell humongously head-over-heels in love with her.

*

Rab squeezed through the bodies as best he could. New arrivals were making a beeline for the trestle table stalls that stretched the short length of the harbor road to join the already established throng shopping for souvenirs: blue-tailed falcon T-shirts, mugs, postcards, tea towels, bird watching paraphernalia, tweed hats, carved canes and wool sweaters. And, of course, the obligatory Western Isles' fare of shortbread, butterscotch, Tobermory chocolate and box-sets of whisky miniatures. But even these were being sold under the blue-tailed falcon label. Business looked good and Rab felt happy for the twenty-five or so stall-holders that made up near-on half the island's population these days. *Make hay while the sun shines, guys...*

"Excuse me... Pardon me," he repeated over and over as he wove his way through the crush. A delicious smell filled his nostrils as he neared a little old lady in black hat and coat cooking fresh sea dabs over coals. Garg's version of fast food, served in a buttered bun with ketchup and going for three pounds a pop.

A hefty slap landed between his shoulder blades. He turned around with difficulty, hugging his folio to his chest in the crush, and found himself looking into ink-black eyes. Cold but glinting mischief, and the smile beneath not wide enough to be convincing. "Calum, how ya doin'?"

"Grand, Rab. You'll be up in the glen?" The two had to pitch-up over the crowd.

"Sure. In a while." Then he spotted the eider duck under the fisherman's arm and nodded to it. "Good job."

And so it was, the life-sized bird having been exquisitely carved in wood and painted shades of white, black and green. Its face markings reminding him of a clown's. When it came to carving, Calum was known to be as expert with his knife as with his fists.

The men had struck an uneasy alliance after Calum had knocked his lights out all those months ago. But the price had been for him to come clean to Greda and her man about the shit he was in. The Russian mob after him for the twenty-five mil' he'd magicked into a Swiss bank account. He told them about Frank Holt's disappearance, the dead taxi driver and the murdered kid in the alley. Everything.

His story must've sounded so alien to them next morning in the parlour of his mother's tiny crofter's cottage. And when he was through, he felt he'd defiled the place, and brought a shit-load of trouble to the island's doorstep. And to compound his self-disgust, at the mention of his multi-million embezzlement, he'd seen no dollar signs in their eyes. In Greda's, all he'd seen was disappointment.

Late that same night, he and Calum had talked the whole thing out while getting wasted in Mrs. Drum's.

Before they'd gotten too juiced-up, both agreed the islanders needed to be warned Karpos Brunovich and his goons would probably come looking for him. They'd have to be prepared for any threat to their families.

And he had to hand it to these people, for when the Russians *had* turned up they'd taken the danger in their stride and there'd been little fallout. Except for Dugald's grandson, little Zac, getting roughed-up by the bastards. He swore next time he'd make Stink Bug pay dearly for that, because there was no doubt in his mind the mobster would be coming for him again soon.

When he and Calum had gotten to falling off their stools time at the bar, they'd made booze-fuelled plans together which had made them laugh until they couldn't see through the tears. Drunken plans. Plans to save the island. Plans for Rab to save himself, which, incidentally, entailed him staying put on Garg for the time being. Crazy plans, for sure, but back then he hoped some of them would stick. And now, with the place humming with bird lovers, it was good to see some already had.

"See ye, then," Calum shouted over the din, his smile still lacking something.

"Yeah," Rab said, checking his watch, "Soon."

He watched the swarthy fisherman side-wind away through the crowd in the direction of the harbor. What plans did that guy have for *himself*, he wondered, certain that however long he stayed on Garg he'd never truly trust the guy.

*

Becky sat crossed-legged on steps in the harbor wall to get her breath back and to rub her ankles.

Her arrival could've been a little more dignified on reflection, she decided. Jesus, what an idiot. She'd blown any chance now of keeping her head below the radar when her plan had been... well, okay, hands up, she never had a plan, but keeping her arrival low-key might've been sensible. And to have taken time on the mainland to get kitted-out for the terrain. Boots, at least, dummy.

Thinking of dummies, what was it with the ducks? From where she was sitting she could see what must've been a couple of local women, chatting, comparing their model ducks. One of the birds looked to be made from plastic soda bottles. The other, drinks cans taped together... and was that a kid's sneaker for a head? How crazy was that?

Then a guy walked by with a duck tucked under his arm. His, though, was nothing like the womens' or Stanley, the shepherd's. It was better made. Less amateur. Brightly painted.

Its owner had a tattoo emblazoned on his neck. A gold earring. Dark, spiky hair and jet-black eyes that undressed her as he swaggered by. The cold stare she returned had no effect. He simply grinned then joined a handful of fishermen nearby mending nets. He must've smart-mouthed something to them because they turned in sync to scrutinize her and laughed a laugh devoid of humor.

She looked away and feigned interest in the crowded

market opposite, when something tugged at her elbow. It was the little boy she'd just seen singing with the other children. He wore a Yankees baseball cap under the hood of his sweater, which looked kind of odd this far from home. He'd been the one collecting with the bucket.

"What d'ya want, Kiddo? I gave already."

"Ye've gull shite on yer jacket, missus," he said, pointing to a splat of the stuff on her shoulder.

"Shit!"

"Shit, shite, as ye like." *Mmm… another smart-mouth.*

He beamed up at her with large, limpid eyes that put her in mind of a *Platycryptus undatus.* An American tan jumping spider. "Thanks," she managed, rummaging in her pocket book for a tissue. She found one and set to wiping off the mess.

The kid, meanwhile, had dropped his spider gaze to appraise her legs, for God's sake. Her tone went for school-mam.

"Was there anything else, young mister?"

"Um… no, missus… I just…" His face was reddening fast.

"What's your name?" she said, scrunching the tissue and scanning around for somewhere to lose it.

"Um… Zac."

"Well, Um Zac, maybe you can tell me where I can find…" But when she looked back the little spider boy had gone.

*

The miss-matched tables and chairs out-front of the Boathouse Cafe were taken-up with birdwatchers. Rab noticed several fiddling with their cell phones. Ridiculous they couldn't leave the things alone even when they were no good for making calls.

"We've sold fifteen o' these in the last week," Elleen Dunlop was saying with pride as she leafed through the falcon paintings in his folio. The same Elleen who'd hugged and kissed him good-bye a quarter century ago at the top of the cobblestone hard.

Her sister, Mary, turning from clearing a table of tea things, smiled and said in unison with Elleen, "You'll soon be rich, Rabbie!"

In their mid-seventies, these two would ordinarily spend their days spinning and weaving with wool from the island's meagre sheep population, but had commandeered the deserted lifeboat house in order to sell refreshments during the present tourist boom.

Though being born a year apart, strangers found it hard to tell them apart. Matching ginger wigs with tight buns, bifocal spectacles and identical floral pinafores made telling who from who close to impossible if you didn't know them.

He watched Mary glide away with her tea things toward the building's high double-doors on which several of his paintings, mostly of the blue-tailed falcons, were displayed higgledy-piggledy without frames. Most marked-up at twenty to thirty pounds. Not great dough, but steady. And all of them signed *'Tim Santry'* for the sake of anonymity. His dad would've approved, he reckoned. Not so much of the pseudonym but that he'd taken up painting again.

He'd been thinking a lot about Charlie lately, recalling a time when he'd feared he was turning into his old man. These days he wondered if he'd ever measure up to him.

Elleen, still flipping through the pictures, paused at a watercolor landscape. It depicted the forested southern tip of the island, bathed in a golden sunset.

"Ah, Rabbie, ye bring out the beauty in all ye see."

"Well, I'm seeing you right now, Elleen."

"Ha, away wi' ye," she chuckled, "We're closin' early, as ye well know. Be off, now." Then taking a wad of his finished paintings, she ruffled his hair and traced her sister's footsteps into the shadowy confines of the boathouse.

*

Zac had kept his distance in case the lovely lass spotted him tagging along behind. Which had become more difficult with the stalls packing-up early and the beak sniffer crowd thinning-out. At one point, though, he'd been close enough to hear her address one of the stallholders.

"Excuse me," she'd said, "do you happen to sell butterscotch?"

Jesus. Typical tourist or what? But he forgave her, of course.

The stallholder was out of the stuff and had told her to come back the day after tomorrow. She was moving on now with her luggage in tow, the sway of her narrow hips causing her small but fantazmically formed buttocks to roll one against the other.

She perused souvenirs and junk on the stalls as she neared the Boathouse Cafe. Then stopped in her tracks to steal a glance over her shoulder, causing him to dive under a trestle table. Which was no bad thing, actually. He could stay stooped and make his way beneath the market stalls unseen. A ruse, by the way, which came with the unexpected bonus of 98p in dropped change.

By the time he reached the last trestle and keeked out, she'd stopped to ask directions from Constable Finn, the only copper on the island, mounted, as he was, on Sherlock, his grey-dappled pony.

Word had it the Northern Irish policeman had been transferred here from Ulster during The Troubles for the sake of his nerves.

He was sitting to attention in his saddle now, stomach sucked in, doing his best to impress the lass. A tall order, Zac reckoned, what with his baggy, frayed uniform looking like it'd seen better days in a black and white film.

The wassock was pointing back the way the lass had come, grinning like a numpty and sending her away to Mrs. Drum's by the looks of it.

A shape caught Zac's eye and he turned to focus on Rabbie chatting with one of the Dunlop hens outside the cafe. Rabbie had always told him to be on the look-out for Russkies and Yanks, but this one was surely no threat to him, was she? There was about fifty feet between she and Rabbie, he calculated. Maybe he should warn him. Grass the beauty up just to be on the safe side.

She was on the move again, anyway, heading for the pub, most like, her legs coming close to his hiding place, looking smooth and nice to touch. He shot a glance back at the boathouse where Rabbie had disappeared.

Something started to niggle and nag in the back of his mind. He turned to peer out at Constable Finn again and that's when it hit him. All the while the lovely lass had been getting directions from the copper, he'd only had eyes for her. So he'd totally missed the model duck under the mounted policeman's arm. It wore a shiny peaked-cap with a chequered band, a miniature version of its owner's.

Shite-a-roony! Zac hadn't even made his yet!

*

She pounded the desk bell on the bar for what must've been the tenth time to no avail. Okay, she hadn't expected the Four Seasons with porters and bell-hops but a sign of life would've been good. Mrs. Drum's bar-room showed less evidence of human habitation than the *Marie Celeste* during a fire drill.

There'd been a hand-written 'CLOSED' notice on the street door but surely that wasn't there to deter prospective residents. Anyway, she'd booked. In her mom's maiden name, admittedly, but she *had* booked!

She scanned the room. It looked rustic and cosy. Smelt of old beer but in a nice way. She peered through the gloom to a window which looked onto the harbor road. Beyond, birdwatchers were making their way down the ramp to board the ferry for Mull, she supposed.

Damnit! She hit the bell again. Still no one came. Out the little leaded window, she watched as a rainbow-colored cart passed by drawn by a tan and white pony. The vehicle was crammed with the kids she'd seen singing earlier and they were all nursing ducks on their laps made from trash items. She crossed the room to get a better look.

Locals were filing past in the same direction carrying… yup, dummy ducks. A little old lady in black hat and coat struggled to keep up with the others, pushing her duck along in an antiquated baby stroller.

"Right. That's it," she announced to the empty room, "You got me." She abandoned her luggage and headed for the door.

*

Rab was pleased. It was a good turn-out with thirty-seven entrants so far. The predominantly rough-made models were bunched and bobbing in the narrow burn, high up, where it sprung from Ben Wrath's navel. The color-flecked Jetsam strained against a taught rope pegged from bank to bank. To the uninitiated, the stream might seem to have fallen prey to fly-tippers.

The islanders were grouped either side of the starting line, their excitement so infectious he caught himself grinning like a kid. Everywhere there was smiling and laughter. At times like these, it struck him, young or old, we were all children.

Greda was kneeling near-by, helping the school kids place their ducks in the water, and making sure they didn't fall in. Their teacher, Emily Tonbridge, was keeping her eye on her brood from the seat of the school's multi-colored wagon. A needless worry as most of their moms and dads were here too.

"Please, Rabbie, ah forgot mah number!"

He looked down to discover little Lizzie Drum peering up with eyes convinced the World was about to end. He peeled a green sticker, black-markered '38', from a roll and stuck it to the girl's proffered duck. Its body was a soda can with a large potato for a head.

"His name's Tattie," Lizzie beamed, "He's a grand swimmer."

The bird didn't have a hope in Hell. "Well, he certainly looks like a winner!"

She smiled up at him with a small face that shone like the sun. He smiled back, holding out his cloth bag containing the duck race takings so the girl could drop in her coins. They seemed too big for her fist and he felt bad accepting them. But, hey, business was business. Lizzie turned and ran down to join her parents at the waterside.

A slow hand-clap grew out of the hubbub. His eyes met

his sister's and he gave a sharp nod; the signal for the off. Greda tugged the restraining line free, giving-up the flotilla to the burn's impatient current.

At first, the models moved as one but then separated out as they nudged against moss-covered boulders or got caught in small eddies out to the sides. Some were just better made, he guessed, more buoyant or streamlined and so found their own course, stealing a march on the rest. A warm contentedness came over him as he remembered racing his own duck on this burn. Back in a time of innocence. A happy time. His happiest, even.

*

"Shit, shit, damn and shit..!" Climbing the gravelled cliff path hadn't been so bad but now she was in the rough, her kitten heels were sinking into the soft ground and tangling in coarse grass. She removed the damned things to make the going easier then, reaching the brow of the hill, flopped on her backside to take a breather.

The blue sky had given way to a blanket of dense, low cloud and a cold breeze had strengthened as she'd climbed the hill. But physical exertion was doing a fine job of warding off the chill.

She took-in the lime-gray mountain and the valley below. The handful of tiny white, stone cottages dotted about. Some in ruins and none looking particularly habitable in such bleak surroundings. Jesus, how could people live in a place like this?

She heard them before she saw them. Excited whoops and laughter. Her eyes zeroed-in on the culprits below; two groups, strung-out either side of a stream. Locals, young and old, having a total whale of a time, running along and egging-on their ducks in some kind of race. *Mystery solved, Dumbo.*

She found herself laughing too as she gathered up her shoes and padded barefoot down the hill, dodging rocks, and heading for the action. She reached the stream just as the excited islanders filed by, oblivious of her presence, cheering-on their model birds. She recognised a few: Stanley, Zac, the spider boy, the mounted cop (still in uniform!) and the swarthy fisherman with the striptease eyes.

The stretch of water grew wider here. And rockier, making the way hazardous for the ducks. Several were breaking-up and sinking, or getting stuck among submerged boulders, themselves becoming obstacles for those behind. The survivors, though, were on course for the beach, where the stream fanned-out and gushed white over brown and orange kelp-clad rocks.

She felt an uncontrollable urge to join the locals in a dash for the finish line, but a shape drew her eye to the opposite bank, causing something hot and aching to swell in her throat.

Amid a group of excited locals, strode Rab MacBain. His dark mohair coat eight months the worse for wear. Straggly hair, now and face unshaven.

She'd waited an age for this moment, she realized, all

the while wondering how she'd react when it came. But before she even had a chance to, Rab was joined by a beautiful young woman with Pre-Raphaelite hair and pale skin that shone with youth. The two embraced. Then Rab lifted the girl and spun her twice around. Their laughter became distant as the ache in her throat moved up to sting her eyes.

Her body had turned rigid with cold and she watched through a haze as the two set off again, running along the bank, hand in hand, the perfect couple, playing-out the closing lines of a cheesy Mills & Boon.

Chapter Seven

His Hawaiian shirt had no tail which meant the cheeks of his ass were exposed. But that wasn't the worst of it, of course, because the scarred remains of his crotch was also on view and the two black Jamaican cops standing across the table from him couldn't tear their eyes away from the place where his dick should've been.

The one on the right, the stocky one chewing gum with a stubby hand resting on his holstered sidearm... was that a smirk beneath his cap's shiny peak and aviation shades? Was the little fuck finding this funny?

The tiny, windowless room felt oven hot. And airless. He tried not to flinch as a bead of cold sweat trickled down his spine, into the crack of his backside, and down the inside of his leg to the pants and shorts concertinaed at his ankles.

It had become obvious the bitch had screwed him the moment he stepped off the plane. She hadn't even been on the damned flight. How'd she pull that, by the way?

Next thing, he'd been fuming into his cell phone as he'd strode toward the check-in desk for the next flight out to Europe.

"The skirt stiffed me... yeah, Kingston fuckin' Jamaica.

I find out you put her up to this, Hammer, I kill you with bare hands!"

He'd thrust his passport and boarding pass at the male check-in clerk. The latter's radiant smile had instantly vanished on examining the documents, his eyes darting shiftily to his left.

Karpos had been in mid-flow on the phone. "You tell Uncle Fedor I back on track, ya heart? Nothin' stop me now!"

That's when there'd come the sickening sound of revolvers being cocked behind him, accompanied by the low growl of a large sounding dog. Then the mutt had let-loose and barked the place down, drowning out the steel drum muzak jangling from ceiling speakers.

There'd been a collective gasp from onlookers before they'd dived behind bench seating. The cell phone left his hand and exploded into fragments on the hard tile floor. He'd turned all the way around, reaching for the sky like he'd seen in cowboy shows, to be confronted by gun barrels trained on him by the clowns now with him in the room. Oh yeah, along with the Alsatian mutt (more like a fuckin' wolf!) off the leash now and sitting three feet away, panting with the heat and eyeing him up for brunch.

What the hell time was it, anyway? He'd lost all track of time.

He glanced down at his open Samsonite on the table, its contents heaped and knotted after the cops had been through it. The last time he'd seen his aluminium case containing his surveillance goodies it had been with the Gordon woman. Maybe that wasn't a bad thing given the crap he was in now. His eyes flicked to the taller cop.

"An anonymous Fax ain't enough to cut ice where I come from, buddy," he blurted, "Like I told ya, dope ain't my thing".

They'd been looking for cocaine. The bum tip-off had been sent by the Gordon slut for sure. Another lousy waylaying tactic.

"I American! I got rights! You better get me on the next flight out before I sue your black ass along with laughin' boy's here!" The wolf gave a low growl through yellow teeth.

The cop jerked his head at the animal. Looked back at Kapos. "Be cool, mon. Me tink Annabelle here, she be bustin' far yar ass." Then he reached into a pant pocket and tugged from it a latex glove. He stretched it a couple of times for fun and let it snap back.

Karpos felt his naked buttocks clench tight. He rose to his full height and swelled out his chest. "Oh yeah? It take more than you freakin' fairies to get near me with th..."

At which moment the door opened and the hugest black cop in the world ducked into the room, dwarfing everything in it. His partner tossed him the glove, which he proceeded to work a fat mitt into. The stocky punk-ass blew and popped his gum, then sniggered as the new arrival squeezed Lube from a tube onto a middle finger.

Karpos stared at that oversized digit, his guts churning, his face red and burning. "I fuckin' kill the bitch!" he spat, a nanosecond before Annabelle, the wolf, was up on all-fours, teeth bared and snarling.

"Not *you*, stupid!"

*

"You tell Uncle Fedor I back on track, ya hear? Nothin' stop me now!"

The call had ended abruptly after a snatch of excited barking in the background. Bit odd, that, thinking about it.

Hammer lost the phone in his golf slacks and turned to Fedor Brunovich, sitting next to him in the back of the crime boss's limo. The latter's sleepy, turtle eyes fixed on his with a question.

Hammer hid his anxiety behind grinning veneers. "A hiccup. The girl gave him the slip is all. He's on top of it now."

He prayed Brunovich would buy that because, in actuality, his blundering nephew hadn't sounded like he was on top of anything other than his thumb up his ass.

And what in God's name was Becky thinking? Hadn't she got it yet? You just didn't screw with these people. All he could hope was that she knew what the hell she was doing because it was damned obvious Fedor Brunovich was rapidly losing patience. Forget his prospective ten mil' commission, Hammer had started to feel the tightening of a noose around his neck.

Back when he set up the Merlin account, he'd thought

it expedient to charge Rab MacBain and Frank Holt with its administration, made sure they alone possessed the codes to the Banco Confianza account on Grand Cayman. Best practice, security-wise, he'd told them. He'd been covering his own ass, of course. There'd be no trace, digital or otherwise, that would ever lead the FEDs to him. In the event they did come sniffing at his door he could safely plead ignorance. Not a wise move in retrospect, he had to admit, and if Becky Gordon failed to come up trumps on this, he'd be feeling that noose tighten for the very last time.

The old man responded to the news of his nephew's 'hiccup' with a wet snort. Turtle language for, "What a surprise," then turned to peer out the window, where the West Bronx lumbered by due to slow traffic. At this rate, the Van Cortlandt Park golf course was still a good half-hour away.

Whatever, it was a bit late in the day to start playing eighteen holes, for his liking. He couldn't see Brunovich even getting half-way around the course, anyhow. But that's what the old bastard had ordered and, right now, he called the shots.

The goon at the limo's wheel, the one with the mole, Matvy? He caught the guy's eyes scrutinizing him in the rear-view mirror but, for the life of him, Jeffery Hammer couldn't read what they were saying.

*

"It's a tie, Rabbie. Twenty-seven and twelve," Dugald announced at the mouth of the burn where the winning ducks lay stranded in the rocky shallows of an ebbing tide. The islanders thronged around Rab and Greda, chattering and panting from exertion.

Rab watched as Dugald retrieved the models and held them aloft for all to see.

"Aye, twelve'll be mine," Calum called as he pushed his way to the front of the gathering. Rab could see that, sure enough, one of the models was Calum's expertly carved creation. He smiled at its joint winner; a shampoo bottle with a limp piece of sodden cardboard for a head.

Zac, Dugald's grandson, suddenly squeezed out from between Constable Finn and Elleen Dunlop, pointing to the sadder duck. He was wearing the faded Yankees baseball cap Rab had given him. "And that's mine! Number twenty-seven," he said, his voice breaking with excitement.

"A tie, though. So who gets the prize?" called Rab to the crowd as Greda handed him a reed cage containing a white farmyard duck. The plump bird nipped at his fingers through the woven bars with an orange beak.

"Toss fer it," Calum piped up. Zac gaped up at him in horror while islanders muttered among themselves.

Rab took a step toward the fisherman. "And what would you do with the bird, Calum?"

"Wring its wee neck 'n' stick it in the oven on a nice, low heat."

"Quack," objected the duck, which brought chuckles

from the crowd.

Rab looked down at the boy. "And you, Zac?"

"I'm nae gonna wring its neck!" came the indignant response. A cheer went up. Zac was well-liked.

"I say we toss fer it!" insisted Calum over the din.

Rab shot him a side-ways glance. "And I say it's for me to decide." He handed Zac the caged bird to applause and murmurs of approval.

"Me *mam* can wring its neck and stick it in the oven!"

That earned the kid a roar of laughter, before the islanders dispersed and went in search of their models strewn along the kelp-clad shore.

Calum all but snatched his carving from Dugald. Greda, at Rab's side, called after her man's retreating back. "Dinnae be such a grump, Calum! Away wi' ye! Sorry, Uncle Dugald."

"Nae matter, lass," said the old man as he proffered the shampoo bottle entry to his grinning grandson.

"Nah, ye're alright, Granfer. It's proper shite, anyway."

Rab felt Greda's hand squeeze his. She smiled, pecked him on the cheek and headed for the slope that would take her up onto the cliff path. Dugald followed and Zac turned to join him, struggling with his caged trophy. Rab called after him. "Who's the greatest baseball player that ever lived?"

The boy turned back, his grin widening. "Based on what?"

"Home-runs."

"Hank Aaron holds the record at seven hundred and

fifty five, but Babe Ruth's yer man. Greatest all-round player e'en wi' his career home-run record finishin' at seven hundred and fourteen. Am ah right, now?" All rather odd sounding, thought Rab, coming from a young, heavily-accented Garg Islander.

"Smart kid." He flipped him a fifty pence coin, which the boy caught one-handed, winked and went on his way.

Rab wouldn't know if the kid had his facts straight; he'd never taken much to sports. All he knew was the little fella hadn't had Charlie Whistler's *Pocket Book of Baseball Heroes* out of his possession since he'd given it to him. The thought brought a smile.

Emily Tonbridge, the school mistress, stepped up. He nodded a greeting and handed her the cloth bag of race money.

"The school will spend it well, Rabbie."

"Towards a computer, right?"

"Aye, there's nae need fer our young ta get stuck in the past wi' the rest o' us." Her eyes twinkled. She touched his cheek and moved away, and that's when he spotted her.

His breath caught. He tried to swallow but his throat felt full of sand. She was standing fifty yards away along the shoreline; a fish out of water, barefoot and clutching her shoes to her chest.

*

Becky found him sitting on a crumbling tomb near the

cliff edge, where centuries' old gravestones looked ready to topple into the sea. Perhaps there was a church or chapel here once, she wondered, now out there under the waves.

He had his back to her but she knew he'd sensed her presence. She took her time putting on her shoes, not knowing how to say what she'd come all this way to say. She thought she'd rehearsed the words pretty well as she'd followed him in silence along the cliff path to the ancient cemetery, got them off pat, but now it came to it...

He turned his head side-on and she thought he was about to speak, but no. So she waded in without a script. "You get your cigarettes?" No response. "That's how most of those stories go, isn't it? You know, where the guy says he's just nipping out for smokes and disappears off the face of the planet?"

He swivelled further around to look at her and she searched his eyes for the faintest sign of affection. Finding none, she took a breath and continued, keeping her voice light. Perky, even.

"You made the TV news over here. The blue-tailed eagle thing?"

"Blue-tailed peregrine falcons."

"Whatever. It seems one of your friendly islanders knows your grubby secret. They sent a DVD of the report to Jeffery Hammer. Anonymously, of course. You were caught in the background, coming out of Mrs. Drum's."

"How'd I look? Maybe they'll give me my own TV show." Dead-pan. Humorless. He turned back to the ocean where a myriad of cold, gray sunbeams broke through holes in the pewter sky, God's follow spots lighting a vast stage set for an epic. A bird of prey shrieked above the sound of waves caressing the shore a hundred feet below.

Becky allowed herself to survey the bleak expanse beyond the cemetery, where a flock of little black devils grazed among boulders all the way up to the mountain.

"Your plan was obviously better than our plan," she said eventually. "You're all set up. New life. New people in it." She was thinking of the Pre-Raphaelite beauty she'd seen him with and had to check the tremor in her voice. "Not a lot of trees here but more water than you can shake a stick at, huh?"

She wondered if he'd get the reference to that day on Swan Lake. The day he said how he wanted them to move out into the wide, wide nowhere together. The day she dove in and saved him from drowning. If he remembered, he gave no indication.

"Why have you come?" he said, quietly, his head still turned away.

"To save you unnecessary pain. Not my idea, I hasten to add. Hammer must have a soft spot for you."

"He tell you that before or after you showed him what a great lay you are?"

That came like a blow to the stomach. She felt a prickling behind her eyes. Damn him; she-would-not-cry. "You must know me so well, Rab."

He jerked his head around and for the first time she

didn't recognise the face. It wasn't the new shape of his nose, or that his hair was longer than she'd ever seen it. It was his eyes. Once bluer than the sky, these were the hard, dull gray of gunmetal.

"You forget, I finally made it to your apartment that night," he said.

"I got the message. The feather. Very mature. Thanks."

"So tell me you're not fucking the boss. It's what you like to do, right?"

She was damned if she'd dignify that. How could this man ever have been capable of loving her? Anger took a hold.

"You redirected twenty-five million dollars of clients' money to a Swiss bank account." He turned away. "There's no denying it, Rab, it's all in your file. Hammer followed the trail to Bank Haase, Zug. You've since instructed that bank to exchange it for gold."

She was on a roll now, intent on, at least, getting a denial out of him, because it would contain lies she was certain she'd see through. "It's not there now. Hammer knows that much. So I reckon somewhere on this pissy little island of yours there's a whole pile of the bright, shiny stuff. What do you reckon?"

"That you're still pretty good in the sack. Last time I looked you took shorthand and made the damned coffee."

She let that one go with difficulty. Stick to business, she told herself. "The deal is you tell me where the gold's stashed and Hammer calls off the dogs."

"By which you mean Karpos Brunovich, I take it. Seems I'm not the only one who's made new friends. You screwing him too?"

"Jesus, Rab, what happened to you?"

"How well do you think you know Hammer, exactly? I mean *really* know him?"

"Where do you get off with this moralizing crap? I'm not the thief here!"

He was on his feet and she was strangely fearful he might leave. Sticking to business wasn't working as she fought to hold back eight months of pain and failed.

Her voice came out a cracked whisper. "You think a day has gone by when I haven't thought about you? About what I thought we had? I've replayed every moment we spent together. Every facial expression. Every subtle inflection in your voice, searching for some... some tiny clue as to how or why I began meaning so little to you. Thanks for that, Rab. I haven't felt that special for some time."

He raised a placatory hand. "Becky..."

"Don't you apologize to me. Don't you fucking dare!" She was going to cry, damnit! She took a deep breath which held the tears at bay.

"Go home, Becky. Get on with your life."

With that he turned and started walking. She was on him in three strides, clutching the frayed sleeve of his coat. She prised open his fingers and pressed something into his palm. Rab looked down and opened his hand to reveal a white tail feather. The gesture shouldn't have needed an explanation but she gave one anyway.

"A white feather was long regarded as a symbol of cowardice. Not betrayal. The Four Feathers by A.E. Mason? You should read it, Rab. You'll find you have nothing in common with its hero."

Again, no reaction. He simply pocketed the feather and walked away. She turned and strode to the cliff's edge, tears finally misting her vision. She filled her lungs, the salt air catching in her throat. It wasn't good enough. She'd come all this way and he'd told her nothing. Forget the whereabouts of the damned gold, she deserved an explanation as to why he'd just thrown her aside like a used towel.

He couldn't possibly think she'd been screwing Jeffery Hammer. Like he said, he'd made it to her apartment that night. The lawyer had been out-cold on the couch, for Christ's sake.

Why couldn't he just admit he ran out on her for the damn money? What kind of screwed up game did he think he was playing here? Questions for which she needed only one honest answer. She spun around and went in search of it... only to find Rab was nowhere in sight.

She scanned the open terrain and saw only grazing sheep. How could he have vanished from view so quickly?

Then she noticed it: the rear of a squat, tumble-down structure which had seemingly grown out of the crumbling remnants of the cemetery's dry-stone wall. Covered in moss and lichen with a grass-turfed roof, it was easy to miss amid clumps of tall nettles. Probably a shepherd's shelter, she thought as she headed for it.

She now knew exactly what she was going to say to him. The words had come with resolve. No breaking down this time. She deserved answers, right? Damned right!

As she passed through an opening in the wall and rounded the corner of the low structure, she found it was fully open at the front. It housed a lone bench seat: a flat slab of rock resting on rough-hewn granite blocks, but there was no sign of Rab MacBain. He really had vanished. Again.

*

It was the darkest darkness Becky had ever known, out here by the harbor wall. No light pollution, she supposed. What light there was bled from the gaps in Mrs. Drum's curtains and reached barely an arm's length into the damp night air. There was, however, by the building's entrance, one of those old-style red callboxes she'd seen in British movies, but the lame, yellow glow of its light bulb stayed trapped behind its small windowpanes.

The gulls were up past their bedtime, their shrieks accompanying muffled strains of ceilidh music and booze-fuelled laughter escaping from the pub's bar-room. A pair of ponies nickered to one another in the gloom, their reins tethered to iron rings set in the wall. She imagined the animals come closing time, homeward bound in the pitch-black on autopilot, their sozzled masters spark-out in the saddle.

Now in slacks, sneakers and the mohair top she'd at least had the good sense to pack, she felt snug enough against the cool breeze blowing in off the harbor. Oh, and there'd been no sign of the steaming bath she'd promised herself. There was neither tub nor hot water in her cramped room above the pub, though she'd gathered from Mrs. Drum that she could expect hot water in a jug come seven-thirty in the morning. Well hallelujah to that. How do people live like this? she asked herself for the thousandth time. There wasn't even the hope of a cell phone signal on the island for crying out loud.

She sighed a sigh and leant heavily with her elbows on the harbor's granite wall. The last forty-eight hours had taken more out of her than she'd imagined and though the bumpy little bed in her room called sweetly to her, with the racket coming from downstairs, any thought of sleep was wishful thinking.

She looked beyond the harbor mouth toward the Isle of Mull, around seven miles away, where the lights from dwellings twinkled faintly at intervals along its coastline; a costume necklace with most of its jewels missing.

A small fishing boat rounded one of the harbor arms and chugged into the protection of the tiny haven. She could just make out its name on the prow in the glow from its wheelhouse: '*Sea Cry.*' Poetic. She smiled, not wholly unaffected by the romance of this place, until she remembered why she'd ventured out into the cold in the first place and put the smile away.

She straightened and headed for the red callbox. Once inside, its heavy sprung door took its time closing while she emptied her pockets of several pound coins. Mrs. Drum had provided them in exchange for a Citibank-issue travellers' check.

She fed the hungry pay slot with as many coins as she could hold in a fist then punched in the code for the US, followed by a mobile number she'd committed to memory. After several clicks, pops and lengthy bursts of static (the island's telephone exchange would've been installed back in the Stone Age, she guessed) the line cleared and a Russian voice answered.

*

Jeffery Hammer had always enjoyed the sound of his cell's ringtone, it being the opening bars to Verdi's *'La Donne e Mobile,'* from the opera, *'Rigoletto.'* Translation: 'Women Are Fickle.' Which the lawyer found suitably appropriate on this occasion as it was Becky Gordon on the end of the line.

When the call had come, he'd been lining-up for a putt, and with the phone residing in his jacket, which in turn lay on the backseat of the hired golf buggy, it had been the one with the mole, Matvy? who'd answered it before passing it over. He almost snatched it from him and had to calm himself. He went for Mr. Fatherly.

"Becky, is that you, my dear? How nice."

It was the butt-end of the day with the light fading fast and they'd only just made the fifth hole, for Christ's sake. The whole thing had been a total farce, of course. The crime boss hadn't gotten him all the way out here to play golf, anyway. The old man was too feeble even to make the effort. No. This was about 'keeping him close.' Fedor Brunovich may've had that Sasquatch in a suit, Karpos, under his control but Becky Gordon was another matter. She was *his* soldier on the ground and only took orders from him. A laughable notion, if he'd possessed a sense of humor, given the young lady's current shenanigans.

Ergo, while the hunt was on for Rab MacBain's elusive gold, Fedor and his goons weren't letting Hammer out of their sight, paranoid he and Becky might have their own sneaky agenda.

But they couldn't very well sit on him all day long at the office. Too many curious employees and, let's face it, these guys looked more like mafia than the Mafia. So, short of kidnap, this pointless golf excursion, among ludicrous others, had been the mobsters' way of 'keeping him close.'

Yesterday it had been box seats at a matinee performance of 'Les Miserables,' which had proven, indeed, to've been exceedingly miserable. Followed by fun for all the crime family at a downtown bowling alley. An experience Hammer would've readily exchanged for having his balls dowsed in honey and staked to an ant hill. Now at the fifth hole, he tried going for Mr. Calm and Reasonable.

"So, my dear, where are you?"

"On the Isle of Garg. Where'd you think?" Her voice sounded distant, understandably, and the connection was worse than crap.

"How the hell did you get Karpos...?"

"Forget Karpos. He's nowhere."

He tried to stay calm. Fedor and wassisname, though yards away in the buggy, had their ears out on stalks.

"He's somewhere alright. Kingston fucking Jamaica!" Not the calm, voice of reason he'd been going for, perhaps. He took a breath and tried again. "Becky, dear, you know I have every confidence in your abilities, but don't you think it would be wise to..."

She cut him off. "Look. I know Rab MacBain better than anyone. It's why you sent me, in case you've forgotten. You want the gold? I'll get it for you. My way. I've already tracked him down. I'm close." She paused, seemingly for effect.

Excitement fluttered in his stomach. He turned away, shielded the phone from his watchers and lowered his voice. "It's really on the island? He told you that?"

"He didn't deny it. It's an educated guess, okay? I'm the Rab MacBain expert, remember."

She paused again and there came the sound of coins rattling against metal. Was she using a callbox? It would make sense, her cell number had been unobtainable for some time. She was talking again, at a million miles an hour and he imagined her fast running out of change.

"But listen up, Jeff. Once I've gotten you the damn

gold everyone just walks away, understand?"

"Now, wait a goddamn..."

"And you put Karpos back in his cage. Now. Tonight. I want that assurance, you hear?"

He turned around to find Fedor's eyes drilling into his from two feet away. The old bastard had gotten out of the buggy and had hobbled over on his cane. He quickly said, for the old man's benefit, "So you need Karpos called off. Is that what you're saying?"

He glanced at Fedor and raised his eyebrows in a question. Getting no response, he turned away. "Let me work on it, Becky. I'll get back."

He hit 'end call' and slipped the cell into a pant pocket. Fedor's turtle eyes were still on him. He went for Mr. Confidently Optimistic.

"She's close. Anytime now. I told you I could handle this."

It was getting difficult to read the crime boss's expression now with dusk finally upon them. "You know, the girl may have a point, Mr. Brunovich. Perhaps it would be wise to give her some rein, let her do her own thing for a while." And as uncomfortable as it was for him, he went for Mr. Jocular. "Besides, if you brought your nephew home you could get *him* to babysit me on these fun outings."

He punctuated it with a chuckle, just to show how rib-ticklingly jocular he could, in fact, be. It was whilst in mid-performance of this alien activity that Fedor Brunovich delivered a rare performance of his own. He actually spoke. Though, in truth, the single word came out more as a croak. *"Fore!"* was the utterance, and as loud as the old boy could muster. Which was doubly surprising in that, given the deteriorating light conditions, they hadn't seen a single fellow golfer in over a half-hour. So where would this supposed golf ball be going to or coming from?

Then it immediately transpired that the crime boss had been trying his own hand at jocularity, though of an awfully dark nature, it has to be said.

Because the projectile that hammered into Hammer's chest at thirty-three thousand feet per second was not, in fact, a golf ball. It was a bullet from a 9mm revolver trained on him by the one with the mole. Matvy? Yes, *that* little Russkie shit.

The ground came up fast, his face at once pressing into it. Blood seeped out of him the color of a fine *Chateauneuf-du-Pape*, and as it pooled on the manicured turf of which the Cortlandt Park Golf Club was so very proud, something started to niggle in the back of his mind. Oh, that was it; he hadn't gotten around to changing his will yet. Oh, well, it looked like Claudia, his grabby ex-wife, was going to have the last laugh after all.

*

No sooner had Becky hung-up and stepped out of the callbox than she heard the approaching clip-clop rattle and clatter of something horse-drawn. Instinct sent her swiftly into the shadows of an adjacent alley, where she crouched behind a rickety stack of lobster pots. She had no idea why she'd felt the need to hide, but moments later, when she peered out, she was relieved she had.

Her ex-lover was tethering a sturdy looking cob to the pub wall beside the other ponies. The animal was harnessed to a trap; an open two-wheeler and Rab's new best friend, the redhead, was unloading something from its tailgate. Hard to see in the feeble glow of the pub's windows but it looked like a violin case. The girl hugged it to her chest as she moved to join Rab at the pub's entrance, but before they went inside, she must've said something to him because he laughed. It was a nice sound, Becky thought, and one she hadn't heard in a very long time.

*

Ceilidh nights had always been well attended in the pub. After all, Rab mused, where else was there to go at night on the Isle of Garg?

Islanders kept the place going all year-round, of sorts; money had always been tight here but, being Scots, there would always be music and dancing. Except, nowadays, on ceilidh nights, Mrs. Drum, canny woman that she was, sold tickets to the army of bird watchers drawn here by *Blue-tailed-falconmania*.

Tonight, the dimly lit bar-room was heaving with them and there was a steady procession of food coming out of the cramped galley kitchen. All thanks to Mrs. D's recently acquired chest freezer, an endless supply of McIntosh's steak pie and potato ready-meals and an antique microwave oven.

Right now there was a lull in the music while Greda tuned her fiddle to Ol' Wheezer, Emily Tonbridge's ancient harmonium. Greda's guy, Calum, used the break to down a pint in-one and Rab had to give it to him, soused or sober, he was a passed master of the uilleann pipes. The rest of the band comprised a couple of the older kids from the school on squeeze-box, whistle and bodhran, and together they made the kind of up-tempo, soul-wrenching, sounds you just couldn't keep still to.

As he waited his turn at the bar, he spotted the Dunlop sisters with their aged pals at a table nearby. Tonight their pinafores were upstaged by identical tartan shawls. They nodded and smiled sweetly to him in unison, which he acknowledged with a mock salute.

"You'll have yer usual, Rabbie." The landlady called from behind the counter, having to pitch-up over the spirited hubbub.

"Mrs. Drum, you read minds."

"And will ye be wantin' a rock in it?"

Priceless. The old girl still hadn't quite grasped the American idiom. "Ice, sure. Thanks," he said, masking his amusement.

"Well, nae fear, ah'll be right wi' ye," she beamed as she went to serve a bird guy who'd been waiting longer than him.

Young Zac ducked in under the counter flap with a tray laden with empty glasses, his job in the pub these days as dogsbody and general gofer. He was wearing that hood over his baseball cap as usual.

"Hey, Zac. Willy Mays."

"Piece o' pish. Third all-time hitter o' home runs at six hundred 'n' sixty. Earned twelve gold gloves, 'n' was the only outfielder wi' more than seven thousand putouts." He placed the tray down so as to catch the fifty pence piece Rab flipped him.

"You're cleaning me out, kid."

The boy smirked and proceeded to load glasses into the washer. Dugald sidled up, a Scotch on the go.

"His nose is ne'er out o' that damned book, Rabbie."

"It was the old man's. He'd be pleased it found a good home."

"Dinnae get mah wrong, mind. His mam's made up 'cause ye've got him readin' at last. Wi' him bein' a wee bit slow, ya ken?"

Zac had lost his dad a few years back, Rab knew, which probably accounted for at least some of the boy's problems. The aged fisherman leant back, elbows on the bar, and surveyed the room crammed with strangers.

"Beak sniffers," he said before downing the Scotch.

"Don't knock 'em, Dugald. They come bearing gifts."

"Ah?"

"Ready cash."

"Oh aye, their pockets are deep enough, ah dare say." He placed his empty glass on the bar and raised his voice over a burst of raucous laughter from a table nearby. "Listen. Rabbie. We're short in the boat tomorrow if ye fancy comin' out. Usual rate?"

"Count me in, Dugald. I appreciate it."

The old man moved away to join Captain Angus, holed-up in a corner with a full bottle of single malt and a crossword puzzle. Mrs. Drum arrived with his drink.

"Thanks, Mrs. D."

"Slainte," she said, already pouring a pint for a German guy in camouflage.

Business was good but he wondered how long it could last.

Break over, the band burst straight into a foot-stomping reel. '*The Sailor's Bonnet,*' if Rab's memory served, which got people hopping to their feet, and it was great to see most of the men wearing kilts.

His encounter with Becky came back to him and he wondered if he'd been too hard on her. No way, he decided, she'd lain out her position clearly enough up at the cemetery. What mattered now was how he was going to limit the inevitable damage. He reached for his drink but a woman's hand beat him to it.

"Hi," said Becky, scooping ice from his glass onto the counter top. "I like it straight up, remember?" She sipped, scanning the room where the dancing was in full-swing. She had to shout over it. "How's the fishing or whatever you're into these days? Managing to scrape a crust?"

She must've overheard his and Dugald's conversation. He feigned indifference and looked to the stage where

Greda was fiddling at the speed of light. Becky followed his gaze.

"Good looking lady. Talented too, and I've seen how much she likes you, Rab. In fact you're in pretty tight with all these nice folk."

He didn't need this right now. What he needed was time to think. He turned and studied her face, looking for any trace of the woman he once knew. The woman he would've died for once upon a time.

"How'd you think they'll take it," she went on, "when they find out their poor, down-at-heel Rabbie's a lousy fake, just like his old man? You used to be scared you'd turn into him, remember? Well, newsflash. Looks like you already have."

Mrs. Drum seemed ensconced while she served someone nearby, but he knew she was earwigging Becky's every word.

"But hey, don't let me be a party pooper, right?" She raised her glass. "Slanty, whatever," she said before knocking back the liquor and weaving her way through the dancers.

Mrs. Drum scurried over and clutched Rab's arm. "Ah gave the young lass a room. Did ah dae wrong, Rabbie?"

"It's okay, Mrs. D."

'The Sailor's Bonnet' had come to an abrupt end; the dance over. Rab couldn't help thinking, though, that a more dangerous dance was about to begin.

*

The dog stank of sheep dung and was foaming at the mouth. Becky would've sworn it had rabies had it not been lapping frothy beer from an earthenware bowl on the table.

She'd arrived and perched precariously on the end of a bench, tucked in a far corner; the only seat left in the house. The pooch was seated between herself and its master, Stanley the shepherd, whose whiskers were in a worse state than his dog's. The way he was quaffing his own beer, she reckoned the animal could teach him a thing or two about table etiquette.

The revellers had taken their seats to listen to a solo ballad played by a guy on the miniature bagpipes. She'd recognized him, of course, as the fisherman with the striptease eyes and had to admit he was pretty impressive on the instrument.

She looked across at Rab, still at the bar, wondering if he'd follow her over after she'd dropped that firecracker in his lap. Maybe he'd taken her threat to expose him as bluff and bluster. Okay, it was, but it was all she had to work with right now.

Stanley rubbed the back of a grubby paw across soapy whiskers and belched.

She gave him her butter-wouldn't-melt smile. "Hi. Becky. We met on the ferry? Before that I caught you on TV. You beat off those egg thieves, right?"

The shepherd ignored that, just stared into his beer, so she gave his dog a wink and a scratch behind the ears. That got her a growl through bared teeth. From the dog, that is, not the shepherd.

Then the old guy turned to her, his foamy whiskers forming in a way as to suggest a grin in there somewhere. "She says fer ye ta git ta fuck," he said and downed a whisky chaser.

Oh well, it was time she gave good ol' Rabbie something more to think about, anyway. She'd let him sweat long enough.

She rose and squeezed through chairs on her way to the bar, which earned her scowls from seated punters as the fisherman's lilting pipe solo held the room in its thrall. The piece ended to applause as she arrived at Rab's side. He was paying for another drink.

"Don't worry about me, Rab, I'm fine, thanks," she said with a tight smile, nodding to her empty glass. He wasn't offering anyway. He turned his back and leaned lazily on the bar, 'get lost' in anybody's language.

"Yup. Godda keep a clear head for the morning," she said, matter-of-factly. "Early start. Doing a little treasure hunting."

The band tore into another jig, reel, whatever, and she had to shout over it. "Why don't you help me out with that, by the way? Give me a few pointers. Don't be shy, Rab, we're old pals, remember?"

"Gimme a break," he snapped over his shoulder, "This isn't you."

"You're the only fake here, Rab."

He knocked back the Scotch, while around them pairs linked arms and whirled like dervishes.

"Hey, you're pretty good at running away these days," she said, "How'd you manage to avoid Stink Bug when he was here? You and your girlfriend have got a cosy little hideaway somewhere, is that it?"

He turned all the way around, eyes cold but finally interested. "How *is* Karpos, by the way, still hooked on Sopranos reruns?"

"You can ask him when he gets here."

"Great. Why not get Hammer over here, make up a foursome, do dinner."

She toyed with her empty glass for a moment then placed it on the counter. "Okay, I'll level with you, just to smooth things along here. I reckon I've gotten Karpos off your back. For now." He leant with an elbow on the bar, acting casual, but she knew she'd gotten his attention at last. "But one little phone call and, *shazam!* He's on you like syphilis."

Rab's eye-line shifted to the stage, no doubt in search of his beloved. She followed his gaze but the redhead was nowhere in sight. One of the kids had taken-over on fiddle.

"Skipping town doesn't make me a criminal," he said, "Besides, you've only got Hammer's word for what went down. Think about it. How rich do I look to you?"

"Well, I've got an interesting theory about that..."

"And what theory would that be?" a woman's voice cut in.

The redhead had come to his rescue. She was slightly taller up-close and even more beautiful, damn-it, and when she smiled it was like she glowed from the inside out.

"We ha' nae met. I'm Greda. Welcome ta our island."

"Hi. Becky. Lover boy and I were just chewing over old times. We go back aways, but I expect you know that."

"Of course. So, your interesting theory."

Becky sensed Rab's unease as she looked to him for the okay to continue. He gave a reluctant nod and she directed her words to him alone.

"Okay, this poor, down-at-heel Rabbie shit's a put-on, right? I reckon you came here to jerk off with your roots, 'til one day, when everyone's looking the other way, you pass 'Go' and collect twenty-five million in gold."

"Not bad," said Rab, unsmiling, "You should write fiction."

"It's rubbish, is what it is," Greda snapped, "Ye've nae idea…"

"Don't, Greda." Rab cut in.

"I'm nae gonna let this…"

"I said, leave it."

And much to Becky's surprise, the girl did; reining the anger in fast. Greda gave Rab a smile, squeezed his hand and headed back toward the stage. The music had climaxed to deafening cheers and applause. She waited for the din to subside.

"Greda. Nice name." She was damned if she was going to wax about the girl's stunning looks. "You've obviously confided in her. Though to what extent, I wonder," she said, forcing a grin and changing tack. "But hey, it's getting late. Fancy a nightcap? My treat."

"I don't know why you have to do this."

"Neither did I until I got here."

With that she turned, pushed through a gaggle of camouflaged guys and headed for the door marked '*Private*.'

*

"She thinks we're an item, you and me. Can you believe that?"

His sister had finally joined him at the harbor wall, while the last of Mrs. Drum's birdwatchers spilled onto the street, bound merrily for the campsite in the pitch dark.

Greda, still laughing from Rab's revelation, responded with mischief. "Oh, and ye didnae enlighten the wee hen? The poor lass'll be sobbin' into her pillow."

She'd downed a beer too many before closing and was laying the Scots accent on thick to amuse him.

"Ye're a sly ol' beastie, Rabbie MacBain."

"Guilty as charged. So what?"

"So, what's the crack with the lass?"

A good question, and one he didn't have an answer to.

The harbor front was deserted at last. Quiet, but for the sound of water lapping at the foot of the cobblestone hard, and the far-off clip-clopping of someone heading for the cliff path on horseback. Only Sherlock, Constable Finn's mount, remained tethered with Greda's cob. The latter shook his harness, sputtered his impatience. A lone gull, high up, shrieked in response, or just for the hell of it.

"I didn't mislead her intentionally," said Rab, "but if she's got us down as Couple of the Year, that's just tough. I don't owe her a damn thing, and I certainly don't give a crap what she thinks."

That said, he'd already been kicking himself for his behavior toward her, in the bar and up at the old cemetery. Why couldn't he stop baiting her, for God's sake? He should've been creating a cool distance between them, playing for time, not acting like a jilted date at a high-school hop. There was too much at stake here for that. She'd been out to get under his skin and he'd let her.

He stared through the darkness toward Mull, where the island's barely discernible mass mirrored his mood. A lumbersome, tar-black creature floating face-down in deep water.

"It should've been Karpos Brunovich," he whispered.

"I know, Rabbie," Greda said, suddenly sober, "Come. They'll all be waitin'."

*

This really was the eeriest of gatherings. Mrs. Drum had killed every wall lamp in the place except one whose light bulb was seriously on the fritz under a torn, orange shade. It hummed and flickered intermittently in the gloom, casting the islanders as characters in a low-lit horror flick who, though seemingly benign God-fearing folk, every full moon, performed pagan rituals buck naked, drenched head to foot in chicken blood.

Now, where the hell had *that* come from? Rab thought suddenly. Had he really had that much to drink? Maybe it was time to give the hard stuff a rest for a while.

In the real world, the waiting islanders looked up as one and smiled in greeting when he and Greda entered the room. This was the core of the island's community: Mrs. Drum, Large Stanley, Elleen and Mary Dunlop, Constable Finn, Dugald, Calum, Captain Angus, Emily Tonbridge, Zac and his mom, Aggie, from the General Store, and, of course, his half-sister.

They were all seated, facing the stage, with a handful of fishermen and their families; two or three toddlers sleeping on parents' laps, while Stanley's Border collie, Maddie, slept-off a hangover under a table. Rab felt like joining her.

All eyes were on him, though, as he seated himself on the edge of the stage. Calum's eyes, Rab noted, were bloodshot from booze and saying something he couldn't make out in the flickering amber half-light.

These people were the ones 'in the know'; the 'chosen few', and they were waiting for him to speak; to bring them up to speed with the late, unforeseen, arrival of Becky Gordon on their island. But it was little Zac, all wide-eyed and hesitant, who got to his feet and broke the leaden silence.

"Is… is this the time, Rabbie?"

He managed a smile for the kid. "Yes, my young friend. This is the time."

Several of the assembled gazed at the floor. Others looked up, as if able to see through the oak-beamed ceiling and into Becky's room.

Chapter Eight

GETTING through customs at London Gatwick had been a cinch. All the while, though, Karpos's heart had been pumping double-time while he braced himself for any further shitty traps the Gordon slut may've lain in his path. The BA flight direct from Kingston had been the fastest and, therefore, the most predictable way for him to go, so Cupcake could've easily bet the farm on Gatwick being his point of entry into the UK.

He could breathe easy now, he reckoned, as he wheeled his Samsonite toward the arrivals hall and freedom. First he needed to find a bathroom and freshen-up. Get some food down him.

He'd spent the whole flight cramped-up in coach with screaming kids, the works, fuming, as he re-lived over and over the humiliation those fuck-shit Jamaican cops had put him through. *Thanks to that BITCH!*

He remembered a time, a few years back, when he'd been drinking up a storm in McCarthy's Bar, a Mick joint over in Brooklyn. There'd been this faggot comedian doing his thing on a stage in the corner. At one point he'd said about how he'd been cavity-searched by security guys at Kennedy airport, blah-blah-blah. The punch had been something like, "I wouldn't have minded but they don't even kiss ya while they're doin' it." The gag had gone down a scream, though what the hell was funny about it he had no idea.

Right. Wash-up. Chow-down. Then back to business. He now had to get himself an internal flight to Glasgow, but first on the list was getting a new cell phone. No problem there; this was a freakin' airport, right? Cinch.

A couple of dark suits converged up ahead, barring his way to the exit doors. Crisp looking; clean-cut. The younger of the two was black, Caribbean, maybe.

"Mr. Brunovich? Karpos Brunovich?" the white one said with a snotty Brit accent and showing a card with his mug on. Karpos put his age around fifty. Rheumy-eyed and sporting one of those moustaches like you see on queers. His ID showed his first name as Phil. Both guys were giving him shit-eatin' grins.

"Uh... yeah. So?"

"Detective Inspector Hardy. My colleague, here, is Detective Sergeant Huggins. We're Interpol."

"Don't getcha. Into pole what, dancin'?" Now *that's* what you call funny, he thought. Something Tony Soprano might've come out with.

"Just come along with us, sir, there's a good chap." And there came a metallic ratchet sound as his sidekick clamped a handcuff to his wrist. Which Karpos didn't find funny one bit.

*

"Excuse me? Do you sell butterscotch? Pardon me? Hello?"

Zac was keeking out from behind a magazine rack. Tidying the mags was one of the stupid jobs his mam made him do before he went to school each day. At least it gave him a chance to leaf through the tittie mags without her seeing.

Becky, as he'd learned her name was at last night's pow-wow, was at the shop counter, trying to catch his mam's attention. His mam, though, was sitting with her back to the lass, busying herself at the plug and socket board of the old phone exchange cabinet. Even though she wore a headset, Zac knew she could hear the lass perfectly well. After Rabbie's warning last night, he reckoned his mam wasn't the only one who'd be giving the fabulicious lady the cold shoulder from now on.

Becky had obviously been to the market stalls and got herself kitted-out with sensible clobber: boots, woolly top and waxed Barbour jacket. Which was a proper shame as it totally hid her fab-a-rooney figure.

His mam played with a couple of plugs and sockets for an age, it seemed, before finally pretending to notice the lass. She turned and stuck on a surprised look.

"I'm sorry, missus, have ye been waitin' there?" (Certainly no actor, his mam.)

"Uh… no, that's okay. I just wondered if you had any butterscotch. My mom loves the stuff, and I just tried at the market but the guy said maybe not until the end of the week, so…"

Mam formed something close to a smile and cocked her head to one side like a curious parrot. "Then the end o' the week it'll be, madam."

Ha! Good one, Mam. Aggie Moore had never in her life called anyone madam and Becky looked like she knew it too.

Mam then mumbled something about Captain Angus bringing some over on the ferry when he had a mind to, which was a hoot, 'cause he knew for a fact there were six tins of the stuff out in the storeroom.

The lass flashed her a lovely smile all the same, before paying for a map of the island and a couple of postcards. Mam took the money with flared nostrils like it smelt of something nasty.

Becky thanked her, picked up her shiny aluminium case and headed for the door. He ducked back behind the magazine rack just in time, he thought, but she must've clocked him because, as she passed, she paused as if to peruse the women's magazines, and whispered in a smoky voice, "Hey kid. I wouldn't let your mom catch you reading that."

He felt his face flush and his ears glow hot. A condition that worsened after she left and he realised he was still clutching a tittie mag open at the centre-fold.

*

When the aged fisherman had yanked off the tarpaulin

with the flourish of an illusionist performing at Caesar's Palace, Becky had, at least, expected a top-of-the-range Cadillac Sedan with gold-plated door handles, give or take a sequin-bikinied assistant splayed over its hood, but this? Jesus Christ!

The rusted monstrosity appeared to be the rear half of a black London taxi cab crudely welded to the front of a powder-blue 1960s Mini Cooper. Its orange taxi sign was still intact on the roof and its front wheels were considerably smaller than those at the rear. It had to be the hybrid from Hell; something the Adams Family might've driven to a funeral.

Before the tarp had come off, she'd noticed, at a distance, the chalked sign offering a car-hire rate of £20 a day and thought the price reasonable. But for *this* rust-bucket?

"You're out of your mind."

"Take it or leave it, lass, but ah promise ye, it's the only transport on the island unless ye're good wi' horses."

They both had to shout over the screaming of gulls and the gurgling throb of the *Sea Cry*'s bilge pumps. The vessel was moored against the harbor wall, only feet away.

"I can ride pretty well," she said, her lips tight, her voice level, the words twisting on her tongue, "and I can handle a trap or buggy if you have one."

"Nope," said the old boy, seeming to enjoy the sound of the word.

"Then do you know where I can get..."

"Ye've nae a hope in hell, lassie." More words he

savoured with delight.

This was Dugald, the old guy she'd seen talking to Rab at last night's ceilidh, offering him work. Today he was wearing his kilt, which looked kind of odd with his flat cloth cap and yellow wind-breaker. A couple of his similarly attired crew were loading the morning's catch into ice-packed trays on the deck of the boat. To its stern, was a larger vessel; *Morag's Ghost*, whose crew was doing likewise amid nets hung out to dry. No sign of Rab onboard, she noted.

Furtive eyes darted her way amid stifled snorts and hidden sniggers. The men muttered in what she guessed was Gaelic. Several of the older folk had been speaking it in the pub, she recalled.

Dugald tossed her the car keys and she gave him a twenty, along with an icy stare intended to shame the shyster. But he simply doffed his flat cap, gave her a wink and went back to work.

Fuming, she strode up to the vehicle and tugged open its rusted door, almost wrenching her shoulder out of its socket. *Wrong side, Dumbo!*

She kicked the door shut and, resisting the urge to scream, rounded the hood to the driver's side. The crew had stopped work altogether to take in the show, and they weren't the only ones. The crew of *Morag's Ghost* had joined the audience, Striptease Eyes among them, arms folded and grinning like a school kid.

She tossed in Karpos's metal case and flopped into the ripped upholstered seat. At least it was half-way comfortable, though that hardly made-up for the stench of rotting fish and the gull shit-spattered dashboard. How the hell do you get bird crap inside a car?

She got her answer when she went to wind up the open window. No handle. She took a deep breath, put the key in the ignition and reached for a non-existent seat belt. *Oh, just shoot me!*

The engine coughed to life on the fourth go and she saw billowing black fumes in the cracked rear-view mirror. The exhaust backfired, causing her to let out a startled yelp. She grit her teeth and went to put the car into drive… but the bastard thing had a stick-shift!

*

A family of gray seals basked on a granite outcrop only yards from the beach. Rab wouldn't know if the animals were tired from a hunting expedition or simply lapping up the morning's unprecedented sunshine. The warmest weather the island had seen in years, he'd been told.

The seals put him in mind of obese Ottoman princes, luxuriating on low couches. All the picture lacked was a belly dancer and the creatures smoking hookahs. They ignored a couple of black and white oystercatchers in their midst, chiselling limpets and mussels from the rock.

Rab strode along the shale shoreline under the cliffs, close to the water's edge. He felt as tired as the seals looked. The *Sea Cry* had put to sea around 3.30am, barely an hour after last night's meeting in the pub. A straight five hours of fresh air and physical labor had cured his hangover, but had left him in dire need of a soft bed.

Dugald hadn't needed him for the off-loading. The crews of the small fleet would box the morning's catch in ice before it was taken to the mainland on *The Dark Star*, Garg's largest fishing vessel. The fish would make its way to pubs, restaurants, and the like, by the afternoon. The island's proximity made it too far away to get an early catch into Oban's shops and market places.

Back in the days of plenty, and before EU fish quota restrictions, the island's much larger fleet fished closer to the mainland so as to get its haul ashore before sun-up. These days, Calum and Dugald had told him, fishing the old way wouldn't be worth the gasoline.

He'd reached the place where the beach narrowed below the ancient cemetery just as a giant shadow crossed his path. He looked skyward, expecting to catch sight of a blue-tailed falcon returning to its eyrie on the ledge, ninety feet above him.

But instead he saw a bald eagle, its white-feathered hood distinct against the clear-blue sky. An awesome sight, with the creature measuring eight feet from wingtip to wingtip. Leather jesses trailed from its legs, a clue the bird was kept by a falconer. And then it was gone, returning to Greda, of course, somewhere in the Glen. The falconry's raptors needed exercise and his sister flew them as often as she could.

At Christmas, last year, she'd surprised him with a

present. She'd brought out, from under what was once their mother's bed, an early oil painting by his father. She remembered it on Clair's bedroom wall for a time and, according to her, had been their mother's most treasured possession. He wondered why he had no childhood memory of it.

The focus of the picture was a blue-tailed falcon on a block perch in the midst of an otherwise still life composition. A pair of glistening herrings shared the wood table-top with a bread loaf, wedge of cheese and a trio of split pomegranates.

With tiny beads of water on the fruit, detailed wood grain and beautifully drawn bird feathers, the effect was near photographic. Painted at least forty years ago, it could almost be taken for a Rembrandt. Almost, for the self-taught Charlie Whistler had yet to thoroughly master his alchemy.

Clair had also kept a few of his dad's art books, showing not only prints of the Dutch master's work but close-up photos of his brushstrokes. These were accompanied by detailed analysis of the great man's technique. Did Fergus MacBain, even back then, have his sights set on forgery?

He told Greda why he thought the painting had meant so much to their mother.

"Me and ya mom knew where to find 'em. A pair of blue-tailed peregrine falcons. First saw 'em on the island summer of nineteen fifty… oh, I dunno. We were the only ones knew where they nested, mind. It was our secret!"

They'd been just kids, and the secret must've meant something to Clair, because she took it with her to the grave.

Rab was nearing the foot of the glen, where the burn spewed over boulders and onto the beach, the tide already on the rise to meet it. In another hour or so the route he'd come would be eight foot under water, the waves slapping at the cliff's granite wall.

He turned inland on the north side of the stream and began the hot, steady climb towards Ben Wrath. In fifteen minutes, he reached his sister by a dog-leg in the burn, the bald eagle looking heavy and restless on her gauntlet. "Hey," he said in greeting.

"Ah, Rabbie." She placed a tasselled, velvet hood over the bird's head to calm it.

"Heading home?" he said.

"In a wee while, Rabbie. Ah thought ah'd take a stroll into the woods. It's been a few days."

"Sure, I'll tag along."

That soft bed could wait, he decided. It wasn't often he got his sister to himself. The two crossed a wood bridge and headed toward Garg's forested southern tip. Greda was right, of course. It'd been at least four days since either of them had checked on the island's most closely guarded secret.

*

"Come-on-you-lousy-bitch!" Becky pleaded as she

willed the pile of scrap metal to the top of the slope, its gears meshing in agony, exhaust billowing black muck out its rear.

The rusted heap wheezed with relief on making the brow and rattled to a blessed standstill. She cut the engine. Sweet Jesus. It would've been easier if she'd gotten out and pushed the damned thing. And the heat, she thought, wiping sweat from her forehead on a sleeve, where had the heat come from all of a sudden? Maybe some of New York's record temperatures had finally made it across the pond.

Getting hold of her temper, she checked the map (which, by the way, must've been drawn by a complete moron) and surveyed the valley below. Nothing stood out.

She'd checked-out some of the derelict cottages along the skirt of the mountain, searching for trapdoors to hidden cellars, rummaged in the remnants of fireplaces and crumbling chimney stacks, looking for anywhere Rab could've stashed twenty-five million in gold bullion. Christ, what did that even look like? How much space would it take-up?

As she'd searched those tumbledown dwellings in the growing heat of the day, she'd occasionally felt the ghosts of those who'd lived there. Died there, or had simply fled in search of a better life. And she'd found herself feeling strangely sad for them. The ruins themselves, like neglected tombstones, told the story of the island's ongoing demise.

She studied the badly-drawn map splayed over the steering wheel. *Whatever happened to X marks the spot, for crying out loud?*

Damn it! She knew she was going about this all wrong. What's to say the gold wasn't hidden in one of the *inhabited* dwellings? Rab and Greda's place, for instance. She'd yet to establish where that little love-nest was located, but had ruled it out for the time being. Rab wouldn't be that stupid, she'd decided.

Neither could she see him sharing his secret with anyone other than Greda. Then she remembered there was at least one other islander who knew about the gold, of course, because they'd ratted Rab out to Jeffery Hammer. Right now she had no way of squirreling-out the mystery informer. Not without broadcasting who she was and why she was on the island.

The snitch's motivation wasn't even clear. What did they want, anyway, money? Or simply revenge for something Rab had done. Probably the money. Besides, there was no guarantee whoever they were would know where the gold was actually hidden. No. All she could do now was to keep searching, or at least be seen to be doing so. Because, maybe if Rab felt her tugging on his coat-tails, her breath on the back of his neck, he'd make that one mistake that would lead her to the prize. She *knew* him, she kept telling herself. Her ex-lover was not infallible.

The map showed a patch of forest at the island's southern tip but, looking up, she could see no sign of it on the horizon. It must be on the other side of the valley, closer to sea level, she guessed, but the map gave no indication of how far.

Scanning the valley below, she spotted a gaggle of birdwatchers heading inland. She'd passed several this morning, their scopes and binoculars poised for a sighting of anything with feathers on it. It had to be an obsession with these people, she thought. Whatever it was, she didn't get it.

The bird guys below had changed direction and were crossing a little wooden bridge over the narrow stream where the duck race had taken place. Sheep had gathered along its bank, drinking, or in search of cooler air.

The bridge looked solid enough to take the hire-car's weight, she reckoned, but the valley floor beyond was strewn with boulders and... what did they call those things; rocks piled-up in heaps? Cairns? It wasn't an option; her rust-heap would never make it through. Her best bet was to head east to the cliff path where the way south looked clear all the way to the forest marked on the map.

She started-up, jammed the stick into first and headed in that direction. She hadn't gotten far, though, before she was struck by an odd thought. That it was only in Fairyland that there was ever anything at the end of the rainbow. A very odd thought. Unwelcome, so she closed her eyes and dismissed it.

*

A gentle wind had gotten up and it had become strangely chilly, but that wasn't what was bugging her. It was the tall, coarse grass where she lay hidden, rustling loudly in her headphones, amplified a thousand-fold by her high-tech long distance listening device. As a result, she was only able to catch intermittent snatches of Rab and Greda's conversation on the breeze:

Greda: *She canae if she's nae idea...time comes and we're...*

Rab: *...here by the time...too long if Brunovich...*

Greda: *(Laughter) ...gold in the future...*

Suddenly alert, Becky turned the volume up on the device only to get a high-pitched squealing in her ears. She fumbled for the knob and turned it down. She'd hit pay-dirt, damn it, but she needed to get clear of the tall grass but not break cover.

When she'd finally opened Karpos's mystery case the night before, she'd nearly laughed out loud. The listening dish was the last thing she'd expected to find. She'd read its manual and checked its batteries, thinking the gizmo might come in handy if she had to play spook.

Now she couldn't remember if one of its controls activated some kind of filter to deal with foreground interference. Anyhow, it was too late for that and she hadn't had time to attach the recording device.

She'd spotted the lovebirds a quarter of a mile away, approaching along the cliff path from the south. Coming from where, she wondered, the forest? She'd killed the engine and let the vehicle freewheel into a shallow dip behind a row of gorse, then had grabbed the listening device from its case along with a pair of mini binoculars.

The coarse grass had itched through her sweater as she'd crawled through it on her belly. Then, finding a good vantage position, she'd unfurled the dish like a large, circular fan and had slotted it into its pistol-grip. A rifle-mic clicked into the dish and protruded from its center. She'd hurriedly plugged-in the headphones, had taken aim and switched the gizmo on.

Now, she raised the binoculars with her free hand to focus on her targets. Greda was carrying a huge bird on her arm with talons the size of a woman's hands. It had a colorful hood thing with a tassel on its head. So, the girl was a falconer. Was there no end to the little lady's talents? Greda paused to feed the bird something from a pouch at her waist, then she and Rab were on the move again; heading up the slope toward the shepherd's shelter at the cemetery.

She could see the girl's lips moving and hear her in her headphones:

"...as it come's...Nae messin'... just have ta dae what's right, Rabbie. Now if..."

A shriek from a bird of prey echoed across the valley, magnified in her phones. Greda's bird? Then rustling grass drowned-out the girl's words completely. *Shit!*

Something rubbed-up against her left leg! She froze... then felt pressure against her right thigh. Her breath caught. She was about to scream when a voice boomed in her phones:

"Hi! Ve hear it also!" The accent was German.

The grass parted like curtains either side of her and a couple of camouflaged guys wearing grass-tufted baseball caps crawled forward on their elbows, black and green greasepaint smeared across their faces.

The heads and shoulders of four more camouflaged goofs emerged from the undergrowth to join the party. At least three wore headphones and brandished long range listening equipment akin to her own.

The one to her right was pointing to somewhere in the distance, his expression intense, like he'd spotted a convoy of enemy tanks. He leaned close, his voice loud enough to burst her eardrums.

"Fantastisch, ja?"

She snatched off the phones, her ears ringing. He'd probably been speaking quietly, she realized. Following his gaze through her binoculars, she homed-in on a tall, moss-covered cairn around seven hundred yards away. She adjusted focus until a blue-tailed falcon took shape on its summit. An anti-climax, as the damn bird wasn't even tap-dancing.

"Yeah, great," she said with an inward groan.

She panned with the glasses until she found the cemetery. No sign of Rab or Greda. Panned left and right. Nothing. *Fuckit.* Then she spotted Greda down in the valley by the stream, striding inland with the eagle, then whipped back to refocus on the cemetery. *Abracadabra.* What a surprise. No Rab MacBain.

*

The temperature had dropped dramatically as dense, black clouds hurtled in from the west. She'd heard about the weather being 'changeable' in these parts but seeing is believing, as they say.

A drop of water splashed her cheek as she headed for the shelter. It was deserted, so she moved through the gap in the wall to the cemetery, where the headstones and chest-tombs looked resigned to the cold, dark shroud being drawn over them. Rain spattered loudly on the back of her wax jacket. She put up its collar and hunkered into it.

As she wove her way through the graves toward the cliff's edge, eyes darting left and right in search of Rab, she knew there'd be no point in finding him. More talking would get her nowhere. He'd clammed-up and she wasn't going to get that shell open with talk alone. Tug on his coat-tails, she reminded herself, breathe down his neck until he made that one mistake. Maybe he would unwittingly hand her a lever. Something that could prise that shell apart. Something more than exposing him as a fake to the islanders. That threat hadn't ruffled him.

The cemetery whited-out and a clap of thunder split the air. She ran for the opening in the wall through the ensuing deluge, bowed and squinting to see where she was going.

She ducked into the shelter and flopped on its bench-seat, a sodden heap, jeans clinging to her like a second skin. *God, I hate this place!*

More thunder. A blinding flash lit-up the valley. She'd be here a while, she reckoned. No point making a dash for the car, either. With the driver's window jammed open, she'd get soaked in there anyway.

She took-in the shelter's structure. The building looked pretty solid, the dry-stone walls skilfully put together like a jigsaw. No sign yet of any leaks, but she wondered if a grass-turfed roof held-out in this kind of weather.

Then, looking at the bench itself, she realized its seat was a gravestone. Aged and weather-worn, its inscription was barely legible. She could make out a date, though: 1736, and a first name. Mary. The grave it had once marked, along with its occupant, had probably been washed out to sea long ago.

A spider appeared out of a crevice and scuttled down into the gap between the seat and the wall. Arachnids weren't really within her scope of expertise; they weren't insects, but its markings had pricked her interest. It had had a black and yellow striped abdomen, very much like an *Argiope aurantia*. An American garden spider. A bit odd to find one here, she thought.

Her intrest now piqued, she squeezed her fingers into the slim gap behind the seat and tugged. The tombstone slid-out easily over its granite plinth.

And there it was, tucked into a crack. It had curled itself into a ball but its markings were still distinct. Certainly not of the *Argiope* genre, she decided. Probably a common British species. She slid the tombstone out further to get a closer look.

Suddenly, the smell of death filled her nostrils and her mouth dried-up in an instant. *My God…*

Her heart pounding, she fumbled for her cell phone, switched it on and pushed it into the space beneath the slab, where the glow from its screen picked out worn, stone steps descending into darkness.

*

The floor of the tunnel had been flagstoned for about twenty feet before becoming compacted earth. The dirt walls and ceiling, supported by pit-props, looked uncomfortably precarious. Unstable There was no telling how long ago the tunnel had been constructed, but she prayed that if it had held for a hundred years it would hold for a while longer.

The glow from her phone reached barely six feet into the black nothingness, so she made her way forward, one hand feeling along the wall. The smell of decay had become more pungent, forcing her to breathe through her mouth alone.

She paused from time to time, listening out for a footfall; a tell-tail sound of movement. Rab could be down here, she thought. Doing what, though, counting his stolen gold? Why was her heart thumping so fast, she asked herself. Her ex-lover would never harm her, would he? No. So why, then? The anticipation? The thrill of the chase?

The ground suddenly gave-way under her. Before it could take her with it, she spotted something protruding out of the dirt wall and grabbed hold of it. She hung there for a moment until, feeling about with her toes, she discovered she'd simply reached the top of a steep slope.

She let out a breath. Calm down for Christ's sake, she told herself. This really wasn't an Indiana Jones movie, where snakes and poison darts were gonna come shooting out of the walls.

The glow from her phone revealed she was dangling from a corroded, brass handle, sticky and green from oxidation. The instant she realized what it was, it came away, bringing with it the whole side of a rotted casket. She screamed as she fell, her shoulder hitting the floor hard.

Straightaway, she was up, her back pressed against the opposite wall, where she slowly brought up her phone to illuminate the coffin's sleeping occupant.

The corpse was cocooned in a gossamer shroud of spiders' webs and, though the cask's lid had caved-in, she could still make out fragments of lace and stained, yellow satin, toe bones pushing out of a rotted slipper. Shoulder-length, silver hair lying coiled under the webbed outline of an ivory skull and mandible and, as much as she wanted to, Becky couldn't tear her eyes from the collarbone sticking out at an angle, like the corpse had been stabbed to death with it. *Holy Christ!*

Her breathing had become labored. "Sorry," she managed to whisper. She turned and moved too quickly down the slope, hitting her head on a prop and landing on her backside, where she slid to the bottom of the incline on loose gravel.

Recovering, she found herself sitting in pitch darkness and that she'd lost her phone. She felt around for it in the dirt. Nothing. She didn't have to panic, she reasoned. The way out was up the slope. She'd be able to feel her way back to the stone steps below the shelter... but then, as her eyes adjusted to the dark, she saw daylight, barely discernible, twenty feet ahead. She rose and felt her way carefully toward it.

Rounding a sharp bend to the right, she discovered the light's source. A small hole had been roughly-hewn through the rock wall, to the cliff face, she guessed, creating an oasis of daylight in the tunnel. Beyond that, the way was lost to impenetrable darkness.

She pushed her face into the aperture and filled her lungs with clean, salty, air. She exhaled and filled them again. Something moved out there!

She jumped back, startled, eventually, returning to peer out. The opening looked onto a rock ledge where a trio of falcons were hunkered on their eyrie in the teeming rain. Though thoroughly drenched, it was clear they were juveniles, but not full-fledged. She marvelled at the sight. It was strange being so close to them. Delightful, she thought, surprising herself.

There was a bright-blue tail feather teetering on the edge of their home, an adult's for sure. It looked to be within reach so she leant into the narrow opening, stretched, and got hold of it. The youngsters swivelled their heads to watch her, unperturbed.

As she studied her prize in the half-light, she thought again about finding that lever. The one that would crack Rab's shell wide-open, and watched, amazed, as the very leverage she sought materialized in the palm of her hand.

Chapter Nine

GATWICK Airport's cramped interview room turned out to be pretty much the same as the one in Kingston. No air, no windows, but minus the wolf. Admittedly, this was after a night and a long morning in the cells.

This time around, though, had been much more fun. The detectives had been a riot. Regular jokers. They'd removed his cuffs and conducted the whole Q&A shit over tea and cookies. And not piss out of a machine, either, but brewed and served in a china tea service, an heirloom left to DI Phil by his late mother. Cups, saucers, titchy silver spoons, the works.

And the cookies, Jammy Dodgers, as they were named on the packet, were pretty good too. The DI's "absolute favorites," apparently, and Karpos didn't doubt it, judging by the crumbs and red jelly sticking to the guy's comedy moustache.

His black sidekick, DS Huggins, had played mom with the teapot, all dainty like, while Karpos and the DI sat opposite one another, a mini audio recorder propped against a sugar bowl between them.

At first, he just didn't get these clowns. They obviously hadn't seen enough TV cop shows because, from the get-go, they'd been playing Good Cop, Good Cop. Which had kept him on edge for a while, waiting for one of the fuckers to lose the act and turn nasty. Maybe flash a tube of Lube and get him to drop his pants. Didn't happen.

Anyhow, it looked like the tip-off hadn't come from Cupcake this time. His name had popped-up on Interpol's computer as "a person of interest," as DI Phil had put it while helping himself to another sugar cube using a tiny pair of tongs.

"...as a member of a notorious crime family, you understand," the detective had continued. At which point, Huggins, arms folded, back leaning against the door, said he thought his Auntie Pearl had the exact-same tea service, except for the sugar bowl, which was bigger.

DI Phil cleared his throat to get things back on track. His expression had gotten all serious, but like a dad about to give his kid a good kick up the ass but it was gonna hurt him more than it was gonna hurt the kid.

Eventually the DI slid a sheet out of a file and scanned it for a second.

"Mr. Brunovich. Your family is credited by police forces throughout Europe as being perpetrators of, and I quote, illegal gambling, extortion, kidnapping, multiple murder, human trafficking and the enslavement of vulnerable females into prostitution. Rape for gain, as I prefer to call it. Would you like to comment?"

Well, that was about as nasty as it got, and by the end of his little speech the detective even looked apologetic. His eyes had gone all misty, like he was gonna blub, at which moment, Huggins chimed in again.

"And the teapot, guv. Auntie Pearl's has got a slightly different pattern on it; a Chinaman fishing in a little boat. I think the chink's on the cups too, come to think of it. Probably not the same tea service after all, aye, guv?"

This had to be a freakin' act, Karpos told himself. It wasn't until much later, five miles out of Glasgow in his hired Mercedes SUV with a fuck-shit tail on his ass, that he realized exactly how much of a performance it had been. The guys deserved Oscars.

It seemed there was nothing for Karpos to crap his pants about here. DI Phil's list of the crime family's transgressions had been old news. The Brunovich clan hadn't been into any of that shit in years, and Uncle Fedor couldn't be touched for any of it now.

The family had moved on, its business concerns evolving at the same rate as modern computer technology. The good old days, when you had cops on the payroll, bought a judge or put the screws on a government official for protection were ancient history.

Since moving the operation to the States, the Brunovich family had joined the world of organized cyber-crime. Okay, he had no real understanding of how that shit worked, but in one year, the family could make more dough using the Internet than it had made in a decade with its protection rackets, building development scams and whore houses.

The magic of it was that every cent they made from credit card payments they made anonymously. Porn sites, set up and run by the likes of Timur Golovko, operated through cut-outs, blind-alleys with dead-end addresses in Nigeria, Thailand and Ukraine, making them totally untraceable.

Some of the more 'specialist' flesh sites brought in huge bonuses because, once you'd gotten a sick fuck's credit card details, you cleaned-out his account or just plain blackmailed the freak. The whole caboodle managed from deep within a maze of shadows by an army of geeks and tame hackers. And the pervs were gonna go blubbin' to the cops?

Another thing. Internet scams were dreamt-up on a daily basis, the good ones raking-in several thousands of dollars before they got shut-down. That happens, you just stick another one up there in a different guise.

The profits generated by these scams were mega, like with the porn, because the racket was global; targeting and conning the dupes literally in their millions. And the only time anyone had to get their hands dirty was when some up-start wannabe tried to cut themselves an angle, or one of the geeks got a conscience. Or greedy. And then there was the hearse.

Laundering all that dough was the trickiest part. Bogus business fronts like bars, clubs and gaming arcades weren't able to handle the volume of cash mounting up. That's where Hammer, Frank Holt, and that Scottish prick, MacBain, had come in.

Anyhow, none of the above seemed to be on DI Phil's sin list today. It seemed all he and his Interpol pals were doing here was giving the Brunovich family tree a shake to see what fell out. At the same time sending them a message: 'We got our beady eye on you bad guys, so you'd better watch out!' *Yeah? So bite me.*

The tea party ended on a pleasant note; handshakes all-round and Karpos saying how he hoped he and his new cop buddies should do this gig again sometime. Maybe on his way back from his birdwatching trip in the Highlands.

"Interview terminated at 15.22," DI Phil said, reaching for the mini recorder. Then, pausing to scratch his head, he said, "Huggins? I thought you turned this thing on."

"I thought *you* had, guv."

The Inspector personally escorted Karpos onto the plane and showed him to a seat in First.

"Avoir un bon voyage, Mr. Brunovich. And best of luck with the twitching, dear boy." *Twitchin'?*

As the cop turned to go, he grinned and waggled his eyebrows at a hot stewardess with a rack you could stack books on. She looked back at him, kind of repulsed, and Karpos truly felt sorry for the poor schmuck. His moustache was still stuffed with crumbs and shit from his Jammy Dodgers.

*

He spotted the tail, three cars back, five miles out of Glasgow. A dark-blue sedan with tinted windows and one too many antennas. The second giveaway came when it jumped two sets of lights to keep up with his hired Mercedes SUV.

He checked the dash clock: 9.32pm. It had taken him around fifteen minutes to get used to driving on the left but he was on top of it now. He reckoned if he could get away from the bright streetlights he'd have a better chance of shaking the assholes. The Russian killed his lights and zigzagged away from the main drag.

Ten minutes later found him outside a junkyard in an unlit side-street, where he'd parked between a couple of container trucks.

Several minutes went by. No sign of the sedan so, hopefully, he'd lost it. Nevertheless, DI Phil's Scottish buddies had ID'd his wheels, so the time had come to get inventive. He found a tyre-iron and flashlight in the trunk and jimmied open the scrapyard's high, corrugated-steel gates topped with razor wire. Then, dowsing the flashlight, he stood in the dark for a few minutes, holding his breath and listening for signs of life. No dogs. He relaxed.

The beat-up Honda Civic was tucked behind a small brick office. It looked too good for the crusher so he took a chance. It hotwired like a dream. *Badda bing, badda boom!*

He transferred his Samsonite and swapped the Honda's tags with some his flashlight had picked out in amongst the junk. There'd been several pairs so he'd stashed a couple of extra sets.

Following the main route north out of the city again,

he drove a few miles, took a detour and pulled into a crowded car lot beside the River Clyde. The last sign he'd passed had called the place 'Greenock.'

A whole bunch of people were boarding a boat for a night cruise down the river. They'd be away from their wheels for hours, he reckoned, and so waited for the boat to sail before hotwiring a dark-green Nissan coupe. It would be a faster ride until he found something else to swap it with. Overkill, maybe, but it would take the cops longer to join the dots and trace his route.

He stuck another set of junk-yard tags on the vehicle and headed back to the A82. All this shit had slowed him down but he reckoned he'd still make Oban, on the west coast, by midnight.

*

Almost 2.00 in the morning and another busy night in Mrs. Drum's. It was rare for the old lady to keep the place open so late outside Christmas and New Years' but everyone seemed to be having a good time. And, after all, there was money to be made.

Dugald and his crew, Rab was surprised to see, were even socializing with the beak sniffers. They'd spent most of the evening playing cards with the German crowd by the inglenook and, having relieved them of their shirts, were now thrashing them at their own game in a beer drinking contest.

The crew's youngest member, Big Sam Greer, was

proving more than a match for the camouflaged contenders. At six-foot four and weighing-in at three hundred pounds, his face and hands forested with course, red hair, he resembled a woolly mammoth in a kilt. And it was only just dawning on the Teutonic troop that he could drink the Atlantic dry twice-over. The sure losers weren't looking happy.

"Hey, Rabbie, ye shouldna've." Little Zac's face had appeared, beaming through the beer pumps.

"So you got my gift."

"Aye, right enough. Mam just give it mah. It's the raw bollocks, Rabbie!"

Rab, in the guise of Tim Santry, had ordered the boy an alloy baseball bat, glove and a tube of balls from the States. The kid had never handled a real bat, he'd realized when he'd spotted him, a few months back, knocking a tennis ball against a wall with a length of wood.

"Are ye aff ta give mah lessons, Rabbie? That'd be grand!"

Rab laughed. "I'll pitch you a few balls sometime, okay? But I reckon you'll be teaching me, kiddo."

The kid beamed some more then, suddenly remembering something, slipped a hand into the pocket of his hoodie and brought out a folded slip of paper. "By the way, me mam said ta gi' ye this."

Rab took it before the kid ducked out under the counter flap to collect glasses. Mrs. Drum shuffled out from the galley kitchen and placed a folded newspaper on the bar top.

"Angus brought it over, Rabbie. He says nae ta worry ye sel' about the money, just now."

"That's great. Thanks," he said, but it was Aggie's message that most intrigued him for the moment. It was hand-written on a yellow Post-it. A phone message from Angus who was apparently staying overnight on the mainland. The call had probably gotten Aggie out of bed, poor woman.

He didn't have to read far before a sudden blood-rush to the head made him nauseous. Karpos Brunovich was in Oban.

A burst of raised voices came from the inglenook where the drinking contest had become heated. Big Sam Greer and one of the Germans were on their feet. A couple of chairs had gone over and the men were sizing up for a scrap. Birdwatchers at a neighboring table rose as one and moved away to give them room.

"Behave yesels o'er there!" the landlady bellowed. "Sam! Sit down, ye lummox! Any breakages and ye'll be payin' fer 'em!"

The mammoth complied and the temperature dropped at the table as quickly as it had risen.

Rab slipped the Post-it into a coat pocket and tried to calm down. He slowed his breathing and looked to the newspaper for any kind of a diversion. He needed to think.

The paper was yesterday's *New York Times*. The ferry captain occasionally got him a copy when one showed-up in a newsagent's in Oban. He realized the landlady was still lingering behind the counter. She didn't need to hear the bad news just yet, he decided.

"Did you, uh… did you have a flip-through yourself, Mrs. D?" he said, nodding to the paper.

"Oh, aye, wee bits," she said, wrinkling her nose, "Americans, though. Wi' all them universities, ye'd think they'd ken how ta spell!"

She shuffled to the other end of the bar to serve someone, so he opened the paper and turned straight to the financial pages out of habit. Something at the bottom of the right-hand page jumped out and slapped him. Angus had circled the item in ink.

'FBI probe into law firm after senior partner vanishes.'

"Homesick, already?" Becky asked, arriving at his side with a whisky in each hand. He hadn't seen her enter the bar.

"The New York Times," she said, raising her eyebrows, "You get it flown over? How sweet."

He refolded the paper, aching to read the FBI article and accepted the proffered Scotch, hoping it would cure the bad taste in his mouth.

*

Becky watched him knock back the liquor in-one. He looked on edge. A good a time as any, she reckoned, to push him all the way over.

The place was rammed with the birdwatcher crowd again. Not so many locals tonight, she noted, but business must be good, nevertheless.

One of the German jokers from this morning had spotted her and was waving and grinning like a dope. She ignored him and emptied her glass. She put it down next to Rab's and called to Mrs. Drum.

"Same again, please, ma'am, when you have a moment."

The landlady came right over. Her eyes lacked the warmth of the night before. "Will ye be wantin' a rock in it this time?"

"Uh… sorry?"

"She never takes ice, Mrs. D," said Rab, staring at the counter top. The old woman moved away with the glasses. Rab was avoiding eye-contact, she noted. She leaned in close and lowered her voice.

"So. The fish biting today? I hope so, given how broke you are n'all."

He gave a weary sigh. "Why don't you just cut to the chase? Make your point then leave me the hell alone."

Mrs. Drum returned with the whiskies and Rab made no move to pay for them. She handed the old lady a twenty. "My treat, Rab, I know how squeezed for cash you are, poor baby."

He seemed genuinely distracted, fidgeting with the folded newspaper.

"Alright," she said, fixing a stare, "so you don't want to play nice. Fine, then I reckon it's time I took off the gloves, because I can hurt you, Rab. Badly. You think I'm messing, that I'm not capable, but you don't know me anymore."

"You got that right." A mumble.

"So, one last chance, or all your new pals get to know your secrets. I'm serious, Rab."

"Fine. Go ahead. Knock yourself out."

Mrs. Drum returned, plonked Becky's change on the bar-top without ceremony and waddled away.

"But your hidden treasure isn't the only little secret in town, is it, Rab?" She made a show of checking-out a group of fishermen sitting near-by. "But hey, I get it. It's the same old story, right? The island's economy's gone to rat shit. The fishing's non-existent and there's barely a cent coming from the sheep. So, why not have a stab at tourism? Why not? Great idea."

Rab made a point of looking disinterested. He topped-up his Scotch with a drop of water from a jug.

"The thing is," she went on, "Garg hardly has the sun-baked beaches of Hawaii, or the dreamy architecture of Florence or Athens. So, where's the tourist attraction?"

He remained unmoved. Surely he could see where she was headed.

"Come on, work with me, here," she urged, "Where's the hook, Rab?"

No response. He was behaving like a sulky kid, refusing to eat his greens.

"Well, that's okay, sweetie, because the hook's right here." She dipped into her pocketbook and brought out the blue tail feather she'd taken from the eyrie.

He glanced at it and his face froze like a stopped clock.

In that instant, she knew she'd hit the spot. She had him, damnit!

His eyes met hers for the first time, the gunmetal in them giving-way to the deep-blue she remembered. They looked young and troubled once more. Quietly pleading.

"Tell me," he whispered, "have you asked yourself why you're really doing this?"

"What do you mean? Of course I…"

He nodded to the newspaper. "Don't you think a multimillion embezzlement might've made the headlines? The financials? Maybe get a mention on Bloomberg?"

One of his famous diversionary tactics, she warned herself. Lame too. Nevertheless, it had put her off her game for a second.

"Jeff explained that," she said. "It was never reported. That kind of news spooks the clients. It's bad for business."

"Frank Holt. Remember him?"

"Of course. Jeff had him relocated."

"Damned right, he did. To about six feet under the ground. But, of course, you wouldn't know that unless Hammer talks in his sleep, right?"

"Change the record, Rab. That one's got a scratch in it."

"Okay then, you think you've gotten Karpos under control. Believe me, sometime in the next forty-eight hours you're gonna find that really isn't the case. And he's someone who *really* doesn't play nice."

She remembered the bastard's hands stroking her legs.

The pressure of the gun's muzzle against her temple... but how had Jeff put it?

"Karpos will agree, I'm sure, that he was somewhat over-zealous in the execution of his duties at that time."

"You don't know what you're saying," she snapped, "Jeff made it clear…"

"Forget Jeff. The Russian mob put you here, or they got Jeff to send you. Whichever way up, they're really not gonna trust Miss Tippy-tap from the typing pool to pull this off on her own?"

"Fuck you."

The Brunovich's were creeps, no question. Their import/export business was no doubt into all kinds of shady deals. The usual stuff: tax evasion, jiggery-pokery with the company accounts, but the Russian mob? Really? Besides, GHD was a highly respected firm. Jeff wouldn't sully its reputation with anything so distasteful. So tawdry.

"Don't smoke-screen me with that Russian mafia crap, it doesn't hold up and you know it."

"Becky, there-is-no-gold!"

Good try, she thought, but she knew this man. She'd shared a bed with him for almost a year. Did he really think she couldn't see through his lies? He was still talking.

"When's it gonna sink in, Becky? I'm running because, as corny as it sounds, even in the movies, I know too much. And however this ends up going down, if you're not actually working for them, your days are numbered too, believe me."

"That's not your concern," she spat, holding up the feather, "*This* is all you've godda worry about, mister."

He looked away. She followed his gaze, guessing he was looking for Greda to spring to his rescue. But his saviour was nowhere to be seen. She noticed, instead, the eyes of every islander in the room zeroing-in on the feather in her hand, their expressions giving nothing away. The birdwatcher crowd remained oblivious.

"Come on, don't make me do this. The pot of gold, Rab. Where's the end of the rainbow?"

He turned his back and sipped his Scotch. *Unbelievable!* How could he be so arrogant? So selfish? She thought he actually cared about these people. She toyed with the feather for a moment, then downed her drink.

"Jesus. How long did you people think you could get away with it?" She affected a laugh. "When it rains, it pours. Remember that saying?"

He still said nothing as she turned and ambled over to the inglenook.

The German dope's eyes lit up when he saw her coming. He got to his feet, grinning like an idiot and removed his camouflaged cap.

"Ah! This is very goot, ja? You join us, pretty lady, yes?"

The little spider boy was standing close-by, gaping at the feather. He was holding a tray of empty glasses and she helped herself to one.

"Thanks, kid," she said, filling it with water from an earthenware jug. She held the glass up for the men to see, waiting for Rab to intervene. He didn't... and so she dropped the feather into the glass.

A hush had descended over the room and she realized she now had the attention of everyone in it. The Germans were the first to lean-in and watch as inky dye swirled out of the feather to turn the water a vivid shade of blue.

She placed the glass on the table and made her way through a cloying silence to the door marked 'Private', wondering when the self-loathing would kick-in.

*

Zac had managed to lose the tray of glasses on the Germans' table and get safely behind the bar before the volcano erupted. The quake that signalled it started as a low rumble by the inglenook, where the camouflaged numpties had got to their feet, shouting and cursing Granfer Dugald and the lads in their native gobbledygook.

The shockwave ripped through the room so that practically every beak sniffer in the place, even the women, began booing and hissing the islanders. It was like being at the panto but without the funny costumes and the men dressed-up as women.

Zac watched, mesmerised, as the shockwave hit the back wall and returned to its (as Miss Tonbridge had taught the class) epicentre, where Big Sam Greer had overturned the table full of glasses while the Germans swung punches like bampots. Rabbie leaned over and shut the counter-flap with a *bang!*

"Stay there, kid, and don't move!" he yelled before throwing-off his coat and diving into the thick of it. Zac stood on tiptoe to keek between the beer pumps and saw the Dunlop hens going at it like ninjas. Elleen was pulling a woman's hair out, while her sister hung onto an old fella's ears and kicked him repeatedly in the shins.

Large Stanley, meanwhile, had caught a beak sniffer around the neck with his crook, holding him three feet up a wall while Maddie shredded the numpty's trouser leg in a rabid frenzy.

Brave constable Finn came out of the gent's lavy, putting on his cap. He took-in the mayhem and buggered-off back inside.

Zac, never to miss an opportunity, used the diversion to whip a couple of packs of Marlborough Lite from the ciggie shelf and stuff them down his kecks, checked the coast, and swiped another couple of packs.

Back at the inglenook, Sam Greer snatched up a chair and raised it aloft, about to crack the skulls of a couple of Jerries armed with the poker and iron tongs from the fireplace.

The high-pitched clanging of a ship's bell cut through the cacophony like a terrible scream, and had many covering their ears. The battle subsided and the room became quiet. Mrs. Drum muted the bell, fuming, her face as red as a post box. She filled her lungs and bellowed across the bar.

"Samuel Greer!" The big man blushed and lowered the chair to the floor. "Ah told ye ye'd be payin' fer breakages, did ah nae?

"Aye, Mrs. Drum, ye did!"

"Well, take nae heed o' mah, laddie! Ah've a nest egg that'll cover it, nae problem! Tear the place apart if ye have ta!" With that, she grabbed a bottle of *Creme de menthe* (not a big seller) and lobbed it into a group of Dutchmen who'd been sitting quietly the whole time in a corner.

It took a few moments for the old hag's meaning to sink-in, but once it had, it was as if a passing film director had poked his head in and yelled: "Bar-room brawl, take two! Action!"

Because, much to Zac's humongous delight, the madness returned with a vengeance. And even if the legendary *'Battle of the Blue Feather'* hadn't exactly happened the way it's recounted here, it's the way Zachariah Moore would one day tell it to his wide-eyed grandchildren.

*

The latch *clacked*, the door opened and Rab entered the low-lit parlour, his hurricane lamp boosting the room's luminance. Calum looked up from the kitchen table, a sable brush poised above a pot of ink. He acknowledged Rab's arrival with a nod.

Greda put aside the book she was reading and smiled. Hi, Rabbie, you're back early tonight."

"Yeah," he said, placing his lamp on the table and waiting for the fisherman to finish applying blue pigment to the tail feathers of a peregrine falcon. The bird, mounted on a block perch, seemed happy enough to oblige him.

"Are ye okay, there, pet? said Greda, rising from her chair and approaching the table, "Ye look like ye've seen a ghost.

Calum read his expression too. "What's botherin' ye, man?"

He decided not to hit them with the worst of it just yet. "Becky," he said, simply.

"Creepin' Jesus," growled Calum, tossing his brush aside, "What's the meddlin' wee, bitch been up ta now?"

He and Greda listened as Rab filled them in on the evening's events: Becky's conjuring trick and the effect it had had on all concerned.

"Luckily, it didn't come to blows," he added, "but I reckon our guests'll be clamouring to get off the island first thing in the morning."

Calum examined the ink bottle's label in the light of Rab's lamp. Angus coudnae get us the usual," he said, "but ah've been usin' this fer weeks now wi' nae problem."

"We've had nae trouble wi' it, Rabbie," Greda said in support of her man.

Rab thought about that. That day's downpour had

been the first rain the island had seen in a while. *"When it rains, it pours. Remember that saying?"*

That had to be it. Becky must've found the tail feather after today's deluge. He said as much.

"Fair point," Calum conceded, "but, come now, Rab, it was always gonna happen. Just a wee matter o' when."

"It's not the way I would've done it, though," said Rab, taking a chair at the table, "but you've godda hand it to her, she did a fine job of it."

Although it had always been the plan to expose the birds as fakes at some point, they'd meant it to happen in a way that would attract the most media attention, but perhaps it was better this way, Rab was thinking. With Becky being an outsider, the fraud's exposure would have more impact; an act of spite from a disgruntled tourist, perhaps.

Silence fell upon the room as each retreated into their own thoughts. Until, unable to hold back a moment longer, the three fell into fits of laughter.

High spirits prevailed as dawn appeared through the window and they planned their next move in what had become something of a game. A game that had another level yet to be played out.

Rab killed the mood, then, by showing them the item in *The New York Times* he'd at last had the time to read. It told of Jeffery Hammer's disappearance and probable murder. He let the couple digest that before following it with the contents of the Post-it note.

Rabbie. That fat Russkie bastard's back like you said he'd

be, throwing his weight around in The Crab 'n' Tackle!
Angus.

"So, my friends," said Rab, looking to the window where dawn had blossomed into a fine morning, "Act two. Enter Karpos Brunovich."

Chapter Ten

KARPOS descended the rusted, iron ladder set in the side of the granite wharf. He stepped onto the deck of *The Wayward Lass*, shrugged-off his backpack and threw down his bundle of bungee rope. He'd reckoned twenty foot would be more than enough for the job.

He knew he was overdressed in such fine weather in black commando pants, matching polo-neck and boots. But this was his essential night-climbing gear, and he liked to be prepared way ahead of an operation.

He detected the strong scent of gasoline and, looking about him, saw nothing to inspire confidence. The fishing boat showed more than just signs of neglect. He couldn't see an inch of paintwork that wasn't peeling, metal fixtures that weren't badly corroded, and what areas of the deck hadn't been crudely patched with tar and canvass looked to be awash with... yeah, spilled gasoline.

The tub's skipper, Mikey MacCullen, squeezed his bulk out of the wheelhouse, scratching at his dark, matted beard. It struck Karpos the guy cared more about his boat's appearance than he did his own. His pants and wool sweater were so ripped and worn, it had to be the grease stains holding them together.

"It's ye sel," the guy said, without enthusiasm.

"Who the fuck else it gonna be?"

The skipper's grubby hand moved from his beard to scratch his crotch. "Dae ye have mah money?"

Karpos had arrived in Oban before midnight as predicted, had torched the stolen wheels in woods outside town and had hiked the last mile. He'd signed into a hovel calling itself a guest house under a false name and paid with a cloned Mastercard, curtesy of Timur Golovko.

By 1.00am he'd found The Crab 'n' Tackle, probably Scotland's roughest drinking hole, where you'd expect to find it in a coastal town: right on the seediest, most run-down stretch of the waterfront.

Country and Western blared from a juke box inside. Some dumbass trucker bleating on about a trailer trash cowgirl who'd gone done left him for a rodeo clown. He was truly shocked that anyone would listen to that whinging crap outside the US.

A half dozen lowlifes nursed drinks at the bar, hunched on stools in a fug of stale booze and body odour. After a spell of being ignored by the clinically obese bartend, he'd figured it time to make his presence felt.

"Hey! Chubby Cheeks! How 'bout a beer over here?"

The ass-wipe made like he was deaf while an overweight bum sitting close-by gave a snort and mumbled something to his muppet buddies. His accent was impenetrable but Karpos reckoned he'd gotten the gist: 'Loudmouth, commie bastard.'

He took a few moments to marvel at how certain words could be universally, even instinctually, understood no matter the speaker's native tongue, then head-butted the dumb fuck, splitting his nose wide-open and dropping him like a sack of chopped tuna.

A cold beer arrived in front of him double-quick, the bartend all smiles and friendly like, while the muppet losers kept their eyes averted. No heroes there, he thought.

Though, there was one old guy, at the far end by a wall phone, that gave him pause. He was paying the Russian no mind, but there was something about him he couldn't put his finger on. The guy had one arm and an eye missing, and had his nose in a crossword book. Which was kind of weird given the time and place. What the hell was it about the old-timer that rang bells, damnit.

Images began to flicker at the outer-most regions of his memory, enlightenment a mere half-dozen synapse gaps away, when the slurred voice of someone stinking of unwashed clothes and gasoline said, too close to his ear, "Nae a bad Glesgae kiss there, pal."

Karpos turned and stared into the deaden eyes of the guy he now knew as Mikey MacCullen; a bottom-feeding ass-wipe in his mid-fifties and skipper of *The Wayward Lass*. He was about to give the fairy a huge fist to chew on when the guy hastily explained the kind of 'kiss' he was referring to. The Russian relaxed, though was still in the dark as to what a 'glesgae' was. No matter, for he'd already decided MacCullen was exactly the kind of lowlife scum he'd come here looking for.

"Ah dinnae get it," the skipper was saying later over a game of pool, "There's a ferry ta Mull and another ta take ye on ta Garg."

"What can I say? I a sneaky kinda guy."

"A grand ye say? Pounds sterling?"

"Cash, sure, how many times?"

He returned his pool cue to the rack after letting the patsy beat him five games straight. When the joint closed around 3.00am, the deal had been struck and handshakes exchanged.

Next morning found him at a branch of The Royal Bank of Scotland where, after firm objections from its manager, (made less-firm by a bribe masquerading as a hefty commission) he arranged a twenty-five thousand dollar wire transfer from Banco Confianza on Grand Cayman and walked out with it in cash minutes later.

Next stop, a Millets outward-bounders' store on George Street, where he'd purchased the backpack, clothes and climbing paraphernalia. And, would you damn well believe it? adjacent had been The Costume Box; a fancy dress place with a mannequin in the window wearing a Spiderman get-up.

That'd be a scream, he thought; scaling the cliff face dressed as the comic book superhero. Given there was a fair chance he'd be recognized on the island this time, he'd gone inside for a browse.

Something to hide his prominent buzz-cut would be a good idea, he'd reckoned, and the place sold several kinds of hats. One in particular had caught his eye. It was a kind of puffed-up tartan beret with a red bobble and a fuzz of ginger hair sewn around the back and sides. '*A must for members of Scotland's Tartan Army*', read the label, whatever the hell that was.

He'd tried it on in a mirror and, though very much tempted, opted instead for a Tweed cap and a stick-on salt 'n' pepper moustache. A pair of wire-framed specs completed the transformation and he'd left the store looking like Lord Limey of Snooty-ass Manor.

"Ah said, dae ye have mah money?" MacCullen repeated, leaning in the doorway of the wheelhouse.

Karpos unzipped the top of his backpack to expose a wad of new notes. "A grand, like we agreed."

Someone else slipped out of the wheelhouse behind the skipper. A skinny little guy around MacCullen's age who probably shopped for clothes at the same charity outlet as the skipper. He had about three teeth in his head and no chin. MacCullen placed a hand on the weasel's shoulder.

"Hughie works fer mah, by the way," he said, his words slurring even at this early hour. "We come as a team, ye ken?"

"Sure," said Karpos, matter of factly, as the weasel edged around to his right, his beady, rodent eyes not leaving the backpack.

"Now, it strikes mah," the skipper was saying, "that a grand isnae a tidy sum between two. Now, *two* grand, that'd be tidy, what dae ye think, pal?"

But he didn't have to think. He threw a lightning,

sideways punch that made contact with what there was of the weasel's chin, sending him over the side of the boat. He gave MacCullen his best Tony Soprano 'don't fuck with me' look. "We tidy now?"

The big man replied, with no trace of a slur, "Nae problem. Hughie loves the watter…"

Karpos spotted movement down by McMullen's knee where a dog had appeared. *Uh-oh…*

"…Tyson, his wee doggie, now, he's different matter. Hates gettin' wet. He'll ha' yer bawbag first."

The mutt was one of those muscle-bound inbreds with stubby legs; head and jaws shaped like an anvil. Its eyes were too far apart and it had a stump where its tail should be. And the skipper might've been right about it not liking water. The sound of its owner spluttering and splashing over the side seemed to be stressing the mutt out big-time.

Karpos frowned. He just had to ask. "What is bawbag?"

The skipper laughed, retreated into the wheelhouse and fired-up the boat's engine.

"I said, what the hell is bawbag?"

Getting no reply, he growled and went to slip the mooring lines, check the outboard inflatable dinghy was securely tethered at the stern, and went to join the skipper. Tyson was growling and giving him the stink-eye as he gave him a wide berth in the doorway. MacCullen steered a tight turn and headed for the open sea with the dinghy bobbing in tow.

They'd sailed a short distance out in silence when

Karpos noticed the big guy's hand reach into a drawer by the wheel. He shifted his weight onto his left foot and kicked the drawer shut with as much force as he could muster. The skipper's wrist snapped like a twig and he fell to his knees, screaming.

The Russian checked the drawer to find, nestling among papers and charts, a Webley MK VI, which he knew to be the standard service revolver issued to British officers in World War 1. Old, sure, but in pretty good condition, and there was a box of .455 slugs with it. *Well, waddaya know. Hi there, new best buddy!*

A swift kick to MacCullen's face knocked the man out cold. He took the wheel, giving the mutt a wary glance over his shoulder. The little shit had remained in the doorway the whole time, its growl deeper now, calculating. Karpos took up the revolver, flipped-off the safety and closed the drawer.

*

There'd been no hot water brought to her room at the usual half-seven sharp. Instead, a hand-written note had been shoved under the door.

Regretfully, due to unforeseen circumstances, the management requires you to vacate your room by 10.00am today. An itemised bill awaits your attention at reception. We hope you've enjoyed your stay.

Mrs. E. Drum (proprietress.)

Becky wondered what the *'E'* stood for. Ear? She couldn't blame the old girl, she supposed, as she jammed the stick-shift into second and eased her foot off the clutch. She took a right turn at the stream and headed inland toward the little wood bridge that crossed it, doing her best to avoid ruts and boulders.

She'd received the cold shoulder, too, at the store, where she'd made a last-ditch to get her mom that butterscotch. No luck with that, of course, and even her number one fan, her little spider boy, had kept his gaze glued to the floor as she'd passed him on the way out.

What the hell have I done, she thought, as she'd taken-in the scene along the harbor road, where the fruits of her infamy had been all too apparent. Very few locals had bothered to set-up their market stalls, and fewer visitors had shown an interest in them.

She'd seen birdwatchers attempting to board *The Mishnish* with rucksacks and camping gear, though the tiny vessel had clearly been overladen. Which Captain One-arm One-eye had been at pains to point out through a crackling bullhorn.

Needless to say, tempers had been running high as the crowd jostled and squabbled to get aboard; the Germans, typically, being the most vocal. The spectacle reminded her of refugees at the end of the Vietnam War, desperate to get themselves airlifted at the Fall of Saigon.

A splinter-group had given-up and had cornered a

fisherman in a bid to negotiate a passage to the mainland. Something she'd probably have to do herself later, she realized, but there was just one thing she had to do before she could even think about that.

Dugald had surprised her when she'd turned up to hire his scrap-heap again. She'd expected the old guy to rob her blind; charge her double, at least, but he'd waived the fee with a shrug and had thrown her the keys. Even more surprising; he'd taken the time to give her directions to Rab and Greda's place. She wondered about that now, as she pulled-up by the little wood bridge. Maybe, like every other Garg islander, he had simply wanted to see the back of her.

She shielded her eyes from the sun and scanned the smattering of whitewashed dwellings skirting the base of the mountain. Rab and Greda's cottage was the last in line to the south, apparently, set well apart from the others. She already knew the track that led to it but the most direct route to their place seemed to lay diagonally across the valley floor and up the other side.

She considered the rough terrain before her; the toppling cairns and rocky debris, and for the first time noticed faint cart tracks weaving a way through. Oh, well, how difficult could it be? She made a wish and drove across the bridge.

*

It was true. Tyson really didn't like the water. Karpos

watched through the wheelhouse doorway as Mikey MacCullen's bullet-ridden corpse bobbed five hundred yards away in the boat's wake. The mutt barking its little doggie heart out, standing four-square on the dead guy's chest as the surf rose and fell. If the fucker had had a tail, it wouldn't be wagging it now.

He could see the Isle of Mull to his left as he skirted the headland and steered due west. He'd decided not to risk using the island as a stepping-stone to Garg. What if people there were on the lookout for him, ready to sound an early warning? No, this way was safer.

The sea was pretty calm, there being no wind to speak of. A pair of dorsal fins cut across his bow. Dolphins?

He checked his phone. No signal. That was okay, though; he'd managed to touch base back on the mainland, waking Matvy Golovko from his beauty sleep around 3.00am NY time. The ass-wipe had chewed him out about that before getting down to business.

Uncle Fedor was not happy on a couple of counts. He wanted results and was getting pretty pissed he wasn't getting any. Karpos assured the Georgian he was on top of it. Only hours away from triumph.

He was heartened to hear the Gordon slut had gotten in touch with Hammer and confirmed the gold was on the island. Then happier still that, as a result, the lawyer, outliving his usefulness, had taken a bullet at long last. Which was a shame, as he'd liked to've offed the prick himself.

Matvy had sounded on edge, though, and when pushed

admitted Uncle Fedor was doubly pissed at the Golovkos brothers for botching the body dump.

New Jersey construction workers had gone on strike, and it looked like the corpse, waiting at the bottom of a foundation trench for a concrete overcoat, wasn't gonna get one in a hurry. So it was only a matter of time before some keen-nosed on-site security guy got a whiff of Hammer's stinking cadaver. Karpos chuckled. Not his problem, he thought, and went over his plan one more time.

If Cupcake had blabbed like he reckoned, the islanders would be ready for him this time. They'd be watching the harbor and beach landing-sites for sure. Easy to do. It was a titchy island. That's why he was going-in the way no one would expect: scaling a cliff face under the cover of darkness. Once a mile off the coast, he'd wait for nightfall, transfer to the outboard dinghy and sink the fishing boat. Cinch.

As he steered *The Wayward Lass* toward the squat, gray outline of Garg, he noticed something. Well, to be picky about it, the lack of something. There was no longer the sound of distant yapping, which made Karpos feel all warm and fuzzy inside. The poor little doggie must be sleeping with the fishes at last.

*

She should've known better. Taking a shortcut across the valley had been a stupid idea. After getting the car stuck in boggy ground, she'd had to spend over an hour and a half gathering rocks and stones in order to make ramps under the wheels. Another half hour to get onto solid ground. And now the damned, useless piece of rusting crap had given up the ghost in the shade of a towering cairn, steam billowing from under its hood.

Becky got out and kicked the door shut in a fury, which caused it to snap one of its hinges and flap at an angle, like on one of those comedy clown cars you see fall apart at the circus. As if to join the act, the hood shot-up in a cloud of steam when she tripped the catch. Sure enough, its 1960s radiator was hissing with rage, ready to explode.

She shoved aside her suitcase in the trunk, rummaged through ripped nets and cork floats and found a plastic oil container.

"Would ya be havin' a bit o' trouble there, miss?"

She straightened too quickly and whacked the back of her head on the trunk door. The middle-aged cop was smiling down at her from his gray-dappled pony.

"What the hell does it look like? Shit! She said, rubbing her bead."

"Looks banjaxed ta me, as yer askin'."

Banjaxed? "Very helpful, Officer, uh...."

"Constable Finn, at yer service, miss," he said in a guttural Irish accent, his smile displaying more gaps than teeth. The guy looked as ridiculous in his oversized uniform as he had on their first meeting, his scruffy mount looking like it might be better employed pulling a gypsy caravan. Realizing she was being unnecessarily snippy, she smiled and softened her tone.

"Well, constable, if you'd really like to help a lady in distress…" She held up the plastic container and tried for butter wouldn't melt.

"This is a no parkin' zone, by the way," he said stiffly, "Have it shifted by nightfall." He saluted, gave the reigns a flick and set his horse clomping on its way.

She watched him go, stunned, as she surveyed the expanse of wilderness around her. Get it shifted or what, it gets towed? What the hell with? Hers were the only wheels on the goddamned island, for crying out loud! She took a deep breath and pulled herself together. Water. The distance back to the stream looked to be about a mile. Rab and Greda's place stood no more than half that at the top of a gentle incline. No-brainer. She started the long climb.

She made it to the dirt track in twenty-five minutes, hot and out of breath. She recognized the two-wheeled trap parked close to the cottage and a stable that probably housed the cob. Chickens pecked and scratched out-front and a goat, tethered to a stake, seemed to be asleep. She spotted an old, cast-iron pump against a side-wall and made a bee-line for it.

Its handle squealed and clanked as she pumped, most of the water missing the container beneath.

"Ye need help wi' that?" said Greda, standing at the far corner of the building. Startled, Becky nodded dumbly. The girl disappeared for a moment and returned with a large plastic container, more suited to the job. She held it under the spout while Becky worked the handle. Once filled, Greda placed it on the ground. She beckoned Becky to follow her past a chicken coop and around to the rear of the property.

The aviary came as no surprise. She knew the girl was a falconer after all. Greda stepped out of one of the cages with a bird of prey mounted on her gauntlet. A peregrine falcon, she guessed. It was beautiful up-close and she felt like she wanted to touch it. It had leather thongs tied to its legs which Greda had hold of. She turned to Becky, her delicate, freckled face expressionless.

"Ye should buy yer mam that butterscotch and go home. There's nothin' fer ye here."

The island's jungle telegraph was obviously more effective than its telephone exchange, thought Becky. "I came to say goodbye."

Greda remained unmoved by the announcement. She went to a door at the end of the cage block and disappeared into darkness with the bird. She re-emerged with a cell phone and proffered it with her free hand.

"Yours?"

And, of course, it was. She'd lost it in the tunnel yesterday and now felt the guilt flushing in her cheeks. "The feather... It was unforgivable, Greda. If I could just..."

"We shall survive wi' the fish and the sheep. It's been our way fer three hundred years."

"Even so..."

"And we've a few canny projects underway that'll have the tourists flockin' back in nae time, nay worries."

The falcon became suddenly restless. It flapped its wings in an attempt to take-off. Greda's eyes shifted to gaze over Becky's shoulder. She turned to see Rab fifty feet away, where the ground rose up toward the mountain. He was carrying a small easel, paint-box and an artist's folio. Odd, she thought. Rab a painter? Since when? He'd halted on seeing her. She lowered her voice to a whisper.

"You love him?"

"Of course," came Greda's reply, and looking into those beautiful, young eyes Becky could see that she did.

Rab discarded his art gear and brought something small and bloodstained from a pocket in his shabby coat. Greda must've released the bird, for she felt a rush of air on her cheek as it shot past her. It flapped its wings twice, glided low to the ground, then swooped up to land on Rab's outstretched arm where it tore at the bloody morsel in his fist.

Her ex-lover beckoned to her, turned and began climbing the steep slope. And so she followed.

*

They'd walked around the base of the mountain until the island's north-west headland could be seen stretching to the Atlantic. She had no idea where the time had gone. They'd hardly spoken on the way.

The sun was low in the west now, the clouds, cartoon-like in a Salvador Dali sky. Rab paused at the top of a rocky outcrop where he launched the falcon into the air. She watched as bird climbed rapidly until she could no longer see it.

"The only sanctuary I had on Earth that night was you," Rab said suddenly, his eyes on the horizon, "Some joke, as it turned out. The mob was on my tail. I was desperate, but I held on to one hope. That you'd pack a bag and come with me. Just like that; destination unknown, future unspecified. I was so sure of you. Sure of us."

She hadn't expected this. He'd opened his shell and the story had come pouring out: Frank Holt's disappearance. The death of a taxi driver and the murder of a homeless kid in an alley. Stink Bug out for his blood because he 'knew too much' about the Russian mob's activities. But there'd been no embezzlement, he'd assured her; the gold, non-existent, simply a ruse by Hammer to get her to assist Karpos in finding him. Some of the bells rang true. Some didn't, but she realized she didn't care anymore.

He was still talking, his eyes searching the sky for the falcon's return. "I thought I'd only have to ask and you'd just give everything up. Life in the City, your job, everything. Screw our original plan, we'd simply leap into the unknown. I was dreaming, of course."

"Maybe our plans are less important than our dreams. Maybe I'd've gone with you."

"No. Dreams are lies by definition. I was lying to

myself. Something Charlie tried to get me to see before he died, but you know what? I don't do that anymore."

The sun was gently slipping into an amber sea, turning everything, even the air, it seemed, shades of orange and yellow. There was still no sign of the falcon.

"When do we get to talk about Jeff?" she said carefully, not wanting his shell to snap shut just yet, but it seemed he wasn't ready for that. Maybe he never would be.

"I asked you once," he went on, "did I look rich to you? Well, sure, I'm rich," he said, gesturing to the landscape where the panorama of lush, coarse grass had turned into a sea of finely spun gold; rocks and boulders into 24 karat nuggets scattered in a pan-handler's pan. "Every blade of grass, every stone, every shaft of light. This is my pot of gold." There was regret in his eyes. And resignation. "This is my sanctuary now."

He moved a strand of hair away from her face and for a moment she thought he would kiss her.

There came the sound of rushing air. Rab put out an arm and the falcon alighted upon it, plumping-up its feathers, eyes alert; the flying ace returned. Rab rewarded it with something nasty from a pocket.

*

The TV in the corner was showing an old movie. 'Whisky Galore', one of Rab's all-time favorites, Becky recalled. It had come to the sequence where, after a cargo ship carrying 50,000 cases of whisky had run aground on a Scottish island, its inhabitants were hiding the contraband from the mainland authorities. Bottles were getting stowed in unlikely places: milk churns, a violin case, under the mattress in a baby stroller, decanted into hot-water bottles etc.

When the movie had been released in the US, she recalled Rab telling her, it had gone by the name, *'Tight Little Island.'* The black and white movie was the kind of gem that made you smile all the way through.

It wasn't Rab watching it now, though. He was sitting opposite her at the table, sketching in a pad by the light of an oil lamp. It was Striptease Eyes, Calum, as she now knew him to be, sitting three feet from the screen in a threadbare armchair.

The DVD collection under the TV she reckoned to be Rab's. Home-recorded copies. These had green stickers along their spines bearing titles in black marker: *'The French Connection', 'The Third Man', 'Local Hero.'* Rab had built-up a similar library back in New York, where she'd watched quite a few with him.

Greda was washing the dinner things at a stone sink. She'd refused Becky's offer of help graciously enough, though no one had had very much to say during the meal. It had been unclear what the Striptease Eyes was doing here. A friend of Rab's, she'd decided, or maybe he helped run the falconry. Whatever, the guy still gave her the creeps. Greda, turned, drying her hands on a cloth and looked to Rab.

"Ah've a few wee tasks wi' the birds, Rab. Ah'll nae be

long. Calum?"

The fisherman rolled his eyes like a 12-year-old, paused the movie and joined Greda at the door. He shot Becky a resentful look before ducking out into the night. Greda's eyes communicated that she was giving Becky space to say goodbye. She acknowledged the kind gesture with a nod before the young woman took up a lamp and left, closing the door quietly behind her

"Keep still," said Rab. He'd been sketching her portrait for a while now.

"Why didn't I know you could do this stuff?" she said.

He shrugged, replacing her question with his own. "So, you slept with the enemy. Terrific. How much did Hammer offer you, anyway? What, three, four percent of the gold's value? That'd be fair, I guess."

She reached for her half-filled wine glass and sipped. *Jeffery Hammer.* What would be the point of even going there? It seemed nothing she could say would stop him picking at that scab. Why waste her breath when they'd soon be out of each other's lives forever? He could pick away 'til it bled, she thought. He was a big boy and she didn't carry Band-Aids.

She pondered the paintings and sketches spread around the walls, noting they were mainly of blue-tailed falcons.

"You have no lobes," he said, breaking the awkward silence.

"What?"

"No earlobes. I never noticed that before. Weird."

She was pleased he'd changed the subject but was

disconcerted by the observation. She felt her ears, rose and crossed to a small mirror over the sink to see what the hell he was talking about. Before she could get him to elaborate, he moved on to something as equally obtuse.

"You still do that question thing with mirrors? How'd it go? 'What was the choice I made that brought me to this?' You said you never got an answer. I used to love that. Gotten any lately?"

She searched for something she could use to switch direction and didn't have far to look. "Jesus. You do this?"

She felt him watching her closely as she studied the painting of water lilies on a pond; the pastel colors, the style. She'd seen the artist's work up-close in New York's Metropolitan Museum and this was definitely no print.

"It's a Monet!" she blurted."

"Nope. It's a Whistler."

*

He hammered the piton home in the granite crack and weight-tested it before attaching a karabina and slipping-in the rope. He jammed a boot into a crevice and pullied himself up another two feet. It was slow going, and even though his head-torch showed the way forward, the footwork had to be pretty much by feel, but hey, he still had it, right? Over twenty years since Mount Elbrus and it had been like getting back on a bike.

The Wayward Lass had sunk like a rock after he'd holed

its hull about a mile out. The slashed inflatable had gone the same way, pulled down by the weight of its outboard. He'd swam the last few hundred yards to the cliff face in the dark. Not easy with a back-pack and a coil of bungee rope looped across his chest.

He'd come to the end of that twenty foot of line, and so, anchoring himself for the moment, he pulled up its dangling tail-end and repeated the process: piton, karabina, pulley and pull. Cinch.

*

And so Rab found himself telling Becky the story of Charlie's unintentional foray into the shady world of art forgery, and his own role as The Alchemist's apprentice. In so doing, he savoured those memories.

Tom Ryan first entered their lives around the time Rab was finishing high-school. A friend of one of Charlie's print worker pals who'd started to turn up at the weekly poker games in their Brooklyn basement apartment.

Tom was a dapper, merry, little man, portly and never to be seen out of his too-tight Harris Tweeds and pink dickie-bow. He had a face and a smile like the Man in the Moon (a nickname that had stuck) and Rab, like his dad, had taken to him straight away.

A dealer in nineteenth and early twentieth century fine art, he worked out of a small gallery in SoHo. The art connection was probably enough for he and Charlie to strike a bond, but the fact Tom was Glaswegian totally

ROBIN DRISCOLL

nailed it for his dad.

Tom had just loved Charlie's work; the technical accomplishment, the perfectionism and historical detail, and was forever badgering Charlie to sell to him. His dad would just laugh and say how he needed to keep his work as a private hobby. No one else even knew he painted, let alone *what* he painted, and that turned out to suit Tom Ryan just fine in the end.

It had all gone wrong over a game of cards. Rab knew at the time Charlie was having money problems. They were behind with the rent and the bills were stacking up. It wasn't until years later he discovered his old man had borrowed from the wrong people to raise the necessary funds to get Rab through law school. He felt bad about that now.

That particular poker night, the pot had become too rich for the rest of the gang and one by one they'd thrown in their hands and gone home. But Charlie knew Tom to be pretty much an amateur at the game, the cuddly Glaswegian seeming to enjoy the guys' company and to not mind losing a few dollars along the way. Thinking back, Ryan must've been in it for the long game because, come midnight, he'd hustled Charlie all the way to a ten thousand dollar marker.

The solution Tom had offered in parting, his smile radiating a friend's regret and heart-felt condolence, was for his dad to hand over the twenty or so forged masterpieces he had stashed away. And Charlie was only too happy to oblige him. It was a quick fix. No harm done. And Tom even covered the rest of Charlie's debts into the bargain. What could be sweeter?

Tom had disappeared soon after. His SoHo gallery had closed and word had it people were looking for him with regard to his own considerable debts.

It wasn't until about a year later that their came a spate of valuable art discoveries throughout Europe. A Henri Matisse in a Parisian basement. A couple of Renoirs tucked away in a Marseilles attic. A Rembrandt in Argentina, reputed to be part of a Nazi treasure hoard. The Man in the Moon had been hard at work, it seemed.

Of course, many of those pictures had since proven to be fakes with modern investigative techniques by authentification experts: X-ray fluorescence mapping and hyperspectral imaging to name just a few tests Rab had boned-up on since. Nevertheless, he knew for a fact that a handful of Charlie's finest works still remained undetected in a few public galleries and private collections around the world.

Becky had listened, as intrigued as much as Greda had been by the story of Charlie's exploits, and when he'd finished, she got up from the table to study the Rembrandt look-alike featuring the blue-tailed falcon. The one that had belonged to his mother.

"And was this picture the inspiration for your Whisky Galore ruse with the peregrines?" She meant painting their tail feathers, of course.

"Yeah, partly, but that picture holds a secret of its own, rooted in the sixties.

"And he never got caught? Your dad, I mean."

"It was a hobby, like I said, and unlike me, he was too highly principled to try passing them off as the real thing," he said with a shrug. "He saw his works as tributes to the great masters, I guess.."

"And you don't, I take it."

He pondered that for a second. "Well, when you think about it, a fake, no matter how good, only has a value because the real thing exists someplace, right?"

She was at his shoulder now. He hadn't noticed her approach. She nodded to his sketch pad. "Can I look?"

"It's not finished."

She leant to inspect the portrait anyway and tilted her head to one side. Her hair brushed his cheek and he breathed-in her scent.

"So. Where does the *real* Rab MacBain exist? I've seen the fake, where's the original?"

He hadn't meant it to go like this. If she'd only left on the ferry this morning with everyone else. She'd gotten herself in deep with Jeffery Hammer, somehow and, whatever she thought she was doing, whatever her motives, there was no way of stopping Karpos Brunovich now.

Sitting there, remembering what they'd had together, savouring her scent and refusing to recall what had thrown them apart would help neither of them. He had a flash of Becky kissing Hammer in her window, and the pain felt no less intense than it did the first time around.

He opened a draw in the table, brought out his copy of

The New York Times and spread it out to show the relevant page. Becky's brow furrowed when she realized what it was she was reading. He adjusted the lamp's wick, as if shedding more light on the words would soften their impact. It didn't.

"My God..." she whispered, her face turning pale.

When she'd finished reading he gave her an up-date. "Finn, the island's cop? He went online at the police house. The Times now says Jeff's body was found on a construction site this morning."

She turned and perched herself against the edge of the table, head in hands, the news sinking in like poison.

"Looks like the mob are tying-up loose ends, Becky. I'm still one of them, and like I said, so are you."

She was staring at the floor, the cogs turning in search of something she'd missed or had misunderstood from the beginning. "Poor Jeff," she said in a small voice.

Rab turned away. "Yeah. I know you two were close."

She looked at him then, eyes wide with incredulity.

*

"Close? Jesus, are you kidding me?"

She'd promised herself she wouldn't dignify his childish assumption that she'd been screwing his old boss but, damnit, she'd held back long enough.

So, out it poured: the hell Rab had put her through that night. The gun to her head, a monster's hands touching her. Hammer showing up and the two finding solace from the violence in a kiss before, Jeff, soused, had passed-out on the couch. She paused, seeing realization dawning in his eyes.

"I didn't go down that hole in the ground after your pot of gold, Rab. I went down there looking for a way to punish you, okay? When I saw how easily you'd started a new life, I had to hurt you back. I never cared less about the damned gold, and if you can't see that then what were we about, Rab? What did we ever have that was worth a goddamned thing?"

He was staring at her like he'd been slapped. Enough. She headed for the low door and grappled with the latch with a clumsy thumb.

"Becky, wait! Karpos was spotted in Oban. He could even be here by now!"

*

Clack! went the latch and suddenly she was out in the dark, her head was spinning. Hammer dead. Karpos on the way. She couldn't think. *The water container.*

She found it by the pump where Greda had left it earlier, and went to leave with it when she heard a low chuckle from somewhere. Say goodbye to Greda or just get the hell out of there? Damn it!

She found the lit kerosene lamp on the ground outside the aviary but there was no sign of Greda or Calum. Then, more chuckling. Gasping. Female. Becoming breathless. A male grunt... and through the wire in one of the cages, deep in the darkest corner against a wall, Calum's lily-white buttocks could be seen thrusting between Greda's thighs. Her copper hair flashed like flames in the lamplight as she tossed her head back and climaxed. Calum's buttocks quivered against one another in spasm while he groaned, his breathing labored.

Greda caught sight of Becky through the wire and giggled like a naughty schoolgirl. Her playmate laughed too when he turned his head and saw her. Without even attempting to uncouple from him, Greda cleared her throat and said, fighting back laughter, "Is mah brother nae goin' wi' ye ta fix yer car?"

"Huh..?" she managed, her gaze shifting to Calum.

"Dinnae look at me, woman; ah'm just her wee bit 'o' rough!" then seeing her eyes shift to take-in the eagle perched nearby he added, "Nae fear, lass, the bird's wearin' its wee hoodie. Cannae see a thing!"

That got the lovers laughing-up a riot, so, feeling more stupid than she'd ever felt in her life, she snatched up the hurricane lamp and hastily made her escape.

Chapter Eleven

He'd fast run out of rock-face and had been scrabbling for purchase in the loose soil layer. He hacked repeatedly at the subsoil, the hammer's spike seeking out places firm enough to take three hundred pounds plus the weight of his backpack. His last solid anchor point was a piton wedged in a granite crevice eight feet below. If he lost his grip now he'd fall that far and dangle in his harness. Not a problem, providing the drop didn't snap his spine.

He paused to take another breather and let his head-torch show him the fringe of grassy vegetation that told him he was six feet from the top. He hadn't reckoned on the soil layer being so damned deep. At least he could see a promising tangle of roots almost within reach. He inched his way up another couple of feet, his heart pumping in his throat, and got hold of the firmest looking of them.

Something screeched and a shape shot out of the darkness and cannoned into the side of his head. Then, whatever it was went shrieking into the night. A fuck-shit bird, he thought, a big one. He let the hammer dangle from his wrist by its strap and checked his face for damage. Nothing, except his eye stung and felt gritty.

The root he was hanging from began to come loose but he managed to get the hammer's spike into something firm before it gave way completely. He was about to toss the root when he realized it wasn't a root at all. It was a human bone. Thigh or upper-arm. His head-torch washed over the dirt wall, picking-out a partial rib cage here, a mandible there. Jesus, he was climbing through a damned burial ground. The dead had never worried him, certainly not their skeletons. But graveyards? They totally creeped him out. He suddenly needed to get this over with.

The end of the bone shaft had splintered to a point so he used it, along with the hammer's spike, to spider-crawl his way up the soil layer. He made it to the top, grabbed hold of a tuft of coarse grass and hauled himself up onto safe ground. He rolled onto his side to get his breath. Yep. I've still got still got it, he thought. Screw *Spetsnaz*. Their loss!

He wriggled out of his harness and let it drop over the cliff edge with the rest of his climbing gear. He wouldn't be making his exit this way. Getting to his feet, he surveyed his surroundings in the weakening beam from his head-torch and, yup, it was a cemetery: crumbling headstones and chest tombs, broken crosses cloaked in ivy.

He needed to change out of his wet clothes, but as he leaned down to unzip his backpack, something caught his eye twenty feet away. One of the chest tombs had become weirdly silhouetted against an unearthly, orange glow.

Then the temperature seemed to plummet as a huge apparition rose up in the light and floated toward him. *Fuck-shit!*

"Ye haven't been upsettin' the wee birdies, now, ha' ye?" the phantom boomed, holding a light up close to its huge, silver head.

Karpos relaxed. The asshole was human, and when the guy got up-close he saw he was old with a face full of silver whiskers. He was carrying a kerosene lamp and brandished a shepherd's crook. Bigger than Karpos, yeah, but that wasn't gonna be a problem.

The shepherd placed the lamp on the ground and straightened, breathing heavily and looking as mad as hell.

Karpos saw the move coming a mile-off and ducked as the crook swished over his head. He crouched, snatched up his spiked hammer and sprang at the giant, his shoulder crashing into the guy's sternum. That sent the old-timer reeling backward to land on his ass against a gravestone, gasping for air.

The Russian swung the hammer at his head only to miss and take off the top section of the gravestone. He raised the weapon again, but before he could bring it down, a large shape flew at him out of the darkness.

The image of a giant fruit bat flashed in his head as sharp teeth crunched through his sleeve and into his wrist, the weight of the beast knocking him to the ground. He struggled to get free but the teeth wouldn't go away. They sank deeper and shook his arm like it was a plaything. He screwed his eyes shut, but it was no good, the Afghan hounds were on him again, tearing his flesh off in chunks while women laughed behind their *burkas*. He screamed, wanting to just give-up and weep.Light from the shepherd's lamp flared in the beast's eyes, and Karpos returned to his senses. His attacker was just a clapped-out sheep dog; mangey looking, like its owner.

The Russian managed to pass the hammer to his free hand and brought it down on the mutt's head. The animal went limp and rolled over; dead as it gets. He tossed the hammer and studied his arm, where rivulets of blood ran out of his sleeve and through his fingers. There was no time to staunch the flow because the old man had come-to and was staring at the dead mutt, fury in his eyes. He struggled to his feet with the aid of his crook looking ready to pounce, but Karpos beat him to it. He dropped his full bulk onto the loser, grabbed him around the throat with both hands and squeezed. The shepherd choked a couple of times but got out a futile threat through clenched teeth.

"Ah'll ha'e yer stinkin' bawbag ye Russkie bassa!"

Karpos loosened his grip. He just had to ask: "What in damn hell is bawbag?"

The shepherd's crook had somehow gotten sandwiched between them and the old guy yanked hard on its shaft, bringing the hooked end crunching into the Russian's testicles. Karpos let out a howl and fell back, clutching his balls in agony.

Meanwhile, the shepherd had gotten hold of the chunk

of broken headstone and went to smash it into Karpos's kneecap. The latter blocked the blow, prised the lump of stone from him and brought it down on the old guy's head. Once, twice, and once more for luck.

Ditching the blunt object, he looked about him for witnesses and, seeing none in the dark, took a deep breath and retrieved his backpack. His head-torch had died at last so he tossed it and snatched up the shepherd's kerosene lamp. He held it over the bearded giant for a moment, noting that his eyes were open and cloudy like he'd seen on dead fish.

The broken section of gravestone by his head boasted a weather-worn legend: *IN LOVING MEMORY.* Hilarious!

He dragged the bodies, man and mutt, into a clump of stinging nettles and concealed them under ferns and ivy before heading into what was left of the night, the dead man's lamp swaying at his side.

*

"Shit…shit…shit…" she muttered as she made her way down the slope, lamp held high, her arm aching with the weight of the water container. *Damn you, Rab!*

He'd never once hinted that he had a sister. They must've been laughing at her all this time. Rab, Greda, Calum, everyone!

She had to get the hell off this damned island, but that couldn't happen until tomorrow now, of course, and then she remembered she didn't even have a bed at the pub. Damn it, she'd sleep in the car! But where *was* that useless heap of junk? She'd reached the towering cairn where she'd left it; walked around it once more in case she was going mad, but it wasn't there. Had it been towed away? What little energy she still had seeped away into the dirt underfoot. She dropped the lamp and container and sunk to her haunches, her head in her hands.

Why did these people hate her so much? Oh yeah, she'd dropped a feather into a glass of water and wrecked the island's economy. It couldn't have been worse if she'd poisoned their livestock and burnt all their homes to the ground.

She took a long, deep breath, determined not to cry. The glass in the lamp had shattered where she'd dropped it and the flame had gone out. It was so damned dark, she'd lost all sense of direction. Had she circled the cairn twice, or three times?

She looked for a line of lighted windows where she thought the base of the mountain should be. That, at least, would give her some bearings. No luck. Then she spotted a light... only it was on the move; heading toward her; a lamp swaying at someone's side. Who would be out here this late? A local on their way home from Mrs. Drum's, maybe? Whatever, this wasn't a good feeling.

She backed away around the cairn, treading carefully so as not to disturb loose boulders and crouched down. Hopefully, whoever it was would pass-on by. She listened hard, the blood rushing in her ears so that she couldn't hear if the owner of the lamp was getting closer.

She risked peeking around the tower of stones, and watched, as a circle of light washed over the patch of grass where she'd been. Then the circle shrank, as if the lamp had been placed on the ground. She could feel her heart pounding as she strained to hear signs of movement, every sinew in her body preparing for flight.

As she rose, her foot nudged a small stone, knocking it against another. The resulting sound was like the single *clack* of a castanet.

That did it. She turned and ran... straight into powerful arms that clamped tightly around her so that she couldn't move. She tried to scream.

"Becky! It's me!"

*

Rab felt sick to the stomach as Becky gave him a blow-by-blow account of her night in Hell. The beating from Karpos. The sexual assault. The more he listened the more he hated himself. How could he have screwed up so badly that night? And he knew, deep down, that he was *still* screwing up, because Becky needed to know what was going on, and right now he needed her not to. Karpos would pay, though, he promised himself that much.

For now, he held her close, lying at the foot of the cairn, stroking her hair, honey-colored in the light of his lamp. It didn't help that she didn't blame him for what he'd put her through, only that he should've trusted her. Should've come clean about laundering money for the Russian mob. And that there could be anything between her and Hammer was madness, he realized now.

She rolled onto him and kissed him, slid her hand under his shirt and stroked his chest.

"Becky? You need to get off the island first thing. You've godda promise me."

"Okay."

"Angus will have the ferry heading out around eleven."

"I know."

She could even laugh about Greda turning out to be his sister. He'd explained how it had been news to him too, and she'd said she was pleased Greda was in his life. She liked her, she told him, a lot.

She bit his ear and nibbled his neck and he felt a familiar stirring. And, as if she knew the effect she was having, she placed her hand there, gently at first and then firmly.

They made love, rolled up in his coat, the ecstasy washing through him, displacing all the bad thoughts and fears and sadness and regret, and he felt more loved than he'd ever felt in his life. "I never deserved you," he whispered, beginning to doze.

"You got that right." And then she was asleep long before him.

*

She woke to find herself alone, wrapped in his frayed city coat. The Great Houdini had done it again.

She sat up and leant back against the cairn, the coat around her shoulders, and took in the view down to the ocean. A carpet of cold mist clung to the valley floor, edging imperceptibly, like glacial ice, all the way down to melt in the sea. The sun would soon burn it off, she guessed, raising her face to catch its warmth.

She could hear bleating sheep and spotted them grazing along the far-off stream. A lone skylark twittered its manic melody high-up. The island was a beautiful place, she decided at last, admonishing herself for ever thinking people were mad to live here.

A car engine coughed to life and she swung around in time to see Rab step out from behind another tall cairn a hundred yards off, waist-high in the mist. He raised the empty water container and waved. She laughed until she ached. Something she hadn't done in a long time.

*

Becky brought the rusted heap to a standstill alongside the *Sea Cry* and she and Rab got out. Its crew was standing in a gaggle by the harbor wall. Clearly, something was up. Raised voices. Dugald pacing back and forth. The group parted when she and Rab approached.

"Where in God's name ha'e ye been, Rabbie?" said Dugald, his face flushed with rage.

Stanley was sitting on steps in the wall. He was wearing

273

striped pyjamas which poked out from under his maroon coat and had a large gash in his forehead below blood-matted hair.

"Jesus, what happened?" said Rab, placing a hand on the old man's shoulder.

An elderly woman Becky had seen before was cleaning the wound with ointment and a linen cloth.

"How bad is it, Elleen?" Rab asked, his voice taught with guilt.

"Nae good. Concussion, ah'd say," replied the old lady, "and the quack nae this side o' the pond 'til Wednesday. And can ah get this hairy lump ta stay in his bed? Can ah buggery."

"Sam Greer found him first thing. Took him fer dead," said Dugald. "Maddie's in a bad way tae."

Stanley raised his head at that and pushed Elleen's hand away. "She's a tougher wee bitch as ye'll ever find. She'll pull through, bless her, or ah'll swing, damn it!"

"Mary's lookin' after her, she'll be fine," Elleen said for Rab's benefit, then to Stanley, "Keep still, old man, how can ah clean ye up?"

The shepherd told his story then, wincing at every tender dab of Elleen's cloth. He'd been on lookout at the cemetery where he'd been attacked in the dark, his assailant having scaled the cliff face, it seemed. He'd put up an impressive fight, he assured everyone, describing the battle in detail. He put his hand to an angry rash on the side of his face.

"An' the sack o' shite dumped mah in the stangers!"

"Stinging nettles," Rab translated, then pressed him for a description. Failing that, a clue to the attacker's accent.

"He was a Russkie, alright," boomed the giant, "Had ta ask mah what a bawbag was! Ah showed the bassa wi' mah hook!"

That got a huge laugh from the crew. Rab helped Elleen get Stanley to his feet and two of the crew volunteered to get the old folk safely back to the Boathouse. Rab squeezed the shepherd's arm in parting.

"I owe you big-time, Stanley. I'm sorry."

"Just skin the fucker fer me, Rabbie," he grunted, "and fer wee Maddie." Then he let the men lead he and Elleen away.

Becky looked toward the harbor where the ferry was docked. A group of birdwatchers were complaining loudly at the top of the hard, looking pissed but with no one to take it out on. Rab noticed them too and checked his watch before looking a question at Dugald.

"Angus got pished on the malt last night," said the skipper, "Fell off his stool. The Mishnish'll nae be sailin' 'til tomorrow now."

It wasn't lost on Becky that she'd been ignored by everyone present since she and Rab had arrived. As if reading her thoughts, Rab walked her away a few paces.

"Look. Some heavy shit is likely to go down pretty soon. I want you kept out of it."

"I'm already in it, Rab, so don't tell me what I should or shouldn't..." He cut her off.

"Go see Mrs. Drum. Tell her I sent you. Do this for

me, Becky. We'll talk when this is over."

She saw there was no point arguing with him. "We do need to talk, Rab. You know that."

"Becky. I'm not… I'm not gonna turn out to be one of the good guys when this is over. And if anything happens to me, you've godda get yourself to the mainland. There's a hotel in Oban. The Columba, near Calmac Ferry Port. Put up there for a night. Two, tops. If I don't make it, promise you'll fly home."

"But Rab…"

"Promise. I've written stuff down. There's an envelope. Greda has it. It'll clear-up the mess I've made… and am about to make. Understand?"

"The Columba Hotel," she said, letting the name sink in.

"Right."

"Then what?"

"Like you said. We talk."

"Okay."

What else could she say? She kissed him, retrieved her suitcase from the trunk of the car and headed for the pub. She wondered if it was too early for three fingers of Scotch, no ice.

*

"Now?" said Dugald, as soon as Becky was out of sight.

"Now," replied Rab.

The skipper nodded to his crew and the men went to work, each knowing what he had to do. The antiquated iron winch was near-on a century old and, bolted into the top of the harbor wall, looked too rusted and beaten up to function. Nevertheless, it had been kept well lubricated and rotated smoothly on its plinth to swing its crane arm over the water, two guys turning its dual-handled ratchet wheel.

Samuel Greer was already in a wetsuit. He donned his face mask while Dugald checked his oxygen tank and regulator. Satisfied, the skipper slapped Sam on the shoulder. The boy placed the regulator in his mouth, sucked hard and jumped from the wall, flippered feet first. He was soon lost in the depths of the harbor's soupy brine beneath the shadow of the winch.

Rab signalled to Constable Finn in the wheelhouse of *The Midas Touch*, a small fishing vessel moored out in the harbor. It was the boat Rab used to fish on with Dugald and his dad as a child. He smiled at its name, now, given the job it was about to do.

The cop waved back, started her up and began to pilot her toward the spot where Sam had gone down.

One of the fishermen yanked the pull-cord on the winch's gasoline motor a couple of times and soon it was putt-putting plumes of black smoke. A brake lever was released and the winch's iron hook lowered slowly into the water on the end of a steel line. Five minutes later, a cluster of bubbles heralded Sam's return to the surface. He gave a thumbs-up and the winch was put into reverse, its steel line instantly under strain.

The hook rose out of the water, bringing with it a thick rope net, bulbous and bedraggled with kelp and weed. The load it held was partially encrusted with limpets and barnacles. A couple of pink crabs gave up the fight and dropped back into the water. The two oblong wood crates, though, were discernible through the rope latticework, as were the stencilled black words on their sides: BANK HAASE, together with a ten digit serial number.

*

Becky hit the bell on the bar top for the third time, wondering what kind of reception she'd get from the old lady when she finally showed. If she showed.

She hoped to God Rab knew what he was doing. He was hell-bent on facing Karpos. She'd never seen him so sure of himself and it scared her. He seemed to have the backing of the islanders and she was heartened that many of the men looked capable of handling themselves.

She was about to hit the bell again when she noticed that scratching sound again from the birdwatcher at the end of the bar. The guy had been nursing a coffee, she'd noticed, and was probably waiting, like she and everyone else, for Captain One-arm One-eye to wake from a booze induced stupor somewhere.

Scratching...

The guy was filing his nails, she realized. Weird.

"Excuse me, sir? Did you happen to see where the landlady went?"

He swivelled his bulk around on the stool to face her, scrutinized her through spectacles under a flat cap and smiled a familiar smile below a not very convincing moustache. The disguise was a joke. A scream caught in her throat and she thought she would urinate.

She made a dash for the street door but Stink Bug was on her at once, clamping a huge hand to her face and forcing something hard into her back. Her teeth found a finger and bit down hard. The Russian let out a howl and adjusted his grip to squeeze her windpipe. He dragged her backward through the drop-hatch, along a passage and out into daylight, smashing her head into a door jamb on the way out.

"Please…" she managed before they both cannoned into a log pile. Karpos rolled her on her back, sat astride her and put a revolver in her face; so close she could see the bullets in their chambers. The bastard leant close to her ear. Hot, wet breath. Spittle on his lips.

"Hey, you don't write me, you don't call. What, ya don't love me no more?"

"Please, Karpos, don't do this…"

"Shhh… you know I kill you."

"Yes," she whispered, the weight of him crushing the air out of her.

"So. Ya fuck-shit boyfriend blab where gold is?"

"Please, there is no gold. He gave me his word."

"Wow, his word." He slapped her hard. "Where is

piece of shit?"

He cocked the weapon against her temple and her whole body jerked violently in response.

"No!"

"Dé jà vu, sweetheart."

She kicked out at a stack of lobster pots nearby, causing the tower to topple and collapse on them. Karpos swatted them aside in a rage to reveal little Zac, hunkered against a wall. He had a smoking cigarette in his mouth which dropped from his lip as his eyes widened in terror. The Russian grabbed him by the scruff and brought him to the ground.

"Get off mah, ye bear-shaggin' bassa!"

Karpos shook him and clamped a hand over his mouth. Moved the gun across and aimed between the boy's eyes. Becky struggled under him but he sat more heavily on her so that she felt her ribs pushing against her lungs. He brought the kid's face close to his. "We meet again, little one. Ya gonna do the right thing this time?"

Zac gave a sharp nod, his eyes wide. Karpos loosened his grip for a second, then spoke in a squeaky voice while working the kid's jaws open and closed like a ventriloquist's dummy: "Please don't let him shoot me, pretty lady... please don't let him hurt me."

Becky played along: "Everything's gonna be okay, Zac, just hang on in there..."

"That's right, little shit. The pretty lady's gonna say magic words that make all this scary shit go away."

There were tears streaming down her face now. "You

don't need do this, you know that. Please, Karpos." The gun had moved back to her face.

"Time's up, cupcake." He threw the kid aside. Zac scrabbled to his feet and ran. "See? I can be nice guy when I want. He probably gone to get his mommy, so now you talk fast!"

"Okay, okay… the last time I spoke to him… Rab, he said…"

"Keep goin'."

"He said…" A clanging thud rang out and remained ringing in the air. The Russian's eyes rolled into the back of his head and he slumped sideways. Becky looked past him to see her little spider boy brandishing a shiny, alloy baseball bat. "Jesus, Zac! That ball left the field!"

The kid smirked, though she could see he was trembling.

"Help me up," she pleaded.

The boy took her hand and got her to her feet. She needed to find Rab. Warn him of the danger, but Zac tightened his grip and tugged her towards the other end of the alley. "Ah have ta sound the siren. It's mah job, missus! Come on!"

They'd soon skirted the rear of Aggie's General Store to eventually emerge down the side of the Boathouse Café, where a World War II air-raid siren was bolted to the building's clapboard wall. Zac grabbed its handle and turned it with both hands. The wailing sound it produced was ear-splitting, the wood-framed boathouse seeming to serve as a massive sound box, amplifying the noise a thousand-fold, so that Becky had to cover her ears.

Elleen appeared at the front of the café, drying her hands on a towel. She bellowed at the top of her voice. "Where, Zac? Where to?"

In the same instant, a mirror image of the old woman appeared at her side; identical hair, apron and specs.

"The harbour!" Zac yelled in reply.

"The harbour, Mary!" Elleen yelled to her doppelganger.

"The tea trays!" shouted Mary in earnest. The couple grabbed a tin tea tray each from a table and scurried away along the harbor road.

Soon, the siren's wail brought other locals to the vicinity and, oddly, several were carrying pots and pans. A fisherman appeared with a marching drum and an elderly lady Becky recognized, wearing a black hat and coat, went by with a large tin tub in a baby stroller.

"Zac! Will you be okay? I need to go!" she yelled in his ear.

"Rabbie said ah was ta keep ye away from the harbour!" came his reply. "Please, missus, stay close so ah can keep ye safe!"

Jesus. Who was the adult here, Becky found herself thinking.

*

Karpos came-to feeling something sharp pressing against his throat. He went to move, but putting weight on his arm hurt like hell. He'd managed to patch the dog bite with a bandage from his field kit, but it still throbbed with pain. A rabies jab would have to wait. The back of his head, too, where he'd been whacked, felt ready to crack open like a soft-boiled egg.

"Dae nae move," came a voice, "or ah'll dae ye like a stuck pig!"

Fair enough, thought the Russian, the blade to his neck was probably more important than the pain in his arm. "Who the fuck...?"

"Shut it."

He felt a sharp sting to his upper lip as the bastard ripped off his moustache. The knife left his throat and he turned to look at the guy. Black spikey hair. Ring in the ear. A tat of a fish on his neck. "Do we know each other, friend?"

"Nae in the flesh. Ah'm a sort o' pen pal, ye ken?"

He thought about that for a second. "The Khad rat."

"Come again?"

"You the snitch."

"Aye, ten out o' ten. Ye want MacBain?"

"I want the gold."

"Ah'll take ye ta 'em both. But it'll cost ye, mind."

"No kiddin'." He sat up slowly so as not to spook the rat and thought about reaching for the Webley in the dirt nearby. But the guy scooped it up and pocketed it before he got the chance.

"Fer safe keepin' ye understand," he said. "Easy now, fatso."

Once on his feet, the ass-wipe headed to the mouth of the alley. Karpos caught up and grabbed his arm.

"Not that way," he snapped. He needed to get his backpack from the bar. He paused before stepping through the pub's side door. The air was suddenly split by the wail of an air-raid siren.

*

Becky had made her way to the harbor, where islanders thronged along the wall, brandishing pots and pans, cookie tins, tea chests; all manner of junk, and she pictured satisfied customers on their way home from a yard sale. Odd, she thought. Eccentric. Islanders were still arriving in numbers; so many faces she hadn't seen before.

She spotted Rab almost at once, standing on the deck of a small fishing boat in the harbor itself. She waved, frantically trying to get his attention, then froze when she saw the cargo in the rear of the vessel. Two oblong wood crates. Words stencilled along their sides: BANK HAASE and a row of numbers. The name on the prow: '*The Midas Touch*'.

*

Lizzie Drum had tracked him down. Like him, she was on school lunch break.

"Lizzie! Take over from mah!"

"Wot, turnin' the handle?"

"Aye, ye daft Jessey. Come on!"

"Will ye come ta mah birthdee?"

"Huh?"

"Tamorra's mah birthdee."

"Yeah, yeah, cool, I'll be there. Take the handle!"

"Will ye kiss mah?"

"What, now?"

"Tomorra."

"Uh... yeah."

Lizzie took a hold with small hands, stood on tiptoe and turned the handle with all her might. The wailing dipped for a moment then rose as the daft wee hen got it up to speed. He checked over his shoulder as he went to see her adoring eyes watching him go.

*

Once at the harbour wall, Becky found herself jostled left and right by excited kids from the school. They'd arrived brandishing plastic buckets and large wooden spoons.

She looked back to *The Midas Touch*, where Rab seemed to be having trouble getting its engine started. The sight of the wood crates on the vessel's deck had brought a wave of nausea, and she couldn't shake Rab's words from her head: *"Becky. There-is-no-gold..."*

She shifted her gaze to the mouth of the alley beside Aggie's General Store, but saw no sign of Stink Bug. Was he still out-cold where she and Zac had left him?

Oh my God! The bastard was standing in Mrs. Drum's doorway and her stomach began to churn. Had the Russian spotted Rab in the boat yet? She followed his eye-line. It didn't look like it. She panned back and saw Calum emerge from the pub and pause at Stink Bug's side. The two exchanged words, and as they did so, a light went out in Becky's mind and a slide show flashed up a procession of pictures in the dark.

Flash! Jeff's office during a heatwave. *Flash!* Close on a brown, letter-sized envelope. *Flash!* A plastic DVD case with a distinctive green sticker along its spine, *'Hammer'* written in black marker. *Flash!* Calum watching a DVD from a collection on a high shelf. *Flash!* Home-recorded copies, green stickers along their spines: *'The French Connection', 'The Third Man', 'Local Hero,'* their titles written in black marker. Lights up. Show over.

Becky watched, sickened, as Judas lead Karpos through the growing multitude to a rusted iron ladder set into the harbor wall. Those who'd spotted the Russian were yelling and hurling curses. Then all hell let loose and a deafening tumult assaulted her ears. A thumping, jangling, clattering din, as ladles beat pots and pans, and spoons bashed trays and hammers beat tin tubs while sticks beat buckets and metal clanked and clanged. The whole island had turned out with anything that made a noise.

She spotted the old lady in black hat and coat bashing her galvanized tub with a length of copper pipe, and Stanley, the walking wounded, back by popular demand

and ballooning maroon cheeks into his tartan bagpipes. *'Scotland the Brave'* if you could make it out over the God-awful racket. The Devil had the best tunes, her mom had always said. Well, this brouhaha certainly had his name on it.

Calum and the Russian had reached the bottom of the ladder and were boarding *Morag's Ghost,* Karpos looking disconcerted by the ear-splitting din, and Becky was sure he'd realized, as she now did, that this was a collective admonishment aimed at him. They were sending him the message that Rab was not alone; that they were standing by him. Great, thought Becky, that's really gonna save Rab's ass.

The Midas Touch was heading for the harbor mouth, its valuable cargo clearly on show. Karpos had seen the crates too, for he was leaning forward at the prow, his jaw jutting like an enraged figurehead. Calum gunned his engines, his boat clearly in pursuit now, throwing up white spume in its wake. A harem of gray seals parted to let it through while gulls swooped and shrieked a protest of their own.

Becky looked on as a feeling of helplessness enveloped her, tears pricking her eyes, her throat aching as the incessant din labored on. She searched the crowd and eventually spotted Zac. He was belting an upturned trashcan with his baseball bat and cursing at the top of his voice; no longer the bashful, tongue-tied youth in a hoodie. She fought her way toward him through the mounting chaos.

*

The thrill was in him again. Zac remembered the last time he'd taken part in the Rough Music. The day the island won its independence.

The Mishnish moored where it was now; at the bottom of the hard. Granfer Dugald fronting-up to the eighth Laird of Glencruitten, the island's landlord, the men head-to-head on the ferry's deck. The swine, erect, aloof, nose in the air, dressed in full Highland regalia: kilt, sporran, silver-buttoned barathea jacket and tamoshanter.

Two bookish lawyers, his oily-haired creatures, in the stern running their bespectacled beaks over a large sheaf of dusty legal papers. And the population of Garg belting out the Rough Music loud enough to cause the earth to quake and the sea to boil.

Then Dugald gobbing into his palm and shaking the hand of Glencruitten's spawn. The crowd cheering, many in tears, and Large Stanley putting aside his pipes to bellow a farewell blessing:

"Up yer shitty arse, ye thievin' son of a whore!"

A Mexican laughter wave rippling around the harbour wall and *The Mishnish* taking the whore's son away, the demon slain, never again to suck the lifeblood from these shores. And so history repeats, as Miss Tonbridge would tell the class, with Rabbie leaving the harbour with a different kind of demon on his tail, gnashing at his princely mantle.

Zachariah Moore smiled at yet another tale he'd be

telling his wide-eyed grandchildren in years to come.

The lovely lass magically appeared at his side and he blushed when her lips brushed his ear. She yelled above the pounding din.

"We have to do something! We have to help him!"

"Ah cannae, missus! It's as it should be! It's our way!"

The lass turned to the crowd as if searching for faces she might know. "Isn't anyone gonna do something?"

"But we are, missus!" he cried, "We're dealin' wi' it! Rabbie's not just our friend! He's family, ye ken?"

"He's my friend too, Zac, and you all making this stupid racket isn't dealing with anything!"

He looked down to the hard, beyond *The Mishnish*, where a small, flat-bottomed boat bobbed, tethered to a buoy. He and Lachlan, a younger kid from school, used it to go lobster-potting from time to time. The lovely lass followed his gaze, then, without a word, grabbed his hand and guided him through the crowd and down the cobblestone hard.

In seconds, they were in the boat. He loosed the mooring line, started the outboard and headed for the harbour mouth as fast as the craft could cut through the incoming tide.

*

The Midas Touch was faring well against the incoming tide. Rab looked back to shore to see *Morag's Ghost* leaving the harbor. Time to reign in the throttle, he reckoned, and slowed the boat to around 40 knots. He checked around the wheelhouse, making a mental note of where everything was. The flare-gun, ready to go, in its rack above the wheel. The jerry can by the doorway, its lid unclipped and loose. The crowbar resting on the crate.

He pushed back the throttle some more, but not too much. He didn't want to drift too far to the south. He gunned the engine just enough to bring it back in line. The Rough Music reached him on a gust of wind, reminding him why he was doing this. Survival was the main goal, of course, and something else. Something a lot less tangible.

He had the island's backing, and for that he was grateful. And then he thought of Becky last night under the cairn. The feel of her body, smooth, warm and familiar to his touch. Would she ever forgive him? Christ, he hoped so. After all, he was her dragonfly, her Blue-eyed Darner, and he was hunting on the wing.

Checking through binoculars, he could see *Morag's Ghost* fast approaching. Karpos at the prow. Calum at the wheel. Would the Russian be armed, he wondered, and checked the flare-gun for the umpteenth time. Then the fuel gauge; both tanks showing full.

A headwind was getting up, once more nudging the boat's nose to the south. He straightened-up and lashed the wheel. He could hear the sound of his pursuers' grumbling engines gaining against the percussive roar from the harbour, intermittent on the wind.

He let-out the throttle for show as *Morag's Ghost* sped

into his wake, a mere twenty yards to his stern, then killed the engine, leaving his vessel dead in the water. There was a distinctive marker buoy bobbing in the sea off the starboard bow; dayglow orange with a green stripe around it. Rab noted its position. To drift south of it would have the boat come aground on the shelf of an oyster bed. Not a good idea any day of the week.

Calum's larger craft was now open to come hard around to collide with Rab's hull. And that's exactly how it went down; the boats bumping and rolling away from one another.

Karpos was over the side in a flash, his boots landing heavily on the deck. Rab turned from the wheelhouse and the men's eyes locked. The Russian spoke first. "Twenty five million in gold and ya couldn't afford fuck-shit haircut?"

"Hey, Karp, ol' pal buddy, welcome aboard. Jesus, you on vacation? Well, you're in luck; the weather's been pretty clement for the time of year."

The hitman gave a snort. He eyed the wood crates and a broad grin broke across his pumpkin face. He snatched up the crowbar, as Rab knew he would, jammed it under the lid of the top crate and jimmied it open... "What the damn hell..?" he almost squeaked, staring at the pile of rubble before him. With a roar he slid the crate aside where it dropped and splintered, sending rocks and boulders clattering across the deck. He hurriedly jimmied open the second crate but what he found didn't make him any happier.

"Looks like the price of gold just hit the deck, huh, Karp?"

Karpos sprang at him, crowbar raised, the veins in his neck fit to spring a leak. He swung wildly with the tool, missing Rab's head by a mile. Rab brought his knee up hard into the guy's groin, causing the goon to groan and stagger back.

He stole a glance at *Morag's Ghost* where Calum had remained at the wheel, his face impassive. It looked like his sister's man was keeping out of it. Good decision, he thought, as Karpos came for him again. He stepped back as the crowbar smashed through a wheelhouse window, then hopped aside when the big guy careered through the doorway, shards of glass crunching underfoot. Karpos brought the crowbar round in a wide arc this time only to embed its hook in a crossbeam.

The wood splintered as he yanked it free and lunged forward to pin Rab against the helm. With a growl, he brought the crowbar up fast and caught Rab under the chin. His head snapped back and he felt his jaw dislocate. His legs crumpled under him and he hit the deck. His vision was blurred but he could still make out the jerry can by the doorway and shot out a foot toward it. The can went over, dislodged its lid and spewed gasoline across the deck.

Karpos spun on his heel to see the gasoline spreading like a malignant stain, the fumes eye-watering in the enclosed cabin space. Rab rammed his heel into the hitman's shin, causing the guy to yell something in

Russian and stagger back, giving Rab time to pull himself up and snatch the flare-gun from its rack.

The giant's eyes grew wide at the sight of the flare-gun inches from his face. He backed-off to the side as Rab wheeled around him, making for the doorway on unsteady legs, the flare-gun unwavering in his fist. The men stared hard into the other's eyes, gamblers daring the other to show his hand… until Rab finally did. The flare-gun coughed, sending a blazing tail of hot sparks into the wheelhouse. The fumes caught instantly, turning the deck into a carpet of dancing flame.

*

Zac's little boat skimmed the waves; a hurled pebble slapping across a wide pond. Becky shielded her eyes against the spray, straining to see ahead where the two boats seemed to have rendezvoused. That was just too weird, she thought, had Rab's engine stalled? She could see no one on either boat. Where was he, damn him? Had the bastards gotten to him already? The signs weren't good. She focussed on *The Midas Touch* just as smoke began curling from its wheelhouse.

Suddenly she couldn't breathe, her heart pounding in her ears. Only fifty feet to his boat, now, and what the hell did she think she was going to do when she got there? "Zac! Get between them!" she yelled.

The boy obeyed and manoeuvred the tiny craft to Rab's portside, its fibreglass hull slipping easily into the slim gap, as Calum's vessel seemed to drift away a little as if to accommodate him.

Becky closed her eyes for a moment, willing her head to clear and think rationally. It didn't work; she was boarding *The Midas Touch* and nothing was going to stop her. She grabbed hold of one of its rope fenders, hauled herself up and strained to reach a rusted grab rail.

*

"Zac!" yelled a voice he knew. He craned his neck to see Calum glowering down from *Morag's Ghost*. "Are ye mad, ye dobber? Geta way safe! Go!"

Zac shrugged, accelerated and shot forward through the narrow gap between the prows. He wasn't going far, mind; he'd never abandon the lovely lass in a million years. He swung around to the right, came back off Rab's starboard bow and slowed to a standstill, his outboard idling in anticipation.

*

Becky scrambled over the rail and fell awkwardly to the deck, gasoline fumes catching in her throat. She could see flames licking the ceiling of the wheelhouse and billowing black smoke. She clocked the smashed crates too, BANK HAASE branded on their sides, and the boulders strewn over the deck, the meaning of the scene clearly apparent.

Karpos had Rab pinned against the opposite rail, a crowbar pressed across his throat, the latter gagging, while he fought to break free. She crawled and rummaged through the boulders until she found the largest, then sprang and smashed it into the back of the Russian's skull.

Karpos yelled out, twisted around fast and back-handed her across the face. She slumped back against the wheelhouse, hardly able to see through the pain, but her vision cleared soon enough for her to see the bastard deliver a hammer blow to Rab's stomach, then another to the face. And another, and another, until she couldn't make-out his features through the blood.

"Get off him, you bastard! He's had enough!" she screamed, the words lost in the crackle and spit of burning timber.

Karpos, though, had heard her and turned around, his mouth a sneer, his eyes ice-cold in the heat. He took a step toward her, stubbing his shin on one of the splintered crates. He cried out and stooped to rub the pain away.

Becky saw her chance and made a dash to help her lover, but before she could reach him, the world slipped into slow motion and she watched in horror as Rab arched his back and disappeared over the side.

Karpos stumbled to the rail and stared down at the water. "Fuck-shit!" he bellowed and spun around, a new plan forming in what passed as his brain.

Becky was already backing away, feeling the heat on her back as she got too close to the wheelhouse. The Russian hurled the crowbar in a rage, which narrowly missed her head and clattered across the deck. Three strides and he was upon her, his arms outstretched, fat fingers inches from her neck, when, *WUMPH!* a fireball plumed through the wheelhouse doorway, the blast putting the big man on his back.

Becky watched, unmoved, as he writhed on the deck, his upper-body a flaming torch. In seconds, though, he'd torn off the smouldering jacket and had staggered to his feet. *Morag's Ghost* had remained alongside and Becky squinted through the smoke to see him leap the gap and land onboard with ease. He was screaming words at Calum as the vessel turned and headed for the open sea.

Rab! She dashed to where he'd gone over but saw no sign of him in the water. Zac shouted something from his little boat but she couldn't make it out through the noise of the fire. He was adrift some way off, excitedly pointing to an orange buoy bobbing in the water twenty feet to his right. What was he trying to say, that he'd seen where Rab went down? She searched the water's surface for bubbles but saw none.

A picture from the past came to mind and stopped her breathing whilst filling her heart with dread. *Oh my God... he can't swim!*

There was no time for an elegant swallow-dive, this time. She jumped into the ocean feet-first, headed for the striped buoy Zac had indicated, jack-knifed and disappeared below the waves.

Visibility was poor as she pulled herself downward toward the seabed, scanning all around her. The water was cold and her shoulder muscles soon ached with cramp, but giving up wasn't an option. She spotted the buoy's anchor rope and used it to tug herself further into the depths, her lungs protesting, her ears aching with the increasing pressure. Where the hell was he? There was still no sign of bubbles and even if there were, the water was clouding fast with rising silt.

She needed to breathe. Just a few seconds more, she told herself... just a few seconds... She grasped the rope tightly and tugged herself deeper into the murky soup. *Just a few seconds more...*

Air forced its way out of her lungs and before she could stop herself she'd inhaled through her nose. Pain erupted behind her eyes as she fought not to take another breath. It was no good. She was going to drown. Guessing which way was up, she righted herself and kicked and kicked until she eventually broke the surface.

Zac's hand clamped around her wrist and pulled her into his boat where she lay on her belly, alternately spewing and sucking in oxygen. *Oh, Rab.* She felt suddenly tired. Tired of everything. Too tired to even grieve. Zac gunned the outboard and headed back to shore. Neither uttered a single word.

Becky looked back at *The Midas Touch* in time to see it explode into a hot, orange ball, sending tendrils of flame into the air. In its aftermath, all that remained of Rab's boat was scattered flotsam; ten thousand flickering candles bobbing in an ornamental pool.

*

Becky gathered Rab's coat around her and leant back against the chest tomb at the cliff's edge, her knees tucked under her chin. The diver had been down under the *Sea Cry* for over twenty minutes now, the clock on her useless cell phone told her. Probably due to the poor visibility she'd experienced herself when she'd gone down.

The harbor had been deserted by the time she and Zac had moored-up by the hard, and she wondered what the islanders thought they'd accomplished with their pathetic show of defiance.

Her cheeks were stinging though she'd stopped crying an hour ago. She put it down to the chill wind on her face. The sun had died with Rab, it seemed, the sky closing its gray, iron doors. She realized she was shivering in her still sodden clothes and so slipped her arms into the coat's sleeves and clasped the bulky garment to her.

The diver resurfaced, waving an arm, and soon a body rose from the sea at the end of a winch line. She caught a flash of lightning on the horizon and waited for a crack of thunder that never came.

*

Karpos watched through binoculars from the stern of

the snitch's boat as the prick's lifeless body was brought up. It was cut from the winch cable and laid on a box. One of the crew checked for a pulse before helping the island's cop get it into a body bag. He'd seen enough and so returned to the mystery man at the helm. "Hey, whatever ya name is, get me fuck out of here."

"There's the wee business o' remuneration, Mr. Brunovich. Wanna settle now? Ah dinnae take American Express, mind." The fisherman removed the Webley from a pocket and toyed with it while letting-out the throttle and steering toward Mull. Karpos eyed the revolver, grunted and unzipped his backpack. "I ain't exactly satisfied with the outcome of business, just so's ya know," he said. "And there's people gonna gimme shit when I get back."

"Ah'm sorry ta hear that, fella. Still, ye've been lucky. Ye have yer health."

Karpos really didn't like this guy. He placed fifteen wads of new notes on a shelf by the wheel. "Fifteen grand. That's it. I need the rest."

"There's a lot of folk back on that island that'll nae be happy wi' *me*, by the way."

"Your problem. Now, step on it."

*

Constable Finn had zipped Rab into a body bag. The diver had climbed into the boat and its skipper, Dugald, Becky assumed, was now motoring the vessel back to the harbor. She got unsteadily to her feet and headed for the gap in the wall.

*

Captain One-arm One-eye had seemingly risen from the dead and had *The Mishnish* ready to sail right on time. There'd be plenty of room, Becky noted, as she watched a handful of birdwatchers climb aboard.

She was about to wheel her case down the ramp when Zac came running from the direction of Aggie's Store, a brightly colored parcel under his arm. He arrived, panting, and handed it to her. "Ah got 'em with mah own money," he said, his face flushed, his ears pink. "Butterscotch. Fer yer mam, ye ken? They were nae cheap, by the way."

Becky knelt and hugged him. "You're my hero, young mister," she whispered, and when she released him he had tears in his eyes.

"Will ye be comin' back, missus?"

"No, Zac, I won't."

"Okay." The word was barely audible.

"But you look after yourself. Promise me?"

"Ah'll be goin' up the big school in a couple o' months."

"Well, that's great!"

"Aye. It's on Mull."

"That's wonderful. Look, you can always write me, okay? Greda will know how to get in touch," she said and kissed him.

"Okay," he managed, blushing some more, before running back to his mother's store. She'd miss him. There was a lot here she'd miss, she realized.

"Becky?" It was Greda. The girl approached clutching a fat, tan envelope. "It's nae as colourful as wee Zac's, ah'm afraid."

She looked tired, like she hadn't slept in days. She handed Becky the package. "Rab wanted ye ta get this ta the name on the front, there. A man in Canada, by all accounts."

Seeing Rab's handwriting caused her throat to constrict and her eyes to well. She took a deep breath and tried not to cry in front of his sister. The package was addressed to Assistant District Crown Attorney Grahame Warrick, and the address was of a government building in Ottawa.

"Uh… okay…"

"When yer man gets it, stand back, 'cause all manner o' shite's gonna hit the fan, believe mah."

She stepped forward and kissed Becky on the cheek, smiled a beatific smile, then turned and headed for the cliff path. Becky wanted to call after her and ask about Calum, but thought better of it. That was an ugly dog best left sleeping, she thought. She descended the cobblestone hard with her suitcase and did her best to think of home.

Chapter Twelve

KARPOS flew into JFK after a gruelling seven and a half hours cramped-up in coach. Before that, he'd spent a very unpleasant afternoon in Glasgow with his old pals, DI Phil Hardy and his stooge, DS Huggins. No china tea service this time. No Jammy Dodgers. Just too many damn questions; the DI pushing him for proof of his 'twitching' in the Highlands. Jesus, the guy had to be nuts. That had been three hours of grilling, no handshakes and no fond farewells. He was just glad to see the back of the clowns.

Matvy and Timur were there to meet him with the hearse. No brass band or Welcome Home banners just, "Hi, phantom dick, how's it hangin'?"

Timur opened-up the back, explaining they had a job to do before they could drop him at his uncle's place. He took his Samsonite from the trolley and threw it in the rear of the van. He went to slam the doors when something hard jabbed into his lower back.

"Get in," came Matvy's voice, "Uncle Fedor said to take you any place you wanna get."

The Georgians hefted him inside and locked the doors. The first thing that hit him was the stench of dog. His bowels loosened. His bladder was soon to follow when he spotted dark shapes moving in the half-light. A pair of Dobermans by the looks of them. A picture flashed in his head. Not of Afghan hounds, this time, but of Tony Soprano, driving and listening to Deep Purple's *'Smoke on the Water.'* He'd always loved that scene, because Tony had been so happy. Really getting off on the track, until the stupid CD got stuck.

The animals came at him out of the gloom, but before he felt their teeth ripping into his throat and abdomen, he had time to obsess on his one regret. Okay, Fedor Brunovich had raped his mother; an ignorant Chechen whore, but why couldn't he just once have recognized Karpos as his son? Claimed him for his own, just once? His life might've turned out a whole lot different. Better, maybe. His torn jugular spurted his short and tragic life up the wall of the van while his intestines were dragged out onto the floor. *Badda bing, badda boom! Smoke on the water, fire in the sky...*

*

She retrieved what there was in the mailbox and took it inside. The jog had done little to loosen her up but hopefully a steaming hot shower would do that. She thought about coffee, then remembered the percolator was packed away in one of the boxes out in the hall, waiting for collection the next morning. She had little left to pack now; kitchen stuff mostly, and bedding, of course. Settling for bottled water, she prised off the lid and took a swig. Luckily her Long Island condo had come fully-furnished, so it was just her possessions she'd be taking home to Virginia.

She'd had a call that morning from Donna DeMilt, her college chum in Standing, who assured her that her spare room was ready and waiting in the stable block. Lovely Donna; always there for her when things got tough. A week earlier, she'd heard from Dr. Jon Mahoney; an aging family lawyer and an old friend of her late dad's. He had a small firm in Standing and needed someone to take over the brunt of his work for a spell. He'd received a professorship from the University of Virginia and been invited to join its law faculty. She'd have to sit the Bar exam again, of course, but that was no biggie.

Moving back to sleepy Standing would have its benefits, she was sure. Not least she'd have time on the weekends to help-out her mom at the winery.

She checked her mail. Utility bills. The phone company sorry to lose a valued customer. A half-price token promising a meal for two at Molly's Diner, and a flat, tan Jiffy bag that the sender had practically cocooned in parcel tape. Damn. She'd packed the scissors already.

She'd duly posted the thick envelope Greda had given her to Canada her first day back, and it hadn't taken long before she'd gotten a visit from the FBI.

Special Agent Peter Farley had flashed his badge and apologised for her recent loss. Apparently the envelope's contents had been forwarded to his Bureau by Assistant

Crown Attorney Grahame Warrick, and had contained a statement by Constable Finn describing events up to, and including Rab's drowning. The cop had logged the time of death and an original death certificate had been enclosed.

The accompanying material, though, and the reason for the Special Agent's visit, had been a lengthy signed affidavit from beyond the grave. In it Rab had attested to the criminal activities of the Brunovich crime family, giving names, dates and a list of off-shore accounts presently bulging with its spoils. It contained account numbers, amounts and their online access codes. These had been frozen in the light of a subsequent Supreme Court hearing, she'd been told.

Rab had outlined his own part in the laundering of the Mob's millions, citing several hidden subsidiaries controlled by a company called Merlin Holdings. And he hadn't stopped short of implicating Jeffery Hammer and Frank Holt into the bargain.

As if that wasn't enough damning evidence to get Fedor Brunovich indicted, Special Agent Farley was able to list several known and suspected homicides attributed to the Mob family: Jeffery Hammer, Amir Rumi, an Iranian cab driver, Ethan Adams, a homeless junkie found dead with his dog, and Mikey MacCullen, a Scottish national. There were others missing in action, presumed dead, Frank Holt among them, of course.

Karpos Brunovich had been added to that list after testimony from DI Hardy of Europe's Interpol, regarding the Russian's known movements whilst in the UK. He'd been picked up on CCTV going through Immigration on his return to the States and was now thought to be propping-up a highway overpass somewhere. No great loss to the planet, Becky thought.

For her own part, she'd been subpoenaed to appear at a Grand Jury hearing two weeks ago to give her own account of Karpos's arrival on Garg and the subsequent events leading to Rab's death.

Justice Lynne King was reckoned to be a shoo-in for New York's next Senator and had vehemently declared war on organized crime in the State. And if news commentators and law pundits following the actual court case were anything to go by, it looked like Fedor Brunovich and several of his associates were going away for a very long time. In Fedor's case, the very little time he had left.

She eventually found the scissors packed in a box containing underwear. Of course; where else? She snipped open the package and removed its contents: a DVD case with a distinctive green sticker on its spine. One word written in black marker: '*Becky.*' Her heartrate quickened and she felt a rush of adrenaline.

She un-boxed her DVD player and TV and connected them up. She slid the disc into the drive and hit 'PLAY.' Nothing for a while. Just static and white noise. Then a picture. Maureen Anderson and Stanley outside Mrs. Drum's. Maureen going for melodramatic:

"Let's hope Stanley's right about that. What kind o'

world do we live in when the price o' a rare bird's egg costs us all the extinction o' a rare and beautiful species?"

Why had Calum sent her a copy of the same report he'd sent to Jeffery Hammer's office almost a year ago?

Maureen was on the move, the camera panning with her. "The Isle o' Garg first drew media attention last month havin' achieved its independence when its residents bought their own island for a mere twenty million pounds. Effectively freeing themselves from an alleged, and I quote, 'greedy and neglectful laird on the mainland.' And most intriguing of all? The purchase money was provided by an anonymous donor." Becky was having trouble taking this in. And then it clicked. *Well, son of a bitch...* "After centuries of being lowly tenants in the land of their birth, one islander had this to say about their mystery benefactor."

The shot cut to Greda, high on the cliff path, the wind in her copper hair.

"They have restored our dignity and given the island back its soul, and fer this precious gift, we shall be forever in their debt." She turned to look straight into the camera. "Whoever ye are, we thank ye from the bottom o' our hearts."

Close on Maureen, beaming: "A blue-tailed falcon. A warm-hearted multi-millionaire. Is that two rare breeds, I wonder? This is Maureen Anderson on the Isle o' Garg reporting for STV News. Back to you, Eamon." The screen went to static and white noise. Becky zapped it off.

"Every blade of grass, every stone, every shaft of light. This

307

is my pot of gold."

Rab's words came back to her, putting a lump in her throat. She hadn't been able to get the last night they'd spent together out of her head. Then more precious words: *"...but that picture holds a secret of its own, rooted in the sixties."*

He'd been talking about the Rembrandt look-alike. It hadn't struck her at the time, but thinking about it now, how could his father have painted a blue-tailed falcon back in the 60s when Rab and Greda had only recently faked its existence?

She looked again at the Jiffy bag the DVD came in. Something was poking out of it. She reached and teased out a blue tail-feather. The object of her infamy had come back to haunt her and she felt guilty all over again. Then she felt an excited flutter in her stomach. Her eyes located the bottle of water across the room. She hurried to it, dowsed the feather and ran it over the back of her hand. It left no blue smudge.

"So. Where does the real *Rab MacBain exist? I've seen the fake, where's the original?"*

"When you think about it, a fake, no matter how good, only has a value because the real thing exists someplace, right?"

*

She was intercepted at the check-in desk at Kennedy Airport by Special Agent Peter Farley, shown into a cramped interview room and offered coffee. Her passport was confiscated and she was asked to wait. Presently, a large guy, suited and balding, with a pleasant smile entered and took the seat opposite. Even with his size, Becky couldn't help but find him attractive.

He slid a newly minted passport across the table to her. She opened it and checked the mugshot. It was certainly one she'd supplied to US Immigration two years ago, but her name had been changed for someone else's: *Alex Santry*.

"What's this? You're putting me into Witness Protection, that it?" She'd already been told there could be consequences to her giving evidence at that Supreme Court hearing.

The big guy cocked his head to one side. "Call it a wedding gift."

"Uh… but I'm not getting married."

He slid another document across the table. "British marriage license. Congratulations."

Now she was intrigued. There it was in black and white. She was now Alex Santry, married to a Timothy Santry.

"This Timothy guy, he good looking?"

"Prefers to be called Tim. Yeah, kinda. Bit of a ladies man back in the day. Used to be better lookin' before he got his nose bust up."

His accent had a soft edge to it, she noticed. Canadian perhaps. She read the names again: Tim and Alex Santry. Well, it kind of had a ring to it.

"But you haven't explained why I..." she began. The stranger chuckled and straightened his tie.

"Let's just say I'm doin' this as a favor for an ol' beer-buddy." He got to his feet. "Oh, and this meeting? Never happened." He chuckled some more and lumbered out of the room.

*

Sturdy walking boots certainly did better than kitten heels when it came to climbing the cobble stoned hard. No sheep aboard *The Mishnish* this time, just kegs of beer and supplies for Aggie's General Store. Oh, and at least twenty or so visiting tourists.

The school kids were out in force, as she guessed they would be, singing their hearts out at the top of the ramp. She was impressed that they'd graduated to close harmonies. They sounded great.

It was a Friday so she hadn't expected to see her little spider boy. He'd be attending school on Mull, had been her guess, but there he was, ready to spirit her backpack away to Mrs. Drum's. She gave him a hug, then thought perhaps the kid was lingering just a bit too long with his face between her breasts.

She took in the scene around the harbor. The wildlife center had been completed and was buzzing with visitors. Calum's boat had had a face-lift and sported words in tall letters that took up its whole side: 'WHALE WATCHING.' The vessel was packed to the gunnels with school kids from the mainland and wearing bright-yellow inflatable life jackets.

The market had started up again; running the length of the harbor wall and selling what you'd expect, though the blue-tailed falcon brand had been superseded by a smiley cartoon whale.

She wove her way through the throng to where she expected to find Dugald's rust-bucket for hire. Instead, parked where it used to be, was a dark green Range Rover. An 'A' board next to it advertised island safaris three times a day at £20 pounds a trip. No concessions, but promising a snack of salmon sandwiches half-way around.

Dugald strode up, smiling, with Calum in tow. The skipper wore a kilt and a sweatshirt printed with the legend, 'GARG SAFARI TRAIL.' Great idea, she thought. She and Calum got in the rear of the vehicle while Dugald took the wheel.

"Ye had ta be convincin,'" Calum was at pains to explain a few minutes into the ride.

"I see that."

"Not just fer the police, but fer yer own sake. The Russkies would 'o' been watchin', ye ken?"

"Sure, I ken, Calum, but thanks for spelling it out." She wondered if she'd ever get to like this guy.

"We've a wee boat trip planned," said Dugald over his shoulder.

"Sounds good."

"And Greda says she'd like ye fer a stew supper after.

Ah'll run ye up there, if ye've a mind, lass. Nae charge," he grinned in the rear-view mirror.

She grinned back. "Thanks Dugald, that'd be great."

They dropped her outside the shelter at the cemetery, turned and headed back to the harbor. It had been the smoothest ride she'd had on the island to date.

The gravestone slid across its plinth with ease. She took out a pocket Maglite and made her way down the stone steps. She was relieved to find that the grave containing the lady in the yellow satin dress had been bricked-up. "Sorry again," she muttered as she went by.

She rounded the bend to the right, past the open aperture and its oasis of daylight, and continued for another twenty feet, where her flashlight found a heavy oak door with decorative cast-iron hinges. Probably the original, she thought as she turned the rusty handle. The wood groaned as she pushed it open and entered a church crypt.

The vaulted chamber was aglow with candlelight, and the first thing that caught her eye was a canvass camp bed, on top of which was a dayglow orange buoy with a green stripe around it, a coil of rope and a diver's oxygen tank and regulator.

As she moved further into the room, she found Rab seated at his easel, painting by the light of a hurricane lamp. It crossed her mind that there must be some kind of ventilation down here and detected a draught coming from somewhere.

"Well, hello there, Lazarus," she said, her tone light.

He looked up and smiled. "Hi to you too, sweet cheeks. Hey. remember that elephant I was kinda minding for a friend for a couple of years? Liked to sleep on the bed?"

"Uh... Vaguely."

"Lost it. It just nipped out one night to get smokes and never came back. A tad ungrateful, I thought"

"Funny. Reminds me of someone."

"So, I'm just saying…"

"I'll think about it."

*

The *Sea Cry* rounded the southern headland, little Zac at the wheel, standing on a box under Dugald's watchful eye. Rab held her close in the stern as they watched the coastline inch by. The forest at the top of the cliff looked to be quite dense, the trees trained at a slant after continual battering from high winds, she guessed. Rab pointed to an eyrie on a ledge and passed her the binoculars. There was one blue-tailed falcon at home.

"The real McCoy, huh?" she said feeling a strange kind of thrill.

"The real McCoy. You can see why they'd have predators."

"Egg thieves."

"Right, though those mostly get thwarted. Islanders have protected the secret so well even I didn't know about them. Not even as a kid."

"They must've existed here for, what then, half a century at least, if your dad's Rembrandt forgery's anything to go by."

"That's right, and like I said, when Calum had the idea of placing a family of decoys below the cemetery, it worked for us in a couple of ways. It drew attention away from the originals, at the same time triggering a tourist boom. And, by the way, getting STV to report on the birds was also a way of getting my face on TV, seemingly by accident."

"Someone must be well connected," she laughed.

"The TV journo, Maureen Anderson? Calum's cousin on his mother's side. She jumped at the gig, especially when it meant she'd get a second scoop with the fraud's discovery. She'll have a crew back here inside of a week. Needless to say, I'll be keeping my head down this time around."

"Jesus. Is there no end to your skulduggery, Mr. Santry?"

"Afraid not, and with luck, the coverage will have the island enjoying another tourist boom. It all helps." He grinned and did that twinkly thing he did with his eyes.

"If the action at the harbor's any indication, you've got another one on your hands, already."

"Speaking of which, Greda wants to talk to you about running the wildlife center. Said it'd be too much for her with the falconry and all."

"Are you kidding me?"

"No. Really. She got a grant for the project. She wants

you to catalogue the island's bug population; put some displays and presentations together. Fancy it?"

"Well, I'll... I'll talk to your sister."

"She's got a star of the show lined-up, already. It seems the island's playing host to one of Scotland's rarest bugs." He gestured to the clifftop forest. "In amongst that lot we've got Aspens; pretty rare for these parts, and..."

She jumped in. "And rare habitats often come with rare species?"

"In one. See, we've had a few sightings of Six-spotted pot beetles. Don't expect me to have the Latin. Ring any bells?"

"Some. And you're not making this up? This isn't another fake job, a ruse to garner fat research grants, maybe? You can see why I'd ask, Rab," she said with a note of mischief.

"Nope, all on the level."

"Well then, like I said, I'll talk to Greda."

It was looking like she could be sticking around after all, she thought, and wondered if Rab was aware of a certain forged marriage license. She'd have to do a little gentle probing on that score at Greda's over dinner.

Zac slowed the boat almost to a standstill with its starboard side to the island. Rab pointed skyward and Becky looked up in time to see a real McCoy hurtling earthward at a zillion miles an hour and draw a diagonal across the sun. There was a silent explosion as the falcon crashed into its next meal, its victim's feathers erupting like a firework and see-sawing down over the forest canopy.

"Rab? About that elephant."

"Uh-huh?"

She leant her head against his chest and pulled him into her. "Are you sure it's not just gonna show up again one day?"

"Sure, I'm sure." He thought for a second. "Does this mean you'll, you know..."

"Shut up. Still thinking about it."

"How about I let you use my razor to shave your armpits?"

"Okay, deal," she said, closing her eyes and savouring the moment.

Acknowledgements

Huge thanks to all those who helped make this book possible. To Steve Jeanes, who, after reading my first chapters, emailed to tell me I couldn't write. What rot, I thought; I knew how to develop characters and structure stories for TV and film scripts and had done so for several years, I told him over a couple of pints in Brighton.

Steve proved his point to me in under ten minutes. I'd made so many beginner's mistakes. "Even if you were a plumber," he said, "you wouldn't install central heating in your own home without learning how to do it first."

Fair point, I thought, and so spent a year boning-up on how to write pros and discovered how different the discipline compared to scriptwriting. An observation obvious to most, I suppose, but someone had to spell it out in my case.

Many thanks to Hillery Warner BSc. MSc. curator of entomology at London's Natural History Museum. Special thanks to Tom Ryan for coaching me in Western Scottish dialects. And to all those who's names I pinched for my characters, whether they knew it or not. And to Lynne King for her help and encouragement. Big thanks to Deborah Greer-Perry and Peter Farley for taking the time to help with this edit. Any remaining bloopers are my own.

I couldn't resist stealing the line: "If my dog was as ugly as that, I'd shave its ass and make it walk backwards." It was one of Walter Matthau's lines as Max Goldman in the movie, *'Grumpier Old Men'* 1995.

'Rough Music' is my first novel. The story was originally commissioned as a film script but never made it to the screen.

For those interested, you can read about that, and more, on my website: www.robindriscoll.org

And, with that in mind, special thanks to Chris Ide for designing and maintaining the site as well as helping me with social media.

This book version was first published in 2017. Now, with a weeny bit more experience at this book-writing lark, I've revisited and polished *'Rough Music'* for this new edition.

I've since written the first two in my Josie King Mystery Series: *'The Unborn'* and *'Still Warm.'* The third, *'Remote'*, is in progress and hopefully out by Christmas 2019.

Incidentally, this has been a work of fiction and any resemblances to places and people are purely coincidental (except for when they're not!)

And finally, huge thanks to the publishing company, Authors Reach Ltd. They are the publishers of this edition and my Josie King mystery series. The company was formed initially as a writer's co-operative in 2016 by authors Richard Hardie, Catriona King, Shani Struthers, Sarah England and Gina Dickerson to help each other promote their books, but very soon became a Limited Company and a full publisher with the aim of bringing a great variety of books directly to readers through all UK bookshops as well as online outlets.

Uniquely, the company is also owned and run by its founding authors and welcomes interaction from its readers. Other AR authors include Corinna Edwards-College and Veronica McGivney.

All Authors Reach authors have enjoyed previous success and share secondary skills. Gina Dickerson, for instance, designed the layouts and covers for all my books, for which I'm very grateful. Shani Struthers has been amazingly supportive since she introduced me to AR. Richard Hardie is our marketing wizard and if you've seen this book on the shelves in shops, it's thanks to him, especially when publishers don't seem very interested in marketing their books these days.

Authors Reach Ltd. members share the task of promoting their titles through social media, an excellent and often misunderstood tool. You can find Authors Reach at www.authorsreach.co.uk

Thanks again for all their hard work. And thank you all for reading 'Rough Music.'

About The Author

After leaving Worthing Art College in the early 70s Robin, with friends, Pete McCarthy, Rebecca Stevens and Tony Hasse, formed a touring theatre company called *'Cliffhanger.'* Their shows were always comedies and contrived through improvisation.

Years later, while writing for various TV comedies, Robin became a contributor to *Alas Smith and Jones*, then the main writer for *Mr. Bean*; the series. He co-wrote the movies and wrote several of the animations. He recently put scriptwriting aside to write mystery thrillers, which might surprise some, but rather than write comedies, he's chosen to write what he like to read, and that's fast-paced mystery thrillers. As with old dogs and new tricks, he can't help including a certain amount of humour in his work. He and his wife spend their time between West Sussex and West Dorset.

More Books By Robin Driscoll

THE UNBORN
(Josie King Mystery Series Book 1.)

New York's Catholic Cathedral. A treacherous brotherhood hiding in the Black Forest. A Vatican conclave to elect a new pope. Add a dash of comedy and you have the ingredients for Robin's second novel. This time he brings us his engaging Detective, Josie King, as she delves into an underworld of religious fanaticism on a personal crusade for vengeance.

STILL WARM
(Josie King Mystery Series Book 2.)

It's NYPD's Detective Josie King's last day on the force. As farewell toasts are raised, she receives a text-message that stops her breathing. Olive, her one-year-old goddaughter has been kidnapped! Now no longer a cop, and without the department's weight and resources behind her, she doggedly follows the clues the kidnapper leaves for her, determined to bring little Olive home. She knows this is personal. Someone is messing with her head, but who, and why? With the clock counting down, Josie finds Olive isn't the only person close to her being targeted by a monster from her past.

REMOTE
(Josie King Mystery Series Book 3.)

OUT SOON!